Past her reflection,
there spreads a field
half shrouded
Like a world left
unfinished.

ROBERTSBRIDGE

Etchingham

Salehurst

Brightling

Penhurst

BATTLE
Ashburnham
Park
Normanhurst

Catsfield

Ninfield

Crowhurst

Hollington

HASTINGS

St LEONARDS-on-Sea

Fairlight

Fairlight Glen

Bexhill

Brede Place
Brede

R. Brede

Pelham Hill

Northiam

Iden

Peasemar

Playden

Udimore

Icklesham

OWIN

50.949

COUNTY OF SUSSEX.

Scale of Miles.

0 1 2 3 4 5 6 7 8 9 10 11

Author's Centres ◎

Railways _____

Dismantling myself
Blowing away
Like red and white
confetti,
cells

Night brushes over
the burnt out houses
and deserted places

GPS: 0°44'14"E, 50°57'0"N

Scrutineer Publishing

By the same author
The Carving Circle

The Book of Dirt

Gretchen Heffernan

This edition published 2017
First published 2015

Scrutineer Publishing
www.scrutineer.org
info@scrutineer.org

Book and Cover Design:
The Scrutineer, Rachael Adams.
Fonts: Adobe Garamond, Bree serif.
Printed and bound by IngramSpark, on 50lb
uncoated paper.

SCB Distributors
15608 South New Century Drive,
Gardena, CA 90248
United States of America

ISBN 978 0 9956843 9 3

Printed by Ingram

A geographical note. The author has extended
the chalk cliffs of the South Downs to Rye, East
Sussex for the sake of the setting. She has
also shortened the distance between Rye, East
Sussex and Hastings, East Sussex.

Dedication

To Mike, Eddy and Ayla with love and wonder.

The Organic Matters Series

The Book of Dirt
The Book of Insects

Prologue

Once there was a speck of dirt caught inside a universal drift that travelled through great vats of blackness, flamboyant gasses and elemental showers without thought or aim. And whenever the dirt floated over the planet that spun like a perfect marble, it felt a gentle pull towards the swells of blue, soft and serious as a whispered promise, which made the dirt stir. Otherwise it felt nothing and this pattern continued for eons. Then a star exploded and a storm of light with fierce lassoes struck the dirt through the Earth's burning atmosphere, where it began to fully awaken.

The heaviness of the beautiful planet hit the dirt like an anvil and it crashed into the sea. The water was a salve to its burns and the dirt began to experience further flashes of light, of dappled consciousness, surging like currents of electricity on the ocean floor.

It was then that it saw her.

To the untrained eye she was ordinary and barnacled. An insignificant rock on the bottom of the seabed, but the dirt sensed a true magnificence inside her. And it was right, for when she opened her mouth; it saw that she was lined with something silver and luminous, like a soul.

The dirt took a chance.

It plunged into her and attached like a thorn inside an armpit. It was awkward at first, but the dirt persisted because it could feel itself growing and by love, by risk and intervention, it became a pearl, which was more than it had ever dreamt possible.

But the truth about dreams is that once they're believed in, they're already half fulfilled, so faith in impossible things is vitally important. It's crucial if you want to evolve and although the pearl longed to reach its full potential, it had come to a point where it found it could advance no further on its own. And so, another truth was shown to the pearl, the truth that none of us are truly independent of one another, of the world, none of us can act alone.

We need others.

1.

Ansley was at the bus stop when Jude and the Keepers found him, which was ironic, because the busses hadn't been running for years and the village, like most villages, had been deserted since the beginning of The Transformation Age.

He rarely left the safety of the woodland, however, the majority of the contaminated people had died by now, so the threat of attack was slim and he needed paper for his poems. This village had a post office and he hoped the contaminated had spared the stockpiles of paper that he envisioned. There was no longer a societal need for paper now anyway; burning was unnecessary as there were plenty of fires around to keep warm and nobody was left to write letters.

The fires started after the earthquakes had caused the fracking wells to leak methane and not even heavy rains could extinguish their blaze. The pools of fire were a malleable blue, like clouds of Bunsen burners slowly rolling over the land and erupting into yellow excited peaks as they made their way through the soils that fed them. This meant that there were few obstacles to blockade the wind, so it stripped the burnt earth of its remaining soil, substance and life. Only the toughest things held on.

Ansley stared at the blue distance. He was safe in the South Downs with its chalky foundation and absence of methane. He didn't know the inferno intimately, but he was all too familiar with its consequential wind. It's strange. You can never predict the things that will shape you after catastrophe. He wouldn't have guessed it would be the wind, but he felt it, element by element, shaping the world, and his life, anew.

The rain blew sideways and stung his eyes, so he ducked inside a bus shelter to wait out the worst of it. The metal slats were missing from the seat, but the glass on the roof and the sides was remarkably intact, though cracked in many places and grimy. He was watching a raindrop streak down the grime and bounce off patches of mould like a warped pinball, when he saw a light dipping in and out of the dark streets.

At first he thought he was hallucinating the bus twisting into view as a serpentine creature of fire and glass. "No way," he thought, "that can't be a bus." Ansley could hardly remember the sound of an engine, any engine at all, and yet, there he was, at the bus stop with a bus approaching. It was as if the oil hadn't run out and he felt nauseous with déjà vu as he watched the bus slowly drive down the High Street. As it drew closer, Ansley could hear someone shouting promises of food, shelter and clean drinking water through a megaphone. He pulled his balaclava over his head and raised his hand as if he'd been waiting for a ride all along.

An old London bus with only its windows scrapped clean of graffiti, stopped in front of him and opened its doors. Ansley felt the hydraulic rush of warm air and nostalgic scent of diesel. He winced at the acidity. A weak and watery glow lit the strange faces of its passengers. At a glance they were a mix of ages and genders, sharing the sunken cheeks of malnourishment and wide, sallow, motionless eyes. The survivors of tragedy adapt familial traits. By comparison, Ansley felt that he didn't look so hideous.

Only the man with the megaphone was alert and vivacious. He was impossibly tall, wore a top hat, a mauve velvet suit with flared trousers and black cowboy boots. Above him, a metal hook had been bolted into the ceiling and from it hung a huge crystal paraffin-light chandelier that flicked prisms everywhere like shards of broken glass. He stood at the top of the steps and peered down at Ansley, his suit was crawling with refracted rainbows. Ansley was too stunned to think.

"There you are!" the man said. "I hope you haven't been waiting long? There were delays on the M5, bloated cows, wandering lunatics, rabid goats and whatnot, but as they say, better late than never," he smiled and his teeth were clean and white. "I'm Jude," he said as he stuck out his hand. "And you are?"

"Ansley," he said as he shook Jude's hand.

Jude's face twitched with recognition.

"A moment please," said Jude as he turned around, reached up with a tinkling and detached an arm off the chandelier to shine over Ansley.

He started his cross-examination at Ansley's feet and slowly began weaving his way up to his face. The waxy fumes from the paraffin-oil flame of the chandelier arm filled Ansley's nostrils and made his pupils shine the colour of rose quartz.

"Would you mind?" Jude pointed to Ansley's balaclava and with great reluctance; Ansley lifted it from his face.

Ansley looked the other way. He couldn't stand to witness Jude scrutinize his appearance. Ansley was completely devoid of sweat glands and hair. His body was skeletal with elongated limbs and his skull was round with a wide forehead. His chin was abnormally protruded, as were his cheekbones and his eyes were pink with dark shadows underneath. His teeth were deformed. He looked like the mythical dweller of a deep abyss, and in a way, that's exactly what he was, as he spent most of his time in a hidden and dark woodland glade.

He had been born with a severe form of ectodermal dysplasia; a simple step-change in the DNA. His disease had mutated to the extent that it prevented him from being in the sunlight. Exposure to sunlight caused his skin to instantly blister and boil. His parents had learned this the hard way and he had bubble-pocked scars up and down his pale body to prove it.

"I remember you," said Jude. "I let you live."

It was true; Jude had allowed Ansley and his father to live. Many of Jude's Keeper's had felt that Ansley should not have been born and ought to be eradicated for the sake of purity. They called him Dark Ansley and argued that although he hadn't ingested his disease, he was contaminated all the same by birthright, and that this could falter a perfect evolution.

But Jude understood that evolution always began first with a mutation and that species abnormalities were usually the catapults of change. However, the need for a mutant wasn't the reason why Jude had spared his life. It was much more tactical than that. For keeping Ansley alive had helped preserve local superstition and fear, thus enhancing the need for a prophet and Jude's position of power.

There was another reason why Jude hadn't killed Ansley, something closer and personal that he didn't entirely understand. He recognized a fellow outcast. There was something about himself in the boy, something misunderstood that reminded him of his own fall from grace and the lengths he took to prove himself worthy. His achievements had been a strive for acceptance on any level, horrid or holy, and Jude was curious to witness the path Dark Ansley would take to validate himself to his demons.

"So the boy with the contaminated genes has survived," he said. "How very, very interesting."

Jude put the torch under his own chin. His eyes were outlined in thick kohl.

"Won't you join us?" He tipped off his hat and bowed.

2.

Ansley's father had spoken about the Prophet Jude with guarded respect even though he admitted disagreeing with his ideas and radicalism. Still, Jude had treated them with fairness. When the new maps were drawn, Ansley's father's land had fallen within Jude's territory, the only habitable territory in the country, and Jude had allowed them to stay. They would have died without his generosity.

Ansley had never met Jude and felt a storm of gratitude, horror and curiosity as he looked at the bowed head in front of him. It was as bald as his own, yet with a tattoo of an octopus wrapped around it like a bonnet. There were two tentacles that curled around his temples and the air that surrounded him was a womb of terrifying excitement.

Ansley sensed the rules were different for Jude, not merely his ability to bend or break them, but literally different, as though he were breathing from somewhere else. Jude waved the crystal arm in front of Ansley's face.

"Welcome," Jude stepped to the side and allowed Ansley to board the bus.

The wind thrashed the rain against the shelter like a premonition and for a moment Ansley felt afraid to move. That's when he noticed the basket of fruit. It was a selection of apples, pears, grapes and strawberries. Jude followed Ansley's gaze.

"Have I rendered you speechless?" Jude laughed and the wick sputtered. His back teeth were full of metal fillings.

It was true. Ansley hadn't seen so much food in one place in years. His mouth watered at the thought of a strawberry. He had been subsisting on fungi, roots and greens for as long as he could remember and was weak with hunger. His hunger mesmerized him.

"Where did you find it?" Ansley asked as he climbed up the bottom step and looked down the aisle. The bus was half full with passengers intensely eating while the spectral light of prisms bounced off their foreheads.

"Ah! That's my secret, now come in, come in, it's still raining and I'm wearing velvet of all things," he took Ansley's hand and pulled him up the remaining steps. "Close the door," he said to the driver, but the driver stalled and turned towards Ansley.

"Not him," said the driver. "I know him. Recognize the eyes. Used to live in the village, he did, and there's no colour in him, like he's dead, only worse. 'Dark Ansley' they called him. He's a bad omen and I'll not be having him," he said as he tightened his hands around the steering wheel.

His knuckles had the J. U. D. E. tattoo of a Keeper. There were rumours about Jude's personal bodyguards and none of them fluffy and nice.

"I beg your pardon," Jude approached the Keeper and put a pale hand gently across his throat. "You'll not be having him? Did I ask for your opinion?"

The Keeper went rigid and a crown of sweat beaded across his forehead.

"Answer the question," said Jude. His calm manner was harrowing.

"No sir. You did not ask for my opinion," whispered the Keeper.

"Correct. Now let me explain something," Jude pointed the crystal arm at Ansley. "The fact that this young man is alive is proof enough of his worthiness. Remember, we are on the brink of evolution and every survivor adds another rung to the ladder that will eventually spin and lead to divinity. You know nothing. You understand nothing. You would die without me. That's why I hired you. Now shut up." He faced Ansley once more. "I do apologise for this outburst of prejudice, but they aren't vetted for their intelligence as you can plainly see. I am commander here and I wholeheartedly welcome you. Now tell me, where have you been living?"

"In the woods," said Ansley.

"A true survivalist, I like it. So, is there anyone else with you? Anyone at all? Your father?"

"No," said Ansley and the thought of his father dropped through him as though he were an empty well. "No one is left."

"Perfect," said Jude. "Cheer up. Here, have an apple," he said and threw it up in the air.

Ansley caught it in one hand. He looked back at the cold and wet darkness beyond the bus door and the desire for food overtook the fear tightening in his chest. I've lived through worse, he thought, nodded a thank you for the apple and walked to the back of the bus.

Nobody seemed to notice him. They were all too busy slavishly eating. The floor was littered with stems and sticky with fruit juices. This indifference towards his presence felt unusual and pleasant. He hadn't been this close to people in ages and his heart pumped with anxiety. He sat down in an empty seat, crouched low and took a few deep breaths to calm himself. The bus was dry and warm. Be grateful, he thought, and bit into his apple.

So that was Jude. The Great Prophet. He watched him straighten up his top hat. It was strange that such an influential man should behave a bit like a deranged clown, although looks can be deceiving, Ansley reminded himself as he glanced at the window. He pulled up his balaclava and put his cheek against the window's cool surface.

Her mirrored face was staring at his white reflection inside the dark glass. She smiled. And Ansley, like an eclipse, pulled down his balaclava and turned away.

3.

Marianne had watched him board the bus. She often tagged along for a ride when her father was driving on one of Jude's survivor searches. This was not out of adoration for her father for she recognized him as a yes-man and not a pioneer. She was not close to her father and had very little respect for his loyalty to Jude, a man she was acutely suspicious of. However, these excursions gave her a glimpse of the world outside of Rye and she felt a peculiar tug towards the calamity she witnessed. She had heard her father's comments and was curious about this boy that he wouldn't trust.

Could he really be Dark Ansley?

She looked up at his covered face as he passed down the aisle. His eyes reminded her of rabbits she had known, gentle rabbits, not evil at all. She had thought he was an exaggerated fable, a ghost story or something to keep the children out of the woods.

Once her father had told her that he'd seen him mushroom hunting, said that Dark Ansley just crouched there with luminous red eyes, silent as a tree stump and as gnarled. Her father described his face as similar to a mandrake root pulled from the ground, pallid, distorted and dirty. But it was obvious that he'd told her the story to scare her and she hadn't believed him. And now, here he was, a survivor.

She thought of his pale reflection against the black window. It resembled the Japanese lantern she'd released as a child, round and white and internally lit into a moonless night. Her wishes had been innocent then, it was before Jude's Project and the mass contamination. The peacefulness of this time pulsed through her and made her touch the pouch tied around her neck.

The pearl was inside her pouch, nestled and humming.

It placed the idea in her head.

Yes, she thought, he is the colour of my pearl and her chest filled with tenderness at the comparison like a drop of solvent to her apprehension.

Marianne had been ten years old when Jude severed his Keepers from modern society. Food was becoming scarce and raids were becoming common, so they felt grateful to be moving to the safe fertile grounds of

Rye. The disease of fear had spread quicker than anything else and infected the brains of those with healthy bodies. It was a time when every person, diseased or not, had something eating away at their minds. That was five years ago and she'd never felt more alone.

She looked at her father's face inside the convex mirror and watched him while he drove. People could be so cruel and closed to lives they didn't understand.

Would her father ostracize her if he knew about her visions?

If he knew how the pearl spoke to her?

She suspected he'd do whatever Jude told him to do. She decided there and then to be Ansley's friend.

*

Jude picked up his megaphone and the bus jerked to a start. Ansley's balaclava was heavy and wet, but he kept it on for fear of making the girl behind him uncomfortable. He hadn't meant to scare her. Kind people generally smile at him before they involuntarily cringe. It may have been a long time since he'd been around humans, but their responses to his appearance were emblazoned on memory like hot iron against rawhide.

The bus entered a thick gully of hedges and stopped when it came to a crossroads. A directional sign for Winchelsea and Rye stood in front of them like a wooden weathervane. The bus turned towards Rye and soon the rolling fields of the South Downs were visible. In the distance, on top of a hill much higher than the hedge, Ansley could just make out the shape of a watching stag.

There was oil the last time Ansley was in Winchelsea and he and his father had actually driven their Land Rover. They were driving through a field bumpy with rocks and tree roots, when a huge herd of albino deer stepped out in front of the vehicle and stood with authoritative grace.

His father slammed on the breaks and Ansley banged his head against the roll bar. The headlights shone directly into the deers' knowing, blinking faces and Ansley froze in panic. His father slowly took his hand and squeezed it, then reached up and unfastened his rifle from its gun rack. If the deer were infected the smallest provocation could cause them to charge. A herd that size could destroy their truck; their communication to the world.

A few deer approached Ansley's window. His father took aim, but hesitated when he saw that their mouths were free of froth and their hides were without sores and intact. They showed no sign of infection, rather appeared to be peaceful, silvered beasts that seemed to have manifested from the moon. When Ansley looked at them it was like witnessing himself as an animal. His father sensed it too.

"They recognize you as one of their own," he said and lowered his rifle. "Beautiful creatures."

His father often called him a beautiful creature and although Ansley knew the term was derived from kindness, the implication that Ansley was less human and more animal hurt him. Ironically, this animalistic trait that caused his offence was certainly the property that kept him alive.

On the drive home Ansley remembered watching silver tinted rabbits and vegetable patches flash through the gaps in the hedgerows as quick as photographs. He captured them in his memory as the time before the land was entirely contaminated, when nobody could conceive of the windfall of hardship that lay ahead.

That was seven years ago. He shrugged it off; he was a different person now, he knew hunger and death.

Ansley looked out the window of the bus. The tinkling of the crystal chandelier bumped dim shadows up and down the aisle that reminded him of how he imagined spirits might appear. He had been walking for so long that it felt strange to be inside a vehicle. It was the motion of being at sea and even the bruise-coloured hills seemed fluid somehow, as if their wounds had leaked. Ansley opened up his backpack and took out a large Ziploc bag containing a notebook and pen. He opened it up and wrote the lines:

Night brushes over
the burnt out houses
and deserted places
like tar across seeping wounds
will harden the poison in
until it's dry enough to crack,
you.

The pewter rain and the chiming crystal proved a spellbinding combination and eventually, even Jude retired his megaphone and stood, as though at a helm, with the alert expectancy of arrival.

Ansley pulled his hood around his face and watched the world pass. The horizon blazed blue. He didn't know where he was going, but at least he was dry and there was the promise of food. He had learnt to stop anticipating the future and live for the present. "Plans need to be flexible when life is erratic," his father used to say.

It had been two years since his father's death, and still, the image of his work boot sizzling inside the charred crater that had once been their house, could kick against his chest like a timepiece.

The back of the bus was dark. The small moon was behind the clouds. Marianne made sure her father wasn't looking, then quickly slid into Ansley's seat. He responded to her as though she were a wasp. He was shocked at the closeness of her, at her smell of damp hair and faint lavender. He pressed himself against the window, but she only moved closer and whispered.

"Don't you know writing is illegal?"

4.

He nodded his head, yes.

"Did Jude ask you to write something?" He shook his head no.

"So what were you doing then?"

He couldn't speak to her. He had hardly spoken in two years. Words arrived readily through his hands and he wrote them, but seldom did they find their way to his throat. He gave her his open notebook and she read the poem he had written. She closed the book and handed it back to him silently.

"I see," she said. "I see why you'd risk it. That's incredible," she said. "But keep it a secret. You'll be banished, or worse, if you're caught writing something outside of the doctrine. Especially if it's personal," her voice was barely audible and her breath smelled of berries.

She snuck a look in her father's direction and slid back into her own seat. In the window she caught his reflection and put a finger to her lips. Shhh. Remember, she mouthed.

Her presence remained in his seat for a few seconds after she'd left as though she'd moved too fast for her molecules to catch her. It had happened quickly. Why did she care about his writing? Furthermore, why did she care if he was punished?

It hadn't occurred to him that the old rules would still apply. He lived alone and wrote what he wanted. He couldn't believe she had talked to him without gagging. The last female he'd spoken to had been his mother and even she had to hide her revulsion.

The ban on Expressions of Personal Self, or EPS's, was a failing government's desperate act to preserve normalcy through mass conformity. By limiting expression through the written word they hoped to prevent rebellion and turn back the clock to before the printing presses had liberated citizens from the domination of the church. It had worked during the Consumer Age after all. The propaganda started small and stated things like "Contamination is a mental disease that's contagious." Very soon people began to wonder if contamination was contagious from mind to mind and why not? Nobody knew much about contamination and the world had become unrecognizably absurd in a very short time. Anything seemed possible. Soon EPS's were cautioned against and eventually, illegal.

All of this had little influence on Ansley. His father supported and encouraged his writing because he knew it eased Ansley's loneliness, and anyway, they were so reclusive, that there was no chance of being caught. After the government's collapse he assumed there was nobody left to enforce the old rules, let alone catch him.

Ansley watched the castle swell into view beyond the windswept hedges. It was a dour collection of four stone towers whose walls had partially crumpled over time. The word craggy came to mind. A few thin rectangular windows shone like open slashes of brilliance, so that it appeared both foreboding and warm. Ansley was filled with a disquieting intrigue as though he had spotted his name in a life-changing letter and couldn't decide if he wanted to continue reading or not.

If the girl stays, he thought, I'll stay.

The bus parked outside the castle. Most of the passengers were asleep with their bodies stretched across the seats and their heads propped up against the windows. Jude removed an arm from his chandelier and walked down the aisle kicking the soles of their feet.

"Okay, people, that's enough of the formless and void! Wake up!" He pounded on the back of the seats.

Ansley, being nocturnal, hadn't slept and surveyed his surroundings while the others woke. The castle was fortified by a tall stone wall that was falling apart. A spray of the sea leapt over it and shattered across a large puddle a few yards from an ironclad door. Stone castles don't make good rafts, thought Ansley.

He knew Rye; his house had been on the other side of the woodland that encircled the village and he had fished its harbour with his father. There were few places that didn't haunt him with their familiarity. His father was a resourceful man, and functioning by night, meant that they often had only each other for company.

The iron door opened and expelled a tiny man, no bigger than a toddler, carrying a folded coat and an umbrella. Ansley had never seen a man so small and couldn't help watching him. The Keeper let him on the bus. He climbed up, stood on the back of the seat and snapped open a black mackintosh. Jude put it on and the little man jumped up on his shoulders, poised with the umbrella. The rustling on the bus stopped as everyone's attention was focused on Jude and his shoulder escort.

"This is a cherub," Jude explained. "Inside the castle you will find a whole tribe of them. I discovered their existence in the vine-choked wilds of the Amazon rainforest, years ago, when I was a budding microbiologist and they have been my companions ever since. It's true that their baby faces can make them seem beguiling, but they're actually undomesticated beings that are best left alone. They exist to be of service and eventually you will become so accustomed to their presence that you'll no longer recognize it as unnatural. Now, exciting discoveries await you inside, so come along," he said and walked off the bus.

The cherub opened the umbrella and held it over Jude's head like a trained monkey. It was very strange and dreamlike and Ansley felt tempted to run away, but the girl was the first to walk off the bus and follow Jude. Ansley was fascinated, as well as hungry, so joined the others in a silent herd. The Keepers directed them through the iron door and inside the castle hall. It was round and damp. The water moving around the stone sounded like a settling stomach. There were thirty-three of them all together, thirty-three new survivors, packed inside a small room.

Their breath was panting and most of them were emaciated. In his mind Ansley lifted the roof like a lid and saw battered warriors, bone to bone, in a stone bucket. The room was quite dark, but for a single light bulb that sputtered like a candle catching damp. He searched for the girl and when he saw her, his heart sank.

She entered alongside the four other Keepers. The Keeper that had driven the bus put his hand assertively on the girl's shoulder. Their resemblance was striking. How had he missed it before? He chastised himself. She was his daughter, which meant their friendship had ended before it'd begun and Ansley was stuck inside the castle.

5.

The Keepers dispersed evenly along the walls. Their backs were erect and their hands were clasped in front of their abdomens. They were wearing black and silver shiny tracksuits, were well fed and outrageously lavish in comparison to the survivors. The girl disappeared into the crowd.

Jude walked in, stepped up onto a podium that made him at least five heads taller than everyone else, readjusted his top hat and cleared his throat with intent.

"OPULENCE!" He shouted and clapped his hands. "I'm ready for my opulence!"

The room was stunned, but for the digesting walls, and waiting. Then ten cherubs bounced in like circus performers. Nine of them stood on top of one another's shoulders and erected like a centipede beside Jude. The tenth rode on the shoulder of a Keeper who was carrying the crystal chandelier. Number ten lit a cigarette, grabbed the chandelier, jumped up on top of the giant human centipede and held the chandelier over Jude.

White moths dancing inside the stone bucket, thought Ansley, but he didn't dare to take out his notebook.

Jude took a deep breath and relaxed. "You are late," he berated the tiny men through gritted, smiling teeth. "How hard is it to follow me around with a chandelier? I'm the one who has to do all the thinking for goodness sake. All I expect you to do is provide the atmosphere," he said, then faced his audience and readjusted his voice to a higher level. "Welcome to Project Nigh! Now, I know you're tired, but let's just take a moment to look around and greet one another," he clasped his hands and waited for a sufficient amount of time to pass.

Ansley studied the cherubs. They wore soiled togas and had bows with a quiver of arrows attached to their backs. They looked rank and stinky. The one on the top of the centipede didn't seem fazed by holding up a chandelier four times his weight. He seemed unnaturally strong as he blew smoke rings, like little halos, above Jude's head.

Jude continued. "These are the blessed faces of your fellow survivors. I ask that you treat one another with honour," he removed his top hat, disintegrated the smoke rings and took a deep bow.

"Here, inside these sturdy walls, I will provide you with nourishment and rest, but it is up to you to foster companionship," he fumbled for a moment and then lifted his hand and read his palm. "Ahem. Companionship is the cornerstone of this project, for you will be working together, rotating your skills and growing food."

There was a nervous murmur in the crowd. Jude seized the excitement.

"That's right! Food! Alongside this castle is one of England's last remaining uncontaminated fields!" He punched his fist in the air and two more cherubs flew in holding 'applause' placards.

Jude adjusted his purple cravat. The Keeper's started clapping and everyone else followed with an unsteady applause that grew in momentum.

"Thank you," Jude raised his voice over the applause. "Thank you. But the credit belongs to you for surviving. Let me explain. Project Nigh is a simple organization that completely depends on your spirit and cooperation for success. The Keepers and I will shelter and guide you in return for your help in the field. This will enable us to survive the apocalypse together and emerge as a pure, uncontaminated species. It's a simple division of labour that's beneficial to all of us, a win-win," he paused and smiled.

"But that's enough talking for this evening. We are all exhausted and need a good night's sleep. Of course, in the morning, you are under no obligation to stay, but I can't imagine what you'd do otherwise," he cleared his throat and ran a finger across his neck to indicate certain death.

"In a few moments the Keepers will show you to the dormitory, where there are rooms with clean linen for each of you, but first, I'd like to leave you with one final thought to muse upon: if death is natures greatest filter then you, my friends, must be here for a jolly good reason. Think about it. Goodnight and sweet dreams," he said and the cherub centipede dismantled, flew up into a pinwheel formation and held the chandelier above him as he left the room. The Keepers followed.

A bug could be heard tapping against the light bulb. Slowly, the survivors began to acknowledge one another, and because eyes can infer the hearts knowledge, a branch of understanding spread from face to face and linked them to the weight of shared experience. It was a good idea. They could grow food and endure the future together. There would be a future.

Ansley's appearance kept him from being the forthcoming sort, but he too felt uplifted, and peeked out from under his hood. The sense of companionship was tactile. It felt light and unexpected, like a sudden cloud in the room, and for a moment his ugliness was sheathed in the terrible fact that each of them had lived, while the ones they'd loved the most, had not.

He saw her scratching her head. She caught him staring, waved and walked towards him. He looked around for her father, but he was gone.

"My pets," she said about her fleas then laughed a sad, yet resigned laugh, threw back her head and snorted. It was horse-like and strong. "Let's just get this over with and out of the way," she said and before he could object, she'd pulled down his hood, lifted his balaclava and, swallowing hard, studied his face without wincing. "Yep, that settles it," she said of his demonic appearance, "we must be in hell."

He snatched his balaclava back into place and stared at her in bewildered amazement. She was unbelievably brazen and he felt like slapping and hugging her at the same time. She just laughed.

"I like to leave people tongue tied," said Marianne.

The Keepers emerged back into the hall to allocate rooms and hand out keys.

"Go on," she said. "You don't want to be left out. I'll see you at breakfast."

"Are you trying to get me killed?" Ansley managed to pry the words out of his mouth.

"Of course not, why?" She was visibly surprised that he'd asked such a question.

"Talking to you would give your father the excuse he needs to strangle me. He is your father, right?"

"Unfortunately, yes, but please don't hold it against me. And, seriously, don't worry. It's practically a prerequisite that Keeper's are all brawn and no brains. We can out smart him. Besides, you were writing poetry under Jude's nose, which is nothing short of a death warrant. Wait a minute. You're not afraid of me are you?"

"I'm not sure," he lied.

He was completely afraid of her, quite simply because she didn't seem afraid of him, which meant that she might unearth him. He feared the things he'd buried to stay alive, but not so much that he could resist her offer of friendship. He'd never had a friend. He'd only had his father.

"What's your name?" He asked as the two Keepers walked over to them.

"Marianne," she curtsied and approached the Keepers.

She took a handful of keys and began distributing them to the remaining survivors. Every key was tagged with a room number that she read aloud and recorded before she pressed it into each startled hand. Eventually she reached Ansley.

"And last but not least," she said. "Room number thirty," she wrote in the small book.

Her voice was purely secretarial and her cool eyes revealed nothing, as though she were proving to him that she could keep a secret.

"Goodnight everyone," she said and left the hall without glancing back.

"Marianne" he repeated to himself. Marianne. And he felt her instantly become his one word for everything.

Marianne,
All the words are yours.
I imagine they will become a record of how I burned
myself up, like gunpowder inside a firecracker,
just to explode in your sky.
Nobody else has ever looked at me.
Nobody.

*

It was easy for the pearl to bring them together. The maps inside their minds reflected one another like mirrored signals. They each saw themselves as alone, yet strong, with a sense of something greater and beyond their current condition. It is why they recognized one another immediately. That's how it works when humans meet. They respond to the image they see of themselves inside the other's presence. And what Ansley and Marianne saw in one another was the thing they held the most secret, the most private: their shared ability to hear the world's different frequencies. Ansley's gateway was his poetry. For Marianne it was her visions, the very pearl itself.

6.

Their dorm rooms were in a big two-storey extension attached to the castle that hadn't been visible from where the bus had parked. The walls were a blinding white and the hallway was long and austere. The Keeper had explained that each keychain had a number on it that opened a corresponding door.

A large group of them shuffled into the hallway silently looking for their rooms. It felt a bit like checking yourself into a hospital, as it was very clinical and in complete contrast to the stone quirkiness of the castle itself. But Ansley wasn't complaining. Since the bombing, he had been living in a makeshift camp in the woods and now he had a bed, a desk, a closet and his own toilet. This was like being swaddled in luxury.

He opened up his backpack, took out his notebook and immediately wrote down the poem he'd been mentally repeating from earlier. He didn't want to forget it. He placed his lucky rock with the ammonite inside it and a pheasant feather on his desk, which eased the room of its sterility, then kicked off his shoes and laid down on the bed thinking about Marianne.

He couldn't believe she'd pulled up his balaclava and didn't recoil or even flinch. She looked him straight in the eye. Who was she? And what was this place? It was truly bizarre. Jude was an obvious eccentric, but that wasn't what unsettled Ansley, for he sensed a deeper hidden meaning behind Project Nigh and that Jude wasn't being entirely honest. He knew he should leave. That something dangerous was afoot, but Marianne compelled him to stay and his heart raced every time he thought of her. He was too anxious to rest, so rose from the bed and stood by the window.

He had a view of the sea where he once fished with his father. After the floods they had had to manoeuvre their boat around the chimneystacks and spinning weathervanes of the swallowed houses. It had been eerie to think of an underwater village corroding beneath them like a modern Atlantis. It had been an image that had haunted him afterwards, as it seemed to reflect how he lived his life, unseen and buried. Like treasure, his father had said, but Ansley suspected it was more like desertion.

And now the arrival of a tide that was unexpected, a bus, a girl and a trace of hope. Perhaps the worst was over, he thought as he watched the street below, unable to convince himself.

Jude and a group of Keepers walked uphill along a terraced row of workmen's cottages. One by one they entered the front doors and turned on the lights. Electricity was a luxury and generator fed, but God only knew how they powered the generators, waves perhaps, or sunlight? His father had told him there was a community here, a religious sect isolated by its landscape.

Rye sat in between the South Downs and vast woodland. The sea spread out in front of it. Most of the main roads leading in and out had been bombed or earthquaked into rubble and only the lanes that the hedgerows or fires hadn't reclaimed were usable. It was remote and lonely, but perhaps that's why it had been saved. Like myself, he thought.

At the top of the street and perched like a weather-beaten sentry, a manor house looked out to sea. Jude, small as Ansley's index finger, disappeared between two tall entry hedges and moments later, lit his windows. An old stone wall connected his house and the cottages to the castle and its courtyard, so that the whole enclosure formed an L. Inside this L spread the uncontaminated field, beyond which, was the dense woodland where Ansley had been living since the bombing, for he had needed a place to shelter from the daylight.

He watched the dark shadow of Jude move around the manor house. It slowed his heartbeat and made his skin feel cold. All the same, Jude had let them live and Ansley was intuitive enough to know that with his modified genes there were certainly people that wanted him dead. The confusion of genetic disorder and contamination was what kept Ansley secluded for so long.

Contamination had reached the end of its lifespan. Those that were infected now were highly noticeable with sores and erratic twitches. In the final stages, their muscles completely eroded and they could be found slumped into piles, waiting until their hearts stopped. On the one occasion when Ansley encountered a person in meltdown he had to think of them as a fallen boulder. He constantly had to teach his mind to play tricks in order to retain his sanity.

Yet, here they were, a small group of survivors that had escaped the windfall of apocalypse. It felt inconceivable, almost as though it were another hoax his mind was playing in order to believe persisting for a future was worthwhile. It must be worth it, he thought, we must make life worth what we've endured somehow. He thought of Marianne, a purpose outside of his daily survival, she produced in him a small shift of faith that brought his equilibrium closer to balance. He dared to hope. The fires burned like blue faraway cities. How many others were out there? Nobody like her. He knew that for certain.

7.

When Ansley opened the door to the dining hall his chest gave a jolt at the sight of the food spread out on a long table near the kitchen. It was an extravagant breakfast banquet of pancakes and silver bowls of mixed berries, apples, peaches, porridge, fresh bread and jam. It was dark in the room, even though it was morning, as the day was overcast and the windows were narrow and few, so candelabras burned in the centre of each table. The room sparkled with the atmosphere of a party.

There were lots of people eating, chatting and laughing, some he noticed from the bus and others he'd never seen before. His pink eyes flashed from his balaclava like neon signs, but everyone was far too captivated by the food to notice. The selection was intoxicating. He decided to enjoy one thing at a time and sat in the corner, away from the windows, eating a plate of blueberries.

He was tired. The cherubs had sounded their trumpets at seven o'clock in the morning, which was torturous for a nocturnal being. He was going to have to adjust his sleeping patterns, but that would mean spending the day indoors. All the same, he'd been hungry, so he put on his balaclava and walked down to breakfast.

Marianne joined him. Her hair was shoulder length, black and messy. She wore a tee shirt with a picture of a finger up a nose that read 'free handshakes.' She had a nose ring the circumference of a five pence coin. He noticed there was something different about her.

"I cut myself a fringe last night," she said as if they had always been friends. "Do you like it?" She sat down.

"It looks great," he said, trying to be casual but feeling as though he might choke with excitement, first blueberries, now her.

"I didn't realise there were any banks left to rob," she patted the top of his balaclava and he involuntarily smiled. It was a mistake and he sunk with shame as soon as he'd done it.

"Are those your real teeth?" She mashed strawberries into her porridge and mixed it up.

"Unfortunately, yes," he brought his hand up to his mouth.

"What are you? The devil or something?" She took a big bite of porridge. "Ahhh, strawberry," she said with her mouth full.

Although she could be brutally honest, she seemed more curious than disgusted by him and he began to relax.

"No. Nothing so powerful. I was born like this. It's my genes. I don't have any sweat glands or melanoma or things like that. I'm usually awake during the night because exposure to sunlight could kill me. But I heard there were pancakes on the menu."

"Huh," she thought for a moment. "So you mean you don't stink?"

He shook his head no.

"Then we are definitely going to be friends. I don't know if you've noticed, but most of these people smell so bad it makes my eyes water."

"Brilliant," he said and ate a few blueberries. "These are so good! How could I ever go back to mushrooms, weeds and cobnuts?"

"Is that what you've been eating?" Marianne asked.

"It sounds worse than it actually was. My father taught me to forage and spot uncontaminated rabbits. By the looks of things I was one of the lucky ones," he said glancing around at the emaciated faces.

"I know. It's painful to see," she said.

"I keep wondering where he gets all the food? And those dorms. Jesus. I feel a bit like a bribed lab rat." He took another blueberry from the plate. "But these blueberries are delicious, so what the hell?"

"The food is from the uncontaminated field and the greenhouses. We grow it," she said.

"I still find that incredible. How long has it been going on?"

"Years now," she said. "We kept it secret until the population was too weak to attack us or already dead," she took a bite of porridge. "I never agreed with it," she spoke in a whisper. "But now that Natural Selection has taken place, he's promised to share the food with all of the survivors, hence the bus missions."

"And that corrects it?" Ansley was indignant. "That just corrects the fact that you've kept food from starving people?"

"In the beginning there was really only enough for us," she said.

"Lucky you," he sneered.

"Please don't. You have to understand, I'm not like them," she looked in the direction of a Keeper and lowered her voice again, "I don't believe in Jude, I don't even like him. He just completely bewitched my father and there was nothing we could do. It's totally destroyed my family," she stared at her hands in her lap as she spoke.

Ansley had heard that Jude wielded an incredible power over people and many devoted themselves to his doctrine after just one encounter. His father called it brainwashing. Keep your mind clean and sharp, his father had said, because there is always some nutcase that will try to wash it for you. He wasn't going to argue that the fear of contamination made people do completely irrational things, but hiding an uncontaminated food source was criminal. Lives could have been saved.

"I don't really understand why we're talking," he said. "Your father must see me as one of the impure."

"Yes," her voice was conspiratorial, "but he doesn't know anything."

"And you do?"

"I don't think of you as impure. Quite the opposite really," she shimmered with her secret. "You and I were meant to meet," her father walked through the door and she ducked down. "I've got to go."

"Wait, what do you mean, 'meant to meet'?"

"Can you keep a secret?" Marianne asked.

"You're risking us both by talking to me, so, blatantly, yes."

"Good. I'll come for you tonight," she said and stood to leave. "Be ready," she cupped her hand over his like a tortoise shell and walked away.

8.

Marianne was a born clairvoyant and so was easy for the pearl to infiltrate. It simply planted its clamshell at the bottom of her mind and dreamed her into its watery world. These dreams were surprising. It's always interesting what the mind conjures up inside of an abyss. Sure, there were plummets of blue, tentacles and corals, but often, there were dreams of soil and air and skies full of wings with green places to expand in growth. And the mollusc, like a tongue, hummed these dreams to the pearl and it matured inside this song, waiting for its release.

One day, the mollusc hummed Marianne swimming. She was a small girl then. Her laugh was like a faraway church bell reverberating through the water. The pearl knew it'd be safe with her, so it rose as a vision, a bubble from the deep that, every so often, popped in her imagination and lingered like a word that is searched for before it's spoken.

The pearl was patient and hushed. It foresaw her father fishing in the cove and casting his net where the sun glittered on the water like a thousand pearls. And when that day finally came, the pearl was ready for him.

*

The morning her father found the pearl, he'd taken the boat out at dawn and, from the warmth of her bed, Marianne had listened to him leave. She pictured him out there, diminished against the iron sea that corroded the buildings, the houses, shops, museums and the old factory its waters had reclaimed and were digesting. The mists smelled metallic, the air was so thick with minerals that it sat in your mouth and coated your skin like extra cells.

The sea made her think of her Nan. Before the flood her Nan's house had sat on the edge of the shore. It was a squat stone cottage with a black gate like a row of stitches that kept the sand at bay. Her Nan had called it a wart on a smooth sandy brow. Her Nan had taught herb lore to her mother and the two of them together smelled as glorious as a ploughed field.

Marianne pictured the cottage inside its new tidal home, covered in barnacles and sea urchins with little mouths that sucked through her Nan's bric-a-brac, her blue medicinal bottles, Aga and fine bone china. She pictured jellyfish floating in and out of her rooms as delicate as doilies and her green wingback chair, sand lodged and sodden.

They never found her Nan's body, but then, most of the south of England had gone that way, quiet and stoic into the sea. There were a few who rose like bruised balloons, floated and rolled to the New Shore, but Marianne had only a vague memory of those days.

She was still very young when the men who had seen war patrolled the beach with binoculars and spades. She could remember clouds of incense and prayers as constant as wind.

But eventually time had licked them clean, just as her mother had said it would, and now the New Shore was a cesspool of reeds and treasure. The most remarkable things pitched up there, pots, kettle lids, knives, end tables, latches and frames to name a few. Marianne spent many afternoons rummaging through the reeds with her waders and mechanical arm.

It was where she learned to believe in magic, for the New Shore was rife with enchantment, and the day her father cast his fishing net over the pearl was no exception.

She had left the house a few hours after him with a belly full of porridge and a glass jar. The newts were plentiful. She loved to put them inside the jar and watch their thin membrane bellies breathing.

She squelched her way into the valley of the New Shore. She was completely alone apart from a few thin egrets that tiptoed across the bog. A yellow field of black-stemmed rapeseed blanketed the hill beside her, beyond which, the town of Hastings crouched like a brown calcified animal with fires burning all around it. When she entered the valley she could no longer see Hastings and the air grew muddier, thicker, as did the gnats. But thicker still was a privacy that had the glaze of a dream.

A cloud of insects hovered above a rectangular shape cloaked in seaweed. She walked closer. She pinched the seaweed with her mechanical arm and it slid off into two pieces revealing a black cage. A perfect parakeet perched inside it like a trapeze skeleton; truly, the skeleton looked embroidered in the air. The poking end of her mechanical arm just squeezed between the bars and when she touched the bird, it crumbled, turned to power, swirled past the bars of its cage and swarmed through the sky.

She followed it.

Her waders were heavy and the tide was coming in, so whenever she stopped to catch her breath she could feel the water compress the rubber against her legs. She struggled to keep going. The swarm hovered in front of a tall old wood-carved clock that was stuck inside a sand dune. She had walked past it a thousand times, but had never heard it strike, yet when she approached, the clock began to chime.

It's face opened and the swarm entered through a hole in the dial. Moments later the door for a cuckoo opened, but instead of releasing a little bird, a thin silver ring dangled out on the mechanism spring. Marianne recognized it straight away.

It was her Nan's nose ring. She took it from its perch, closed her eyes, winced and pushed it through her nostril. Blood and tears dripped into the seawater and swirled in a circular pattern that glowed. She put her finger in the middle of the circle and it dissolved. She knew that something was beginning, something beyond her visions, something tangible and real. She felt herself altering like a change in temperature. It was a phenomenon that she could not stop.

"What is happening?" She asked because she was accustomed to the world answering her questions.

And so it did.

In her mind she saw the sunken clamshell. It began to crack open and the light inside of it was as bright as a star.

9.

The pearl's cove was one of the only places that remained virtually untouched by the flooding. Of course the water levels rose, but the cove resembled its former self and no debris cluttered its waters. It was a beautiful place to fish. Marianne's father trawled the pearl in on his first cast.

He came back for lunch and handed Marianne the clamshell. She was hanging her wet waders up in the laundry room, so dried her hands on her trouser legs and sceptically took it from him. It was the clamshell of her vision. She was not accustomed to gifts from her father, as they had never been close, and had grown even further apart since his role as a Keeper. But the pearl told him to give her its clamshell. It made its voice as loud as God's.

"It's alright," he met her doubt. "It won't bite."

"Thank you," she said and opened the clamshell slowly.

There it was: the perfect pearl, the exact one that she had dreamed. It wasn't simply white, but pink, blue and cream all churning together like summer clouds. It immediately burned a vision behind her eyelids to express that it was real and her heart quickened with excitement.

"It's a miracle," she said, feeling breathless and light.

"Well," her father said. "You can get a lot from a bit of dirt."

*

"Daddy, it's amazing, thank you,' said Marianne.

Her mother placed bread and honey on the table.

"You're welcome. But…wait a minute! Come here," he took her chin and moved her face to the side. "What have you done to your nose?"

"Stuck a ring in it," she shrugged her shoulders.

"Marianne, that's a defilement of your senses," he said.

Her mother laughed and nearly choked on her tea.

"Oh for goodness sake, Harold, my own mother had a nose ring just like that, remember? And have you forgotten that you once had hair long enough to plait?"

"Times have changed, Janet."

"Times repeat, Harold, but they don't change as much as people do. Now just stop it or I'll be forced to use my photographic evidence against your saintly hood," she said.

"You know we're not allowed pre-initiation photographs, Janet," her father was angry.

"I'm not saying that I have them here, just that I know where they are in the old house. I'm sure nobody has raided your ugly mug," her mother said.

"So you'd actually walk back to our old house just to…"

"Look, Harold, it was a joke. I'm not walking anywhere. Just forget I even said it," her mother interrupted and rubbed her temples.

He grunted and went to the door. The lame material of his shiny tracksuit swished against his legs. He put on his hat and left without saying goodbye. There was a Keepers' meeting every Saturday afternoon.

"Off to meet the henchmen again," said Marianne.

She often teased that they secretly wore antlers on their heads and chanted psalms backwards. She was trying to cheer her mother up.

Her mother once laughed about the Keepers as well but, lately, she had become serious.

"It's important for people to have a purpose, you know. It keeps them ticking," she said and put her hand on Marianne's shoulder.

"Yeah right. But I reckon bee-keeping would be more effective than fanaticism," she said and took a bite of bread.

"I don't like you talking like that, Marianne. Jude's considered a minor God to this village, or what's left of it, and if anyone hears you, well, you'd be guilty of treason," her mother said as she crushed some seeds with her pestle.

"Treason! That's a bit harsh don't you think? You make it sound like a royal court or something. Off with her head!" She used her hand like an axe and chopped off her own head.

"Seriously, Marianne, don't fool around, it's beginning to feel like a dictatorship and it scares me, but I don't know what else to do. Where else would we find food? We can't risk leaving. We just have to bide our time and be careful with what we say."

"I know. I only say this stuff to you."

"Of course you do. Sorry, honey, I'm just sensitive at the moment. It drives me crazy too," she said mixing a tonic on the countertop. "Forgive me," she said placing the blue vial in her jacket pocket, superstitious or not, everyone still wanted her mother's homeopathic cures for their ailments.

She kissed Marianne's forehead and walked out the door. The house was silent. Marianne looked at the clamshell resting on the table. She opened it and saw the swirling again. She got up and walked out into the garden.

Their garden was an herbal pharmacy. Whenever her mother had found an uncontaminated plant she carefully dug it up and replanted it there. Her father called it a witch's meadow, but her mother always reminded him that she was from a long line of herbalists and he knew what he was getting himself into when he married her.

Marianne walked into the potting shed and opened the clamshell again. It was like opening a magic trunk lit from the inside. She touched the pearl with her finger and the very air around it wrinkled, as though it were made of silky invisible water.

What was she meant to do with it?

It reminded her of the fisheye she once plucked out of a mackerel. It had been equally mesmerizing and iridescent. The eye had been stuck inside the fish's head like the pearl was stuck inside the clam's tongue. Mackerel are only beautiful inside their own world, for the vibrancy of their scales begins to diminish as soon as they leave the water.

Marianne loved this type of commitment because, strange as it sounds, it made her think of her future. She had felt compelled to keep the fisheye, so carefully dissected it with her penknife and let its jelly drop in her hand. She replaced the eye with a small sequin of sea polished pottery that she had in her pocket. It perfectly fitted the fish's empty socket and she bid it safe passage.

Her visions were beginning to strengthen and she buried the fisheye in her mother's pharmacy because it had told her that it wanted to live underground. Bamboo grew in its place. Marianne sat next to it and let it whisper over her when she had a problem to solve.

Her mother understood the effervescence of nature. How sometimes when holding a rock, a feather or a bone, its touch could hit your body's water and send a fizz up your spine and through your hair. They shared the awareness that we are each different moulds of the same elements and how we transform depends so much on the voices we acknowledge.

Marianne listened to nature.

Her mother understood the fisheye. Her father did not. He regarded nature as a thing to be tamed or eaten. He thought singing rocks were absurd. She sat beneath the bamboo with the pearl in her hands, listening; she took some twine from the potting shed and threaded it through a small leather pouch. She dropped the pearl inside the pouch and fastened it around her neck.

It lived in the pouch for months and steadily grew in her mind. Strength takes time, like trust. She began to rely on the pearl more and more, spoke to it and held it in her confidence, so when tragedy struck, it was there for her.

Her best friend, Joan and her family went fishing and were lost in a storm at sea. Joan was the only friend Marianne had at the castle. Joan's father had also been a Keeper and they shared a distrust of Jude.

Marianne camped near the New Shore after hearing the news, pitched a tent in a dry yellow field. So many people were dying by the hands of weather or disease. Small poppies burst through the summer ground like blood blisters. She waited and searched for a clue, for a piece of Joan's boat, anything, but the sea had swallowed them whole.

In the evenings she built her own fire. It seemed the only thing alive. The waves crashed and whistled around the lost objects. The waves crashed and whistled around her. The pearl dug deep inside her then, it's light held her bones together as it weaved her back into feeling, muscle by sinew, with the thread of the story it revealed her future. She'd survive and not by submitting to fear. She saw herself standing on a hilltop; her face slowly morphing through skyscapes and ages, yet her eyes remained alert and forward watching.

Marianne could not widen her vision and witness more of her future self, but she was aware that the mind grows its focus and could feel herself expanding with power. The pearl told her that she was worthy of this power and it's the stories we're told about ourselves that matter, that keep us going or stop us dead.

10.

Ansley picked up the paper that had been slipped under his door during breakfast. A sheet of paper, real paper and the back of it was completely blank. He wondered how he could get his hands on everyone else's sheets as well. How did Jude manage to find these things? He must have stockpiles somewhere. He thought of the cherubs. Perhaps they flew around gathering like little minion hoarders. It was a note from Jude:

"Greetings from Project Nigh,
I hope you slept well and enjoyed your breakfast. The food you ate was grown here in our own field and is completely safe. The field is equipped with a polytunnel, heated greenhouse and a harvesting room. I will explain the logistics of your lodging now and answer any remaining questions tonight at dinner.
Here at the castle we like to get straight to the point.
Each of you is expected to work for three hours a day helping with the management of the grounds and allotment. Consider yourselves a lucky stakeholder in the new world. What you are harvesting is your future. You must clock in and out of work. Food is only to be consumed during mealtimes. Breakfast is at 7:00am, lunch is at 1:00pm and dinner is at 8:00pm. Times are exact and food is rationed amongst the Keepers and yourselves, so taking from the harvesting room or the field is considered theft. There are two laundry rooms at the end of each hallway for your use. Each dormitory has been fitted with a barrel of rainwater. It passes through a filtration system and into your bathroom, use your water sparingly and it should last you until the end of the month, when the barrels are refilled. Drinking water must be obtained from the kitchen. Feel free to come and go as you please, but don't leave the village, as there may still be impure members of the species lurking about and cross contamination is punishable by death. No exceptions. Attached is a sermon timetable, and yes, sermons are mandatory.
Love and peace,
The Prophet Jude."

'Cross contamination punishable by death' seemed a bit extreme, thought Ansley, but then, they were living in extreme times. He hadn't left the woodland at all during the Period of Disease. The Disease was a form of BSE that had been incorporated within the cytoplasm of a bacterium, making the prion infinitely more contagious as it could be transmitted from host to host and mutated violently once digested.

Ansley and his father had always grown, hunted or foraged for their food. They were intentionally isolated and their house was only accessible down a long wooden track. When they heard the new outbreak was considered a plague, his father felled loads of trees and let them fall haphazardly along the track, cutting them off entirely. His father was a survivalist, as well as a purist, who believed that food preservatives were a gateway to cancer. This belief kept them alive.

In the woodland they had buried an "emergency endurance kit" containing a cooking pot, rope, flint, stone and cotton wool, a blanket, tins of food, a tarpaulin and a penknife. They remained uninfected and had decided to wait out the plague.

You noticed the eyes of the diseased first; they looked sore, red and blinked continuously, then came the tongue blisters, the memory loss and muscle ticks. Worst of all victims spread the disease by airborne transmission so loved ones deserted the sick as they twitched involuntarily into the grave. People died alone.

Ansley had been collecting mushrooms on the night his house was bombed. Air raids were common in areas of high contamination in the early days as a desperate attempt to isolate and contain the sick. But they hadn't heard a plane in ages as the military's stockpiled resources were raided and the personnel disappeared. Probably just some renegade nutcase pilot, thought Ansley, before he realized something was wrong because the woodland had become completely silent. Then came the shrill mechanical noise and the impact of the bomb like the tremor of a beast underfoot. The rest he tried to block out.

He dug up their endurance kit and built a camp inside wild holly that was growing over a fallen tree like a curtain. It was on high ground, with a sentinel's view over a difficult terrain to navigate with contaminated legs. He saw nobody. Three months, his father had said, another three months and the worst would be over. He notched out the days on a trunk of wood.

All though the summer he waited. His father was right; after around three months, a silence descended the atmosphere, soft as snow, yet thick enough to suffocate, and he wondered if he were the last person on earth.

He ventured out and felt equal measures of relief and trepidation when he saw the lights of candles and fires built by other survivors. How could he approach them? With his appearance how would they believe that he wasn't infected? They wouldn't risk not killing him straight away. He had no choice but to keep his distance.

He was lucky that his father had taught him how to detect uncontaminated plants and exist in nature. His grief was shortened by his need for pragmatism, but nothing dulled his loneliness. His evenings alone showed him that he had been hardened in ways that he cared not to admit.

It was strange to be near people again. He'd forgotten the sound of his voice and the feeling of companionship. What did Marianne mean when she said they were meant to meet? She was coming for him tonight and the thought of this cracked through him like a great thaw. The sun was nothing but a red line of horizon like a string of ribbon along a dark package.

Soon, he thought, she'll be here soon.

11.

He was sitting at his desk writing when the rock hit his window. The electric desk lamp was dim, but a luxury. He clicked shut the brass clasp of his notebook, his most precious possession, as his father had given it to him for his poems. It was black snakeskin with lined paper and wide margins for his drawings. His father had traded an uncontaminated pumpkin for it, which was an incredibly expensive trade as it was a vegetable that retained its seeds.

But he wasn't thinking of that now. He was thinking only of Marianne. He looked out the window and saw Marianne standing on the grass like a phosphorescent mushroom. She smiled and motioned for him to come down.

He grabbed his coat and tiptoed through the door and down the hallway.

"So what's our secret mission?" He asked as he approached her.

She looked serious. She took his hand. "There is a cove I need to explore and I wanted someone to come with me. It's where this is from," she unfastened the pearl from her neck, opened the leather pouch and dropped it on her palm.

It glowed like a sorcerer's orb in the night.

"Is that a pearl?" He bent down to inspect it.

"It's not just any pearl, it's a magic pearl. No. Magic is not the right word. I don't know how to properly explain what it does, you see, I get these visions and I know that it's this pearl directing me somehow, it's like a source. That's it. The pearl is a source," her face glowed over the pearl's light, as though it wasn't attached to her body and she appeared to float.

"A source of what?"

"I'm not entirely sure, but it's greater than I am and makes me feel whole. Do you know what I mean?"

"Yes. My poems give me that feeling," he said, embarrassed to be admitting how he felt about his poetry.

"I knew you wouldn't think I was crazy. It's like having another level of instinct, right? I said we were meant to meet because the pearl told me you were important," she said.

"How does it tell you?" It seemed remarkable that they were having such a forthright conversation and he sensed that there would never be small talk between them.

"It drops a picture inside me that strangles out any other thought or sense. On the bus that picture was you, right now, it's the cliff-face beyond the cove," she said.

"Is that where we're going?" He asked.

"Yes. I have to tell you that it might be dangerous," she said and cocked her head to look at him.

He was strange, but that was just it, he was otherworldly, hence off the human radar and she felt, for this reason, that she could certainly tell him things. Specifically, the things that made her different, like her visions, like the pearl.

When she thought this, the pearl rose like a full moon behind her eyelids. She saw a hole, as a dark eye opening inside a wall of white chalk. Again, the pearl guillotined the image of the cliff through her brain.

"Then I've been warned," he said.

The danger didn't matter. They lived in a world of danger, and anyway, he had the feeling that she knew he'd do anything she asked.

They set off walking. The moon was directly above them and full. They talked until it was too windy for words and silence encased them comfortably. Every so often he turned and watched her face. It was chiselled with determination. He could tell that she was the type of person that fixated on things and when she made her mind up there was no stopping her. He was right.

"It's about a mile from here," she turned and said. They were heading towards Hastings. "Let's stop here for a bit, then walk along the cliff so we don't miss the cove."

She walked to a wind bent tree and sat down on the grass beneath it. It was tufted and encrusted with sand. "I just need a little rest," she said and began pulling the hair at her scalp as though she were trying to rip the idea out of her head.

"Are you okay?"

"Honestly, I'm fine. The image is just so heavy in my head that it makes me feel a little nauseous. I think I just need to eat," she took two peanut butter sandwiches from her satchel and handed one to him.

"Peanut butter?" It had been ages since he'd had peanut butter.

"I know, amazing isn't it? I found it in the castle kitchen cupboard and helped myself," she said.

"Isn't that theft? According to the letter...." He teased and she rolled her eyes.

He told her about how he and his father used to eat peanut butter sandwiches when they'd go night fishing. They had a little dinghy named 'The Worn Slipper' because when it was moored in the harbour it looked like a slipper in a giant's bathtub. The boat was thin enough to feel the power of the tide move beneath them, so they never strayed far from the land. The water then was midnight blue and if squelling were a word, it would describe the night sea impeccably, for it both swelled and squelched against their tiny vessel. He liked to put his hand in the water. Sometimes he would get a fright, pull his hand out quickly and cast his line in the direction of his fear, thinking it must be a fish.

His father had taken him out in the Slipper the night his mother left. He was eight years old and remembered the wind was ferocious against their faces. "The world is against us," his father had said and tacked the sail in the opposite direction, making the wind push against their backs. "Now the world is behind us and that's how fast it happens." Ansley had felt a great meaning pass between them that was both familiar and mysterious like a melody whose words he had yet to learn. He told Marianne about it.

"I know that feeling," said Marianne. "It's the feeling of prediction. That's what this pearl is for me."

They rose and walked the last mile along the edge. "Your arrival also feels like a prediction," she said after a while. "Is it true what they say about you?"

"I don't know. What do they say?" The wind stung his face.

"They call you Dark Ansley and say that your genes are contaminated," she said softly and gazed towards Hastings, its blue flames were rimmed with a brown night.

"I guess it's true. My genes aren't pure, at least not pure as you know it, but that doesn't make me less human." He was breathing so hard that his balaclava was moist. "I'm not contaminated and you don't need to fear me."

"Fear you?" She said with surprise. "I don't fear you. See that glow? You probably already know that's Hastings Blaze. I haven't been close enough to it to feel its heat, but I recognize its burn. It's heartless. Jude has that same burn. You do not. If anyone's impure or to be feared it's him, not you."

The wind lifted and twirled her hair like black streamers, it covered then exposed her face and she looked as though she were underwater. Moon water, he thought and turned to face the sea. The air caught his breath, it was salty and fierce and if he had been able to find the adequate words for a reply, the wind would have shoved them, along with his courage down his throat. So he didn't speak, but the silence filled anyway with meaning and gratitude.

This was their destination. It was difficult to determine where the sky ended and the water began, as both were turbulent and made dark backdrops to the moon's radiance. The cliffs were white, below which, he could hear the waves cracking against the rocks like a whip.

Marianne pointed to the cove and began to undress. She took everything off except her bra and underpants. She stood looking at him impatiently, her hair sticking out like some medusa. He bent down and took off his shoes. His head was spinning with worry. How could he expose his body to her? It was scarred and deformed.

"I'm not sure I can do this," he said. There was bile in his mouth.

"I promise I won't look," she said.

He believed her, but felt a paralysis pour through his body like cement and stood unmoving.

"Okay. I'm sorry I wasn't thinking. Of course you don't have to undress. Just wait here for me," she said and disappeared over the side.

"Marianne!" He ran to the edge and breathed a sigh of relief when he saw her hands clutching tufts of sea grass as she scaled down the cliff.

"Don't worry, I've done this before," she grinned up at him.

He quickly stripped down to his boxers. His body would be hidden inside the water, he thought and at any rate he could hardly let her go on her own. There was brave and there was reckless and she definitely looked the latter. The cliff was cold and moist with chalk like wet sandpaper. He tried his best to scale down it gracefully, but scraped and dropped until he reached the bottom of the rocks. The wind was no longer a freight train and their eardrums went warm with relief.

They walked along the base of the chalk cliff and Marianne ran her hand across its surface. He could feel her thinking and followed her silently. She looked at her hand. Her white palm glowed. They were on the side of the cove that was lit by the moon. The other half was in shadow. She took both hands, rubbed them against the chalk and then all over her face.

She could tell from his expression that her face had turned white. She broke a piece off the wall, licked it and smeared it over her skin like war paint. Then walked to the edge of the sea and screamed. And like a game, the sea threw back her scream, she laughed and screamed again.

"There!" She pointed towards a stack of chalk about fifty metres from the shore. "That's it! That's where we need to go!"

12.

The stack looked as though it were made of marble. Although it had once
been a part of the cove, it had detached from the rest of the cliff years
ago and stood alone like a skeletal finger poking out of the sea. The waves
moved up and down it with great speed.

Marianne looked as though she, too, were made of marble and glistened.
She was speaking rapidly, but Ansley couldn't understand what she was
saying as the sea dwarfed her, drowned her sound.

For a moment, he felt scared and looked behind him, and when he
turned back around he saw that Marianne was gone. His heart jumped.
He searched the waves and found her bobbing up and down as natural as a
seagull, waiting for him.

Come on, she beckoned.

He could see her white rock face and her teeth flashing like barnacles,
of course he dived in. The water was cold and it took his breath away. He
gave his body to it reluctantly. The tide was coming in quickly now and
swimming was difficult. More than once the water went over his head, but
he kept going, kept following Marianne and eventually they made it to the
stack.

It towered above them. She kept as close to the stack as she could and he
mimicked her movements. They swam around it and she pointed up to what
looked like a small cave. She swam to the bottom of the rock, found a finger
hold, lifted herself up and began to scale the wall.

Ansley looked up the wall, like scanning a skyscraper, and saw that
there were natural battered footholds. Thank God, he thought. He kept his
stomach pressed firmly against the rock, it was cold, wet and gritty and he
could feel it tearing the goose pimples on his skin.

Where the hell was she taking us? Little white rocks fell on his head every
time she moved and his eyes were watering from chalk dust. He had to
keep blinking in order to see and the blurriness gave him a sickening sense
of vertigo. He didn't need to look down. He could feel the water swirling
beneath him. It shook the rock and the stack shifted, almost growled, with
its power. He felt it rising as though it were coming after him and wanted to

suck him down.

Marianne's body finally popped over a jut in the cliff and disappeared. He knew she had reached the top. Seconds later he pulled himself up beside her, gasping and clearing his eyes of powder. They stood at the entrance to a small cave. She grabbed his hand and yanked him inside.

"Just look at it Ansley – have you ever seen anything so incredible?" She turned around in a circle and then stopped when she saw him.

He had never exposed so much of his skin before. Only his parents had seen him undressed.

"It's brilliant," he said. "How did you…what?" He could feel her looking at him.

"I'm sorry, I just…" she turned away embarrassed.

"Is it my skin?" he felt very self-conscious and ridiculous.

"No! Yes, but not how you mean it. I mean it's, well it's like this cave. It's like nothing I've seen before," she said, keeping her head turned away. "Ansley, do you mind if I look?"

How could he say no? They were standing half naked in a cave together. It was already excruciatingly uncomfortable, but excruciating in a way that felt soothing as well, like scraping off dead skin. Her voice was so delicate and measured; he could tell that it was a difficult situation for her as well.

"Okay," he said, "but be quick." *Like a gunshot*, he thought, *your eyes straight through me.*

She turned around and circled him staring intensely. He stood completely still. The scars on his body were frayed at the edges like veins in marble. She could see his arteries as well as his ribs. He's nymph-like, she thought and touched his arm. Her fingers were wet and cold but her palm was warm.

"You're really beautiful," she said.

They looked at one another and before he knew what was happening he kissed her, lightly on the lips.

13.

She returned his kiss and then backed away. He kept fluctuating between nymph and monster like a hologram. She couldn't control her sudden revulsion.

"Sorry," she said. "Sorry," she shook her head and tried to dislodge the image.

"It's okay," he wanted to change the subject. "It's too quick. I lost control for a minute," loss of control or not, she'd kissed him back which was more than he felt he had a right to hope for.

They stood avoiding one another for an awkward moment. It felt like hours, years.

"So tell me what we're looking for," he said to change the subject.

"That's the strangest part; I'm not exactly sure what we'll find. I'll know it when I see it, if that makes any sense," she said, grateful to speak about something else.

"It makes perfect sense," he said. Like everything about you, he thought. "Did you even know this cove was here?"

"I've seen it from my dad's boat, but I thought it was just a seabird perch or something, until the vision arrived, like an obsession, like I didn't own my body. I just had to come here, I had to, and as soon as I saw the stack I knew this cave was where I needed to be."

"Why here?"

"I'm not sure Ansley, but it feels right."

"Good enough for me. Let's look around."

He had to admit it was stunning. It was like being inside the fold of a doves white wing. It was conical and narrow. At the top, about twelve metres above them, was a small hole that the moon shone through, illuminating layer after layer of damp chalk, sculpted like wet feathers. On the side of the wall, six metres up, was another hole that was rippled like a knot in a tree trunk. Sea wind blew through them both.

"It's like a giant blowing into a conch shell," Marianne said.

He ran his hand along the chalk. "I thought chalk was too soft for caves?"

"They're rare and shallow. This one won't be here in ten years, maybe even less than that, so we're lucky. Listen," she cleared her throat. "Thank you for coming with me Ansley. It would've been really dangerous and stupid to come by myself and to be honest, I wanted you here. You see, you remind me of my pearl, the colour of you, I mean."

"Well you couldn't really ask anyone else now could you?" he tried to make his voice sound light.

"Yeah. But something is happening Ansley, I can feel it, something big and bold and wonderful."

"Yeah I can feel it too." That something is you, he thought.

"What's that?" She said walking towards a wall sculpted in white undulating waves.

"What's what?" Ansley asked.

"There, wedged into the wall. That's what I'm looking for," she walked up and tried to grab what looked like a crystal fingernail.

"What is it?" He joined her.

"Whatever it is, it's stuck, but touch it with your finger. See? It gives you a mini electric shock!"

"You're right!" Ansley placed his finger on it and jumped backwards. "What is this thing?"

It was as though a knife was submerged inside the wall with only a few centimetres of its blade sticking out. He scraped around the chalk and bits of the wall fell off and powdered inside his hands. Underneath the chalk was a grey stone.

"Let me try and pull it out. Hang on," he tugged and tugged but it wouldn't budge.

"Here use this rock," Marianne said, handing him a chunk of chalk

"Step back," he bashed the wall, both the rock and the wall crumpled, but he was able to wiggle the object free. It tingled inside his thumb and forefinger as he handed it to Marianne.

She rubbed it clean and turned it around in her hand.

"It looks like a black beetle's shell, you know, an exoskeleton, but harder," he said. "Does it hurt to hold it?"

"No, but it feels strange. Like a zinging vibration," she said and placed it in the middle of her palm.

They were both looking at it when it completely dissolved into her hand.

"Oh, my God! Did you see that?"

"Yes! It just melted into you!"

They stood agape looking at her palm and didn't see the water running in until it had already reached their feet.

"Ansley look!" She shouted and pointed down to where their feet were standing in puddles.

The tide was visibly rising over the edge of the cave opening and within seconds the dark water started rushing towards them with force.

Ansley looked up and saw that there were footholds in the walls.

"This way!" He shouted and began climbing towards an opening in the side.

Large chunks of the chalk crumbled under his touch and he fell back against the knee high water. A crack widened and split up the wall. A huge sheet of chalk broke away, crashed into the water and exposed a grey and orange trunk of stone. Ansley rubbed his hand against it. The bark was grainy from the sand, but solid and smooth otherwise.

"It's petrified," he whispered.

Marianne touched the bark and another sheet of chalk dislodged, collapsed into the rising water and uncovered half of the tree. Its mammoth grey branches were veined with swirls of copper orange. The water was waist high now and the tree felt like the gift.

"A petrified tree," said Marianne. "How amazing! Like a ladder, come on, it's obvious we are meant to climb it," she said and scurried up the wall.

Ansley followed. Climbing the branches was easy. The bark was smooth, but ridged enough for finger and footholds. The water rose precariously beneath them and Ansley felt the branches dislodge with his body weight. He was aware that cracks were splitting now in all directions.

"Take it slow," he called up to Marianne, but it was too late.

A massive crack lightened across the ceiling and the top of the cave seemed to suddenly split open.

"Hang on!" Ansley shouted, but Marianne lost her balance and fell backwards into the water.

The chalk crashed and the water levels rose. Ansley took a deep breath and dived into the water. The water was clouded with chalk and Ansley began to panic. Finally he saw rising bubbles and followed them to Marianne's mouth. Ansley put his hand on her arm and pointed towards a hole in the side of the wall. It was the only way out. The entire tree was now exposed and its branches would take them to the top. He thought his lungs would burst. She didn't move. She seemed to be in shock. She began to sink. He flipped around, plunged towards her, grabbed her hand and pulled her up to the surface. He pushed her towards the tree and she found her footing on one of the stone branches.

"Hurry," he said as she began to climb.

He heaved his body out of the water and steadily followed her towards the hole. The sea licked the bottom of his heels and he concentrated on keeping his tongue away from his sharp chattering teeth. Nearly there, he repeated as he fixated on the hole, round and black as an unlit planet.

"When we go through it, move to the side so the water can pour out," Marianne called down to him and he felt relieved that she'd regained her wits.

As they got closer to the hole he could see moonlight coming through it until finally Marianne was crawling through its tunnel of dim light.

"There is nothing to hang onto! We'll have to jump!" She shouted and disappeared.

Ansley reached the opening, pushed his body through it and dived into the sea. Behind him, water poured powerfully out of the hole and pieces of the stack began to split and smash into the sea. They swam and swam until the sea felt calm. Their heads broke the water's surface and they sucked in air. The sea was gently rising and lifted them as they filled their lungs with oxygen. The world was soft now. They were close to the shore where the waves licked the surface like a kitten's tongue. Without speaking a word they turned around and looked at the stack. The petrified tree was sprawling and colossal. The copper threads in its grey stone shined weakly in the moonlight, but the tree felt enchanted, yet dead, as though they'd unearthed a charmed catacomb.

"You saved my life," Marianne broke the silence.

He could see their clothes in the distance. Her eyes had changed. She looked capable of anything.

"It was nothing," he smiled. "An everyday occurrence."

The sky was beginning to lighten in the east as though that part of the world had seen an explosion. The birds were waking up. They bobbed like buoys.

She raised her dripping hand. They both gazed at it.

"That was bizarre," he said.

"Yeah," she whispered. The moon blinked against the water and she put her hand out to touch it.

"Maybe it was going to dissolve anyway, you know, maybe it was made out of, oh I don't know, something soluble," he said and felt ridiculous.

She was completely serious.

"No. I feel it in me. I feel it." She looked him straight in the eye. They were both shivering.

"Let's go," he said and they started to swim to the shore.

He didn't look at her while she dressed. She was in a distant mood, but that was no surprise as they'd nearly drowned. He didn't know what to say. The atmosphere was palpable and words felt inadequate. He couldn't believe he'd only known her a day.

"Maybe it means you're mad," he said, wanting to hear her laugh but she didn't, she was still for an uncomfortably long time.

"Yes," she said finally. "Or maybe it means I'm chosen."

Which was exactly why the pearl had given her this vision, for it knew that once the tree of Genesis was disturbed, the initiation would begin.

14.

On the walk home she kept her hand wrapped around her locket. Fog had fallen, the land was undefined and they seemed to walk above it suspended. The castle poked through a grey cloud in the distance and Ansley felt like he was dreaming. Marianne stopped him.

"Look at the pearl," she said and opened the leather pouch.

It glowed brighter than a searchlight. The haze around it was metallic and they felt, once more, the rapture of the sea.

"That's not natural," he said.

"No, but then, nor are you, nor am I. Look, I don't know how you're connected to this but I'm certain that you are. Promise me you won't tell anybody about what happened tonight?" Marianne said.

"I promise," he said.

They paused together standing just beyond the village. Ansley turned around and looked behind them. In the fog the fires of Hastings were softened to an evocative blue mist that pulsed like the approach of something holy. He touched her shoulder.

"We should go," he said softly.

"I'm not ready to go back yet," she said.

The fog surrounded her voice as though she were speaking underneath a blanket. Whatever they said now would remain hidden and between them.

"Then let's sit," said Ansley.

They sat knees touching knees like the tellers of secrets cloaked in fog. It felt like a chance to safely expose. His face was suffused and peaceful. A barn owl interrupted their stillness and he spoke.

"Have you ever been owl spotting?"

"No. But I'm guessing you have," she said.

He smiled his close-mouth smile, put his hand to his lips and mimicked the owl's call exactly. Marianne held her breath. Seconds later the owl called back.

"He's moving closer," Ansley whispered and called the owl again.

The owl returned the call immediately and a dark shape broke the fog and swooped over their heads.

"My father used to say they were like spirits when we went owl spotting. I remember one time we came across a valley full of campfires," he said.

"Was that during the London exodus?" Marianne cut in.

"Yeah, I must have been really young because it was at the beginning of The Transformation Age, but before contamination. Anyway we stood at the top of the hill and watched the fires below glowing like a field of red tulips against the blackness of the night," he said.

"You're such a poet," she said half teasing, half impressed and he shrugged his shoulders as though he couldn't possibly be anything else.

"My father said that we were all refugees now, every one of us, and I remember feeling this naive perception of happiness because I knew what it was like to live as a refugee in a physical, communal sense. An owl swooped over us, as intimately low as it did just now, then lifted and soared over the fires. He'll be all right, my father said; it's the rest of us that are stuck between waves. The next day two hurricanes wiped out Los Angeles."

"Maybe your father had the gift of premonition," Marianne said.

"Maybe the world sends us warnings we don't comprehend because of the way we've built our vision to accommodate our sense of supremacy," he said.

"That's quite a sentence. I can tell you've thought about this," she said.

"Too much time alone in the woods I guess. But then, there's you. And you foresee things," he said.

"Yes. But I don't believe I'm standing at the top of the mountain, so I look up and not down, which makes a massive difference," she said.

Ansley hummed in agreement, then sat silently thinking.

"I remember a feeling of camaraderie as well. There is always a sense of togetherness at the edge of change. We used to watch satellite pictures of the earthquakes and actually celebrate the leaking oil. It felt as though the worst had happened and although it was tragic..."

"Often change is only precipitated by tragedy," Ansley cut in, quoting the Prime Minister.

"Exactly. There was relief, like humanity had released itself from a sickening dependence and could move forward. Like oil was a drug or something. My friend Joan and I would make plans about how we would become Green Girls, a modern version of Land Girls, and singlehandedly revive the alternative energy industry. We had no idea what was in store.

So The Transformation Age was loss, but also hope, because it felt like a crossroads and at no point did we actually believe that our entire civilization could collapse," she said.

"Prosperity as a coat of armour," said Ansley.

"More like arrogance as a coat of armour. And then the hurricanes," she said.

"And then the hurricanes," he echoed. "And desperation kicked in like a monster at the door."

"Remember that news clip of the mussels and fish living in a sofa?"

"I remember the floating baby bottle," said Ansley.

"Yeah," Marianne looked towards the sea. "That was terrible."

*

After the first hurricane, the residents were instant neighbours. They built water blockades and fortresses and shared clothes. There was a palpable sense of respite. Yes, thousands were dead and the city was devastated, but the majority of people were still standing. You could see them coming out of the rubble like bewildered insects wondering if the rain had stopped. They looked up at the sky blinking. There was sun. There were seagulls. Normal things, so hope ensued.

They interviewed a woman holding a small child.

"We made it," she said, "I was terrified, but I stayed and came through it. It just goes to show that humans are capable of anything."

A few hours later a second hurricane hit. Nobody had anticipated another disaster. The first hurricane had wiped out all of the detection equipment. The systems had failed and this time, there were no survivors, not a single one, even low flying media helicopters were taken.

"Check out those clouds." A cameraman said to his pilot. "They seem to be rumbling or growing or something."

He didn't realize the clouds he spoke of weren't clouds at all, but mounting water. It must have been as if the sky had dropped on them. All the footage is from dislodged cameras. There were no faces, just sounds, first screaming then gurgling waves and the sounds of running water with the occasional appliance floating by or a high heeled shoe. The city was pulped and underwater. Ansley kept thinking of a concrete and steel reef. He saw fish swimming in and out of windows and barnacles attaching themselves in patterns on the pavement.

The H from the Hollywood sign was found in a field in Nevada. They auctioned it at Christie's and for weeks there was hype about how many millions it was likely to fetch, but in the end nobody wanted it because nobody wanted a reminder of how infinitesimal humans were against nature. So the age transformed us from collecting relics and artefacts for huge amounts to valuing survival at all costs.

New York was soon deserted.

The following year the beauty and pharmaceutical industries began to collapse. Without oil you couldn't produce petroleum-based products. Some people rejoiced and heralded this as the return of plant-based healing. Others battled and things got particularly nasty. The pharmaceutical companies had the obvious monopoly and charged extortionate rates for their remaining cancer, HIV and diabetes drugs so only the extremely wealthy were able to prolong their lives, while the others died at rapid rates.

Substitutes were possible and might have been found, but the people were warring and suspicious of one another, so progress was slow and corrupted by greed and desperation. People were commonly killed over eye shadow disputes. 'Maybelline Murders' the press called them.

"Thank goodness the fine people of Los Angeles didn't have to see this day," one woman from Phoenix said about the beauty meltdown. Botox and dialysis were offered on the black market. Bodies were found bloated and pinpricked in alleyways. HIV, hepatitis, TB, syphilis, polio, tetanus, measles, malaria and influenza sufferers took to the streets like a parade of skeletons.

They were protesting the hospital's decision to admit only treatable, curable patients. All others were told to die peacefully at home. They were simply overrun with beauty, disease, self-inflicted wounds or incidents. The stockpiles of antibiotics were dwindling and the super bugs had mutated to such an extent that it rendered the drugs useless anyway.

The food industry was also in a state of collapse. Without oil there was no way to grow, process or distribute mass quantities of food products. How would you operate a tractor? A semi-truck? A freezer? People had to go back to planting and harvesting crops by hand. Locality determined what you could grow and eat. What about those that lived in a desert? What about those that lived in a place where the ground was frozen half of the year?

Airplanes, trains, cars were all out of the question so there simply was no way to transport food. Without food and without medicine half the world's population died during the first year and the majority of the rest were weakened by a state of shock.

Huge groups of people left London and the major cities, they walked in packs down abandoned motorways and old Roman roads searching for land to settle and grow food upon. It was a return to the Dark Ages, but with waterproof camping gear.

However, it was true that despite all apocalyptic expectations there remained in Britain an amazing sense of freedom that prevailed as the people were forced to leave ownership behind. They carried what they could on their backs. The 'what if' was over and the survivors tried to enter the future with a pioneering hope.

This is when they believed they could grow their own food, when food was still relatively plentiful in the western world and could be found, albeit scarcely, in street markets.

Time and again you'd hear people saying things like, "I've always wanted to live off the land," or "I feel this is a chance for society to reprioritize." They knew little. The days of disaster were merciful when compared to the onslaught of contamination that lay ahead.

*

The fog began to lift as an early symptom of sunrise. Marianne and Ansley had talked about so much, the state of the world, but also, more importantly, their dreams and how they were still intact. Perhaps the only part of their psyche that remained intact and that this ability was the human spirits greatest example of fortitude. It's why and how they would survive.

The village unveiled itself and all the houses were swathed in sleepy darkness, apart from Jude's, whose windows burned from the top of the hill.

"No rest for the wicked," Ansley said as they both looked up at the house.

"It's strange, isn't it?" Marianne stood and rearranged the atmosphere.

Back to reality, thought Ansley, but he stood as well and met her eye to eye. "Is that a general comment or are you referring to something specific?"

"I'm referring to him," she nodded towards Jude's house. "I always thought it was strange how a world that is wise with its checks and balances could choose him to forewarn us of contamination."

"It does seem odd, but maybe he's a balance of something else," said Ansley.

"What do you mean?"

"I mean that even virtue needs something to measure itself against. It's how things move forward," he said and she took his hands in hers.

The pearl was a burning lump in her throat.

"It's nearly dawn. You need to go," she said. Her voice was a whisper and he stared at her lips.

"What about you?" He squeezed her hands, unwilling to let go.

"I have something else I need to do. On my own. I've put it off to for too long now," and the way she spoke made him feel as though she didn't want him to ask any more questions.

He nodded. "Thank you," he said. "For tonight and, well, everything."

She moved her face so close to his that he could feel the breath leaving her small and perfect nose. She hovered there for a while and then gave him a kiss on the cheek.

"No," she said. "Thank you," then she turned and ran in the direction of the uncontaminated field.

He stood there for a heart-hammering moment and watched her disappear into the grey dawn. He had to outrun the sunrise. If he weren't so enthralled by love he would have felt the yellow windows of Jude's house watching him like a stalking animal.

15.

Jude sat upright in his 'thinking chair' with a pair of binoculars. The chair had been King Henry VIII's coronation chair and was just one of the many things Jude had pilfered from London during its population cleanout. A good pilfer was in keeping with British tradition after all. And who didn't like to be surrounded by beautiful things? He was wearing a black velvet dressing gown covered with gold embroidered ivy patterns and a black sleeping cap with a gold tassel. It wasn't the only golden tassel in the room. Two others held Jude's mauve silk curtains in place. He put his foot on one of the chair's carved lion heads and began muttering to himself.

"Interesting," he said as he lowered his binoculars. "Now what is the connection between Dark Ansley and that stupid Keeper's meddlesome daughter? Could this spell love?" He recoiled at the thought. "A here and now Beauty and the Beast?"

A cherub stood at the door. He was accustomed to Jude's mumbling interspersed with delirious cackling and knew better than to interrupt Jude's thought process. The room was a magnificent library with carved mahogany floor to ceiling bookcases. There was an oriental rug, a hook for Jude's chandelier and a painting of some dark-haired woman that followed you with her eyes. It unnerved the cherub, but not as much as the bookcases, lined with rows of glass jars. There wasn't a single book in sight. Inside the jars were the little green glowing spirals that Jude affectionately called his glow-worms. The room radiated a sickly light and the cherub couldn't take it anymore. He cleared his throat to announce his presence.

"I know you're there, stupid! What is it!?" Jude banged his foot on the lion's head. "Can't you see I'm thinking?"

"Sir, we have your glow-worms," said the cherub.

"Sir?! What am I? A CEO?! No! I'm a prophet for goodness sake! And soon to be GOD of a new world! I told you I wanted to be called Master!"

"Master, we have your glow-worms," said the cherub.

"Fine, fine put them over there with the others," he said and dismissed the cherub with his hand.

The cherub didn't move. He was tired of being treated badly, tired of the unsavoury, not to mention unhygienic, collecting of glow-worms and fed up with the whole dictatorship business.

"What are you waiting for?" Jude asked, annoyed.

"The magic word," said the cherub, finally putting his fat little foot down.

"You mean 'pleeeease'? Are you serious?" Jude's mouth was full of contempt.

"It would be nice for a change," said the cherub. He knew he was taking a big risk.

Jude spat out a laugh, sprang to his feet and bowed mockingly before the cherub.

"I beg your pardon. Please, please put the jar on the shelf," he affected, walking towards the door and shutting it while the cherub did as he was told.

Jude stood behind the cherub, licked his lips, slipped his human body off and coiled around the cherub. "And now, I shall show you some real magic," he said deliciously. "You dear, dispensable little creature."

*

There were times the perks of the job outweighed the stresses and to be fair, the stresses were simply a product of Jude's overwhelming success. Part of that success was pure luck and coincidental timing.

A few years before the world's oil supply was predicted to run out, Conch Petrol untapped the world's largest reserve of oil in the Alaskan tundra. Up until that point humanity had been begrudgingly preparing for its next adaptation. The discovery meant that there would be enough oil to support the expanding world for another three hundred years. Solar, wind and nuclear energy progress virtually stopped. Petrol prices plummeted and economies boomed. At the same time some boffins at Cambridge University worked out how to efficiently capture carbon and thereby prevent the increasingly turbulent global temperatures. The Greens and the Far Right shook hands and rejoiced. Less dependency on oil meant greater stability in the Middle East and a fairer division of wealth. It's difficult to become radicalized when you are healthy, sheltered and fed. Financially united politicians tend to communicate and there was hope that the leaders could now be effective in sorting out the problem of population control and religious separation. The world wasn't perfect, but it was getting better and the future seemed a promising place. It was a great age of prosperity and so a vast populace completely forgot about energy alternatives.

However, the relief ended when an enormous earthquake split Alaska in two. Over a single month earthquakes spread like a crack of lightening from Alaska, across Canada, then the Middle East and Russia. It was as if the earth was purging all of her oil and there was nothing anyone could do to stop her.

Oil seeped from the earth like a leaking wound and rolled into the ocean like black lava. The effect of the earthquakes was incalculable. Scientists stared at television cameras gape-mouthed as thousands of people, plants and animals died.

Of course the humans went mad, poor mites, thought Jude, they actually tried to collect the oil in buckets. Buckets! Oil covered bodies and leaking methane meant that human combustion happened so frequently that camera crews had to carry fire extinguishers with them.

The Earth's purging was relentless and just after the earthquakes, over half of the agricultural land was found to be contaminated with prions of bovine spongiform encephatlitis; the plague of Mad Cow Disease.

Jude had predicted this event, well not him exactly, rather the scientist he inhabited, and his prophetic power increased with every new field that was found contaminated.

Madness spread and began killing an already compromised population. Suddenly the markets really were empty and farms were completely abandoned. Infected animals had to be dispatched and soil had to be tested before you could plant a single seed, hence food was becoming more and more limited.

At the end of the year all remaining people either died or localized. The organization of vigilante groups began and villages became territorial. The residents of those villages with uncontaminated land were the lawmakers. London was reserved for the outcasts and became an asylum where allotment owners were governors.

Parliament had promised a swift return to steam and coal but after the first year, there simply were not enough people to generate those powers. It wasn't as if one day the Parliament buckled, rather it just dissolved like a lump of sugar in a hot drink. There was no single thing to promise, no single thing to fix, plus everyone was fragmented and the population was drastically reduced. One by one the remaining MP's just walked away, accepting their role as a person who simply needed to eat.

Which was ideal for Jude's plan. Things just seemed to fall into place, and for a while this delighted him enormously, but now it was beginning to feel too easy. He wondered if there wasn't some divine trickery involved.

He needed to keep a close eye on the situation. Should he befriend Ansley or just kill him? If he killed him he may never discover the source of his worry, but if he let him live, he ran the risk of becoming a victim of divinity. He'd done that before and it was excruciatingly painful.

Of course, there may be nothing to worry about. He could be fretting over dust motes and hyperbole, he thought to himself as he curled up in his chair digesting the cherub. Too much brain discussion before coffee, he decided and rang his little bell. Another cherub appeared. They seemed never ending and everywhere, like chain-smoking Oompa Loompas, and Jude found solace in their persistence.

"Business as usual," said Jude while the cherub stared at the bulge in his stomach. Jude was in his snake form and digesting the cherub slowly. "Oh don't mind him, I'm nearly done here and will return to human mode soon. I'll take my coffee early this morning. I think I'd like to drink it and watch the sunrise. And I don't want to be disturbed," Jude said and slid off the chair towards his suit of skin.

It was definitely time to do some investigating, he thought as he slipped into his human disguise.

16.

There was a bit of tilled land at the bottom of the uncontaminated field where Marianne knelt, made a basket out of her shirt and filled it with soil. It was going to be hard to part with the pearl even though it seemed the correct thing to do.

She entered the woodland. The plants were moist with cobwebs and dew. The woodland felt damp and alive as if it had been expecting her and she imagined the forest floor printed with footsteps. It was like following a map and she walked straight to the large beech tree of her image. The tree resembled a living, yet smaller, version of the tree petrified inside the chalk stack and she knew she had been lead there by the pearl.

She used her hands, dug a hole at its base, layered it with the uncontaminated soil and plucked the pearl from her leather pouch. It made a happy little slurping noise, like a root and she closed it inside her warm hand. Goodbye and be safe, she willed it, then dropped it inside the hole and covered it with the remaining soil.

It knew instantly it was where it belonged. Below the ground, a current of electricity cracked all the way to the earth's molten core and every living thing awakened inside its consciousness. This shiver lasted for a mere second, but a second was all that was necessary to activate the new beginning. Marianne felt it like a pulsation.

Through the trees she could see the castle. It was quiet and fantastical. It seemed to throb as though it were in some kind of spellbound womb of amniotic sleep and she knew it was far, far away from her. And when a hand, white and crystalline, drew a curtain from behind her eyes, she knew she could shout and shout and the others would never wake up. Except Ansley, who was already awake.

The image of a stream entered her mind. She looked down and saw that a tiny crack had appeared where she'd buried the pearl and through it a silver gush began to trickle. It rolled up to her toes as though it were iridescent lava.

She bent down and touched it, a dollop stuck to her finger, the water was swirling as the pearl had done. She put the dollop in her mouth. It tasted like pure earth but without the grit. She wanted more. She put her face down to the crack and licked and sucked up all the water she could. She looked down at her bare arms. The hairs on them were glistening silver. She imagined her skin was the soil in which she'd planted a tiny moon. This idea, this notion grew inside her like a white flame, a warmth, a soul.

*

It was amazing how love had been waiting just below the surface of Ansley like a bubble ready to rise. It felt like instinct. Exactly how instinct can return to the body as soon as the body is responsible for its own survival. It seemed that there were unvoiced pulses that he just knew, just understood about her and their conversation.

He went straight to his desk, took out his notebook and wrote:
The thought of her dissolving in me
like salt in water —
invisibly
changing my chemistry.
How I could live
so far beyond
myself?

He couldn't stop thinking about her body covered in pastel white like his, it was the most wonderful thing anyone had ever done for him. It was her sign of acceptance. It was why he'd kissed her. He should have waited, they had only just met, but the timing seemed right and the moment intimate enough to warrant a kiss. She had viewed him with such wonder. Maybe too much wonder, he thought. He wanted to still seem human, relatable, hence worthy of a human love that wasn't derived from pity.

He lay down on his bed and got under the covers. It had been an exhausting night and he ran it through his mind. The pearl, her visions, the dissolving exoskeleton. There were so many things to think about, but he kept returning to a chalk white Marianne with her black hair screaming in the wind. He wanted only to remember and savour that image for as long as he could. It blew up in his mind like a balloon filling all his space and he felt happy.

Marianne, I won't have enough paper for you, he thought. And it was true; his paper supply was running low and soon he'd have to search for more. Thinking of doing that now felt alien and distant. It felt lonely. A few days ago he wished only for paper and food. He feared nothing because all of his fears had already happened.

It took him a long time to understand that there's an aspect of relief in disaster, and that living beyond the worst possible thing without an earthly tie can make you fearless. All of his earthly ties had been dismantled. And now Marianne.

He knew he was probably getting emotionally carried away, but he'd been alone for so long, forever really, so it felt almost completely wonderful. Almost. He was wary of attachment.

This was a difficult world for friendship, for love or any kind of emotional investment outside of your next meal. People and places changed and died frequently. He had known nothing other than the burn of loss, so was dangling between the high altitude of new adoration and the low grovelling of caution.

The sun had nearly risen and the sky was as pink as his eyes. He got up and closed his blinds. He put his hand against the slats and wished that he were different, normal.

Who was he kidding?

The burden between the two of them was one of pure practicality. In the end, even if Marianne, or anyone for that matter, were able to see past his monstrous form, his nocturnal lifestyle would eventually cripple them. How could he put that obligation on someone he loved? And yet, being human and having human desires, how could he not?

He flung himself back on his bed. She had cut straight into his interior, and for the first time, he had felt recognized. He couldn't give that up. They had talked about only the things that mattered. Like his writing and how his poems sieved through him, anything could spark one, a branch shaped like an arrow, a throb of thunder, a word, a sigh. She understood how insight was always changing; bouncing from thing to thing like a tiny, glowing rubber door and through this door they both glimpsed different realities.

He shivered. He was still cold from the sea. His sheets were a little damp. He wrapped up in a blanket and tried to sleep, but kept remembering her face dusted with the white chalk, her arms, her neck. She was wonderful. It seemed just like her to do something like that, impetuous and weird, yet perfect. And she still looked at him without flinching. Not even his mother had done that.

He fingered the middle ring on the pointer finger of his left hand. It had been his mother's wedding band and he always wore it. She had placed it on his bedside table the night she left. It was the last thing she'd touched. He knew this because he'd only been pretending to sleep. She hadn't even touched him.

When he told Marianne this, she had held his hand, which was shocking because most people could never quite believe that he wasn't contagious. He was a mystery to nearly everyone, a ghost.

All around them had been a wild whispering. The sparse leaves on the wind bent trees, the grasses, the distant tide, as though they were required to listen and what they heard was inexpressibly connecting.

He thought of the places on his body where she'd touched him, his hands, his cheek, his shoulder. And how warm, almost radiating her palm had felt, as though it were pulsing. Maybe it was? Maybe it was searching for the crystal exoskeleton thing they had found?

What was that anyway?

He had once seen something similar in shape and reverence. It was in the woodland, only it was smaller and black like a polished beetle casing, but like the crystal fingernail, it seemed out of this world.

He remembered picking it up. It had felt cold in his hand, cold as a rock in the snow, and he dropped it quickly. He didn't like it. It seemed equally mysterious and repulsive. But how could something repulsive feel akin to something that would sink into Marianne?

There was a knock on the door and his stomach sprang to his throat.

17.

"Good morning," Jude said and Ansley nodded a reply. "I see my presence disappoints you. So I ask myself, who else would you be expecting?" He leaned in and winked.

"Nobody, I'm just tired, that's all," Ansley said and yawned.

He hoped Jude's arrival had nothing to do with Marianne. Her father would never let her see him again if he found out about their little rendezvous.

"Of course. Are you too tired to let me in?" Jude asked and Ansley stepped to the side allowing him to enter. "I trust everything is satisfactory in your room?"

"Yes, it's great. Thank you," Ansley said.

Maybe he does know about the cove and he's going to ask me to leave, or worse, thought Ansley. Jude saw the look on Ansley's face and laughed.

"Don't worry! I'm here on a gesture of generosity, so relax," he reached into his dressing gown pocket, pulled out a notebook and handed it to Ansley. "Go on, take it," he said and shoved it into Ansley's hands.

Ansley flipped through it and found it was completely blank. Was this a test?

"It's illegal to write," he said and, although it pained him, handed it back to Jude.

"Oh dear," Jude said, "I didn't think you were so well trained. I hope you aren't doing it just for my benefit. It's true that I punish my Keepers for maintaining personal documents of any kind, but they are of a particular disposition where thinking would be tragic for business. I don't mind you writing. You actually have things to talk about. It could be our secret," he said and crossed his hand over his heart.

"But why?" Ansley asked. "Why are you being so nice to me?"

"Why indeed! I don't know. I guess I'm becoming a softy. But also, I see things in you Ansley. We are not too dissimilar you know. I, too, was banished by my people, persecuted and unseen for my talents."

Ansley was very sceptical and had the sensation that Jude was tricking him somehow but couldn't put his finger on it. Was the notebook bugged?

Was he trying to catch him writing so he could banish him? Jude saw straight through him.

"Stop overanalysing, please. It's just a gift. Pure and simple. The gift of a regular old notebook," he said and placed it on Ansley's desk. "I'll leave it here, use it if you want," he said and opened the door to leave.

"Oh, and Ansley?"

"Yes?"

"I applaud your taste. She's very pretty, but don't worry, all of your secrets are safe with me," he said and pretended to zip up his mouth with his thumb and forefinger.

Jude closed the door and walked down the hallway with a smile on his face. He fully understood that sometimes patience was the hardest work to sustain and waiting with awareness was definitely a course of action. It was how he was formed, eons ago, when the world was dark, yet aware of the light of life and anticipating its spark.

*

In this darkness, water flowed. It flowed and carried particles of clay formed of silicates. These lattices of elemental silicon, along with oxygen, were prolific throughout the Earth's crust and were the embodiment of the Earth's natural world.

There was a stream that curved like a snake, and as the silicates flowed down its waters, some of the crystals became attracted to one other. These attractions lead to adhesiveness, so they bonded themselves together and began to clog the stream. It was an act of defiance that allowed similar lattices to coalesce in a pool, creating an early body of resistance.

Time worked as time always does. And the pattern of resistance repeated itself, as it always does, but through its repetition, it became something new.

The waters dried and the dust particles were blown further down the stream, where they stuck together and continued clogging the waters, making more pools of identical particles of silicate. Replication of the body had begun. Jude's body stirred its awakening with a swirl of dust and that was all for thousands of years.

Then ice formed, ice melted and the lattices, like sinews, were packed together and mixed with trace elements of metal. When the waters flowed again the lattices were joined together in a meandering shape of the stream. And now Jude's body stirred with little ripples for thousands of years.

The long body of water linked the silicates and the pressure of the Earth and the heat of the sun over millennia allowed electrons to flow. This was the spark of electricity Jude's body had been waiting for, as it provided an energy source for life.

Born of the Earth, the Sun and the Water, through the process of natural selection and evolution, Jude, a cold-bodied creature was initiated. Heat allowed cohesion of particles to create his form and neurons to fire for his mind to begin.

But nothing magnificent happens quickly.

He slowly flexed his figure and resisted the wind and rain. He hardly thought at all, it was enough just to be. He pulled more molecules of hydrogen into his being and came to master the empty world of barren elements; carbon, hydrogen, oxygen, nitrogen.

In these days of dark and light Jude did not notice the alternative sparks of life; the carbon-forms, until they had taken a foothold, a bridgehead in the battle for the planet. So when the carbon-forms eventually started to sprout, seed and reproduce, he was happy, for there was company. It wasn't easy being the sole silicon-form of life on Earth.

Before he knew it, he was surrounded by a garden, the Garden of Eden.

He had to admit that the carbon forms were things of great beauty. He loved how they rapidly evolved when compared to his own protracted beginnings. He soon discovered it was all the result of a glorious little helix, spiralled like a screw, and he used it to build his daydreams.

Jude was full of dreams then. He often curled around the base of his favourite tree and basked in its green heat. He'd swirl like a synapse up the trunk and drape across the topmost branch. The stars buzzed above him and he marvelled at how each one was its own sun with an orbit and all the minerals necessary for life. He dreamed of creating his own planet, populated with the beautiful helix, as well as his own shimmering silicates that time would dovetail together, designing something new. Something wonderful and uniquely his to rule.

The trouble was that the carbon forms weren't interested in listening to his dreams or anything, for that matter, outside of their own desires. The ease of their success had made them arrogant. They didn't deserve the helix and their ingratitude grated against him.

His anger started by breaking. That's true for most things though, people and plants, and he didn't think he was special for it. Even then, he'd been around long enough to know that a sense of entitlement was always the beginning of failure.

Adam thought he was something special though, Adam believed himself to be God's greatest gift and things just came too easily for him. For instance, whatever Adam planted immediately grew. Seriously, he just flicked a seed against the ground with no more consideration than you'd give a clipped fingernail and gorgeous flowers grew. It didn't even have to be a seed. He could flick a bogie, or a spit wad or even pee and suddenly something would blossom into a thing of beauty, nourishment or both.

Adam was constantly singing. Jude could hear him skipping and singing through the orchard. At first Jude tried to befriend Adam, but Adam was often so enraptured by himself that he took no notice of Jude, and eventually Adam's voice snagged against Jude's skin like torn metal.

It was the way Adam swayed and swaggered and thought he was better than everybody else that made Jude vow to prove his brilliance. For years he performed menial tricks like eating small animals in one gulp. The carbon forms never clapped, so Jude's tricks became more and more elaborate. He danced and coiled then shot up hissing through the clouds like a red spring, yet even this did not elicit a single round of applause.

It gave him piercing thoughts and he grew fangs. He realized that what he thought, he could become. Isn't that the most incredible truth? But there was no one to share this revelation with and so his disappointment gave way to loneliness.

Then she arrived.

The rumour was that she'd come from Adam's ribcage. She was exquisitely beautiful, brown and golden, as if the sun had shed a tear and created her. Jude wanted to possess her. He wanted to make her do something forbidden.

But first he had to get rid of those blasted angels. They had taken to following him around, clinging to him like flies on crap. He called them his harem. It got their wings all in a flutter, but she loved them and fed them as if they were pet hummingbirds. The angels whizzed around her and sat on her shoulders. There was never a moment when she was alone and the situation was becoming desperate.

Mr. Perfect Ribcage didn't help Jude's despair with his constant singing, planting and celebrating. Every time they'd celebrate she'd have another baby. Babies flew out of her like bats screeching from a cave. She laughed, tickled them under the chin and called them her little cherubs.

When it was feeding time they all stood in a circle around her, clapping their dimpled hands or standing on one leg, and milk shot from her breasts like a fountain straight into their little pink mouths. Then they danced and sang until they fell on the ground, like a pile of cats, and licked the remaining sticky bits of milk off one another's skin. After a little nap, they would share a bowl of his pee-begot-fruits.

It was so pathetic it nauseated Jude. He had to catch his own food. He had mastered, without recognition, swallowing an egg whole. An egg! Never mind a rabbit with rigor mortis. More than once he'd regretted not eating a cherub or two but he got his chance in the end. He decided he would get her to eat one of the forbidden apples. But how?

He travelled to the edge of the garden for inspiration and inspiration came as a weed. To this day botany is a great interest of his. He adored the wayward seed pooped out or blown into the perfect flowerbed like a dirty stranger dumped into a picturesque town. Seeds are also mavericks. He learnt so much from weeds. Namely to lay quiet and root before exposing yourself, sinister planting, and that's exactly what he did.

This weed had thorns and even though he'd never seen a thorn before, he recognized it at once as sharp and poignant. He coiled around it and picked it. It pierced his skin and he knew it would pierce hers also. That night, he placed it beside the tree and waited.

When she woke up the angels were already surrounding the weed. There was nothing else like it in the garden. What was it? Who put it there? Was it Him? Was He trying to warn us about something? Finally, the angels were occupied.

Adam came and left immediately to compose a ballad about it. Eve came with her children twirling and leaping on and off of her like birds on a beautiful cow. She looked at it with her large cow eyes. She picked it up and it pricked her finger. For the first time in her life she saw her own blood, her own vulnerability, her potential loss.

The blood trickled down her forearm and pinged off her elbow before it splat against the head of one of her children. She looked in horror at her bloody child and felt a fear as deep in measure as her love and for a split second she doubted the garden. That was all Jude needed, only a second of doubt, he slipped straight in and planted one of his scales. He knew he had her and all he had to do was wait; wait and study the tree.

He was becoming a masterful serpent as fierce and steady as a maniac's pulse. He curved and moulded around the branches like a gelatinous wave, a lick, and saw all. Scales of him caught on the jagged bits of bark; they nestled in like small eyes in sockets, black as onyx and shiny.

He was all over that tree. The Apple Tree. Every morning all his little scales would light up as the sun emanated and rose. One would assume that the sun burst through the tree but it didn't. It oozed through the tree like a stretch oozes through a body in the morning. It was as if the tree couldn't help but spread its sun and all those little apples lit up like empty bulbs.

They weren't even allowed to touch the apples, but Jude loved them all the same. He loved them with a love as intimately fragile as a spider's web or a throat. He could not help it that he was brutish. He's a serpent, no less, each day he'd push down his brutish heart, like a jerking fish under a hand, and continued his study. He covered the tree as if he were holly or ivy, he was everywhere, he was infesting.

Sometimes all you need is a bit of luck, and out of such luck, she started sitting in The Apple Tree like a soft bird. She'd swing her legs and the apples would gently bounce and sway in time with her bosoms. Her doubt was growing day by day and everyone could tell she was unhappy. Every so often he'd slip into her brain and leave another scale. Now she needed him, her melancholy was like some heat-seeking animal.

He's a reptile for goodness sake, though there is a heat to his venom. His venom was like a cancer in her. She longed for control but that was impossible. It made her desperate. Her desperation had become think and hardened. She spent her time travelling her mind and looking for a way out of herself and back to happiness. Often he slithered to the top of her brain-tree and watched. She looked like a lost minnow.

One day he decided to speak to it.

Listen little fishy, he said, your belly is as round as an apple, your blood is as red as an apple, perhaps its flesh will restore your happiness? Snake eats apples all the time and he is supremely happy. He smiled at her then.

She bit it.
Hook, line and sinker.
"God, I'm good," he thought.

18.

It was Project Nigh's first official workday and Ansley was covering the twilight shift. Marianne wasn't at lunch and Ansley was beginning to wonder if she might be avoiding him. It was frustrating and ridiculous that he couldn't leave the confines of the castle to look for her. Although what would he say to her anyway?

In the light of day, his romantic notions had dwindled to pity. She pitied him, hence her kindness, he wallowed. He understood pity. It felt comfortable to him. He sat at his desk and put his hand against the curtain so he could feel the sun pelting through the cloth. Sometimes he longed to fling back the curtains and bask in the sun's full radiance.

He could hear people working in the field below, the irregular murmur of conversation, the singsong of laughter and the clang of tools. He put his hands in his head and listened to a world he was not a part of. Hunger, molasses thick, poured into him and he filled with it. Marianne was out there.

Desire is a bird in my throat,
I imagine holding her,
dismantling myself
and blowing away
like red and white
confetti, cells,
to love me
would bring her
darkness.

It was true that the villagers had called him 'Dark Ansley' and they were right, he thought; only a monster hides from the sun. He got up, filled the sink with water and splashed it over his face. In the mirror he saw his small peg teeth, pallid skin and absence of hair. She had called him beautiful, but the way she said it had inferred a different, unique and alien beauty, not an ethereal beauty.

He had been a fool to think there was really a chance of something remarkable with Marianne. If she embodied anything, it was sunlight, and he's a human that sunlight could kill. A human version of one of those colourless, formless creatures that dwell in the black bottom of the sea. Only his poems illuminated him. In his mind he was shimmering. Only there, nowhere else, with no one else.

He left the castle at sunset. He wanted to take a walk before his shift started. He wasn't used to being indoors and missed the fresh air. The sky was red and veined with purple like a bloodshot eye. The owls had begun and the bats. He breathed deep the dusk and walked through the field towards the woodland. The wind rolled the leaves into piles.

The beauty of being scentless was that animals were not frightened of you. Woodland had always been his sanctuary. He approached the deer drinking at the stream. Their tails flicked white against the darkening trees. Something in the underbrush was red and foreign.

As Ansley moved closer he saw that it was a nicely folded tee shirt. He picked it up and underneath was a pair of jeans, trainers and boxer shorts. The clothes weren't dirty and appeared to have been recently set down. It was puzzling and Ansley looked questionably at the deer, as they were the only other living creatures present. In response, they blinked at him, alert and graceful. They sniffed the air, acknowledged him with a ripple through their hides, and continued drinking.

Except one. One remained completely still and stared at him with eyes that seemed human. It looked like it wanted to say something.

"Hello?" Ansley said and instantly felt absurd.

The deer didn't speak; instead, it began to quickly fade into a boy. A real boy, about Ansley's age, about fourteen and completely naked. They stared at one another, utterly shocked, and then the boy covered his private section with his hands and took off running.

"Hey wait!" Ansley ran after him. "Wait!"

Sticks cracked beneath their feet. They ducked and swerved around branches. Their breath was synchronized. His hair was a curly blond mess and the back of his head looked like a sheep's butt. Ansley let out a snort of laughter. It caught the boy off guard and slowed him down, not much, but enough for Ansley to bridge the gap between them. He reached out his hand. He could feel the heat from the boy's neck as he lunged forward and grabbed his shoulder. Then. Nothing. Gone. Like a bubble that pops as soon as it's touched. The boy had vanished.

"No!" Ansley shouted and ran back to the stream.

His legs burned. His throat was full of musk and moisture. He spat and caught his breath. Tree shadows pulsed alongside his heart and a breeze shuddered over him. The thump of blood died down in his ears and left him with the sensation of being watched. He heard leaves break cautiously underfoot. The deer emerged from their camouflage. Slowly, they circled him; a ring of eyes and not one of them was human.

"Who is he?" The deer blinked back at him.

Aghast. He looked up at the sky. Stars tucked themselves between black branches, everything was hiding from him. Had he just imagined it?

A large buck let out a single aggressive snort like a gunshot. Ansley turned and sprinted back to the field. He still couldn't believe what he'd seen. Of course he was real. He had touched him. This changed everything. All the elements of Ansley's world were transforming. His heart flung against his throat in spasms, like a creature trying to escape.

Ansley was standing in the field reeling from his experience when Jude approached him.

"Ansley, my night hawk, my bat, my tenant of the underworld, your role is particularly important. Some might say it's demeaning, but I think it's luminescent! Here," he handed him a bucket full of saltwater. "Now on the whole, I want it stated that I'm opposed to genocide, but when it comes to slugs, I say, kill the lot of them. How are you enjoying the little gift I gave you?"

"I haven't touched it yet," Ansley said, challenging Jude because he just couldn't believe that Jude wouldn't prosecute him for an Expression of Personal Self.

"Still suspicious? Aw well, time will take care of that," Jude said.

Ansley took a deep breath and tried to slow his heartbeat in order to regain his composure. Jude was alone and there were no cherubs or Keepers in sight. He wore a gold brocade dinner jacket and a mood ring.

"Look," Jude shoved the ring into Ansley's face. "Green means I'm serene. How accurate. So do you have any questions regarding your cabbage mission?"

"Just one," said Ansley, happy for a distraction from the boy. "What do you want me to do with the bucket when I'm finished?"

"Put the lid on it and shake them all down. Tomorrow night you can toss the remains on the compost heap," he twiddled an imaginary goatee. "Any more questions?"

"Yes, actually," said Ansley. "Are those really cherubs?"

"Fallen cherubs, big difference. Don't trust them. They're like lobotomized monkeys that would eat you if they thought it'd spark their aging process. Even I wouldn't eat you, would I?" He brought his nose down to Ansley's nose. His breath smelled of uncooked garlic and rancid meat. His eyebrows met in the middle and created a single M spread like a child's drawing of a bird, mid-air.

Ansley didn't feel completely sure.

"Now, the night is young Ansley and the cabbages are latticed. I want the bucket full," he said, spun around and marched up the hill towards the castle.

Ansley bent down and began collecting slugs and snails from the cabbages. Their trails glowed like secret ink. There was a rustling from the trees behind him and the deer boy spoke.

19.

"Did he really call you his night hawk? That guy's weird," said the voice.

Ansley spun around but couldn't see anyone. A bit of bracken shook and the boy, fully dressed in the red tee shirt and jeans, stepped out of the woodland. Ansley held his breath. He was real after all.

"Sorry if I scared you earlier. I have that effect on people I accidentally meet," said the boy.

"Then we already have a lot in common. I'm Ansley."

"Hey Ansley. I'm Dex." They shook hands.

Ansley tried not to stare at him, but it was difficult because he was a striking combination of unusual traits. His hair was a long blond shock against his brown skin and his eyes were like two blue stones deep-set against protruding cheekbones. He looked like a chieftain.

"So…what happened? I mean, what are you?" Ansley said.

"I'm a shape shifter," said Dex.

"God, that's… Well, I don't know what to say. That's amazing."

"Well yeah, until you're caught naked or accidentally slip into a grasshopper or something. Although I'm quite good at controlling what I shift into now and, of course, where I leave my clothes. I just wasn't expecting anybody to be there," said Dex. "What about you? Why are you so ghostly looking? Are you ill or dead or something?"

Dex stood above Ansley in a half-sprinting position, as though he were nervous and prepared to flee. Maybe he thinks I'm a zombie, thought Ansley. He should have worn his balaclava, but it was so suffocating, and he had wanted to feel the air on his face. After all, he hadn't been expecting anyone either.

"No," said Ansley, "I'm not dead. Why? Have you ever met someone who is?"

"No, but it could happen right?" said Dex.

"I'm not sure," he shrugged his shoulders, "I guess anything could happen now. But I'm not dead; I was born like this."

"I was born with my condition too, it's called animism," said Dex.

"On the unusual genetics scale, yours is a million times better than mine," said Ansley.

"Oh I don't know. Have you ever wondered what it would be like to be a leech? It's terrible. It tastes like you've been sucking on pennies for a week," Dex looked around. "What is this place? Are you actually growing food here?"

This prospect seemed even more astounding to Dex than the potential that Ansley may be dead.

"Yeah. It's one of the last uncontaminated fields around," said Ansley.

"So you grow food from seeds?"

"Well I wasn't here when this was planted, but yes, I assume so," said Ansley.

"That's incredible," said Dex with reverie.

He sat down next to Ansley on the grass.

"No more incredible than you are," said Ansley. "So how does it work? Do animals just suck you up or what?" Ansley asked.

He was beginning to relax as well. Dex was easy to talk to and seemed relatively normal, considering.

"Sort of. I have to touch them first. My father called it the "DNA exchange". The idea is that once I've touched an animal I can, in theory, shift into its form whenever I want."

"What do you mean 'in theory'?"

"I mean I've nearly mastered control," said Dex.

"So you can decide which animals you'll shift into?"

"Basically, yeah, but at first I just shifted into anything that touched me. It was a nightmare. Flies were the worst," said Dex.

"Yuck, I can't imagine. What about one of these?" Ansley held up a slug.

"Seriously, I don't even want to talk about some of my less glamorous adventures. It was all a part of a steep learning curve that I'd rather put behind me now, thank you very much," Dex interrupted. "Let me help you with this," he bent down and started taking slugs from lettuce leaves.

"Isn't that murder for you?" Ansley asked.

"Well, I'm not sentimental. I'm keen for our species to evolve and that requires eating. It's the food chain and all of that. Slugs will always be around."

"Point taken," Ansley laughed. "So how'd you learn to control your animism?"

"Three things: Practice, ritual and meditation," said Dex counting on his slimy fingers.

"Ritual?" Ansley was sceptical.

"Ritual," said Dex.

"What running around naked under a full moon or something?"

"Yes and bleeding goats."

Ansley just stared at him.

"It's a joke! A joke, it's not like a crazy cult or something. It's just making the effort to breathe and repeat the same thing again and again."

"Sorry, life has been turned upside down lately and I guess I'm at the point where I'll believe anything. Ritual sounds like relaxing really," said Ansley.

"Kind of. Kind of like alert and focused relaxation. Once you can do that, you can begin to train your brain."

"Right. Are you a wizard or something?"

"No. I wish. My family were Druids generations ago but I just do my own thing now," said Dex.

"I didn't realize there were still Druids around."

"Nobody is around, and the ones that survived, live in caves and eat moss," said Dex.

"Seriously?"

"No, I'm kidding. Honestly, I've never met a single Druid that wasn't technologically advanced."

"So what, like cloaks and iPhones?"

"Yeah something like that," Dex said. "Not like you. This is Rye village right? I heard you were a bunch of crazies shut off from the real world. Sorry. I hope I didn't offend you, but you don't seem, you know, fanatical or odd in any way. Apart from looking like a vampire, lurking around the woods at night and picking slugs from cabbages, but that's just normal in my book."

"My father never paid much attention to what Jude said," said Ansley.

"Who's Jude?"

"Mr. Night Hawk. He's the leader around here, the one who gave me the bucket. He calls himself a prophet," said Ansley.

"Ah," said Dex, as if that explained everything.

"My father always said that our house happened to be close to a village run by a fanatic. We've never had much to do with the village, or other people for that matter and I am not exactly parish council material. I can't be in the sunlight. That's why I'm so pale."

"Are you serious?"

"Yeah. It keeps me pretty reclusive."

"I know what that's like. Imagine it, playing football with your friends, sliding in for the perfect tackle then, whoops, you're one of these guys," he held up a wiggling snail. "No offence," he told it and threw it into the bucket.

"Has that really happened?" Ansley asked.

"No, but it could have in the early days, and that's why I keep my animism a secret, not everybody would understand. They'd think I was a freak of nature and want to run tests on me or something."

"Probably, but I have to say, you are a bit freaky," Ansley teased.

"Thanks, that means a lot coming from one who resembles the walking dead," said Dex.

"Anytime. I settled into my freakiness ages ago," said Ansley.

"Good for you. Now all you need is a corpse bride and a little haunted house," said Dex.

"Yep and all you need is a cage to control your inner animal," said Ansley and they both laughed.

"You are the first person to recognise me, you know, in animal form," said Dex. "I couldn't believe it when you spoke to me. How did you know?"

"To be honest, I'm not sure. It was like I could sense a human inside the deer and that it wanted to speak. I don't know. Nothing like this has ever happened to me before so I'm still having a hard time believing this is real."

Dex put his hand on Ansley's shoulder. "Take it from someone on the other side of reality and forget about real," he said.

"What do you mean?"

"I mean animism is just one wave, one actuality amongst thousands, millions, churning around the place. What's visible is not all that there is, by a long shot. Take atoms. Atoms existed long before we discovered them right? That doesn't mean they were untrue before we recognized them, does it? It's the same with realities," said Dex.

"The last couple of days have been a true testimony to parallel realities, believe me. I can accept that idea now because of the things I've experienced," said Ansley. "Maybe that's why I was able to see you?" Ansley stopped picking snails and mused for a moment.

He felt tied to a plan he had yet to comprehend and compelled to tell Dex about the cove, but stopped himself. It had been a private experience and he'd sworn to secrecy about the pearl.

"That's probably just your brain catching up, which is why you need to question everything. I mean everything. And especially the things you're told are absolutely true. You need to keep evolving, mate. A few of us can kick start a species. Who knows? Maybe ten thousand years from now everyone will be able to shape shift or, God help us, maybe we'll all look like you. Whatever the case, we'll be as similar to the species we'll become as we currently are to chimps. The future is wide open," said Dex.

"That actually sounds quite hopeful," said Ansley.

He stood and stretched his arms up to the black and blue sky. It was the time of night where everything was completely quiet. His favourite hours.

"Of course it's hopeful," said Dex. "There is always room for possibility. Think about it. We feed from the earth until we deplete her and then she feeds from us and when she spits us back out again, we take a new form. We could be anything then, bacteria, a sycamore, a grasshopper, an angel. In that way the world is economical and where there's economy, there's intelligence and where there's intelligence, there's hope. But I'll tell you what," said Dex, "for you to see me, means something's changing. Something big."

That's exactly what Marianne had said, thought Ansley.

20.

Jude had always wanted his own world, but this pipedream was fraught with many obstacles that it seemed unobtainable. Until now. He knew there was a world hidden somewhere around the cove, so that problem was nearly solved, but there were other problems, bigger problems that needed consideration.

He had his form, sure. He had his special attributes, doesn't everybody? But at the end of the day, he was a crystalline creature at heart, without DNA, without the helix of evolution. How could he quickly grow a population without that beautiful merry-go-round of transformation? He was becoming impatient and wanted fast shaping life inside his rock and crystal world. Only the strongest would do. Only the survivors.

He secretly called the castle his Petri dish. Since his time in the garden he'd always considered himself an amateur biologist really, plus who knew the earth better than a snake? Heck, even his body host, Simorg, had once been a microbiologist and that was no mere stroke of luck, it was carefully planned.

Simorg Wright hadn't always been a religious zealot, but was once a promising scholar with a propensity towards the radical. In fact it was a radical idea that got him laughed out of academia. He wrote an article stating that bovine spongiform encephalitis (BSE) would eventually contaminate the ground making it unsuitable for plant growth because anything grown in it would eventually contain the prion protein.

At the time, scientists were unfamiliar with the particular protein transfer his host was speaking about, and as is often the case, they abolished him from their sight so they didn't have to think about something nonconformist. After his embarrassment, he moved into a council house in the small fishing village of Rye. He thought the sea air might do him some good.

His neighbour, Mrs. Eleanor Murphy, decided straight away that he wasn't, as she put it, dealing with a full deck and that it was her civic duty to keep an eye on him.

An hour later she was ringing the bell of his house, cursing him for taking so long because she hadn't worn her orthopaedic shoes and standing on a step was pure murder.

"Yeeees?" He opened the door.

He was very tall. Jude preferred tall hosts as it allowed him to stretch out his snake body, but Mrs. Murphy certainly didn't approve. Well, that height is just ridiculous, she thought, plus he had an academic's unkempt bushy brown hair. He reminded her of a skinny topiary wearing headphones.

"Are you going to take those headphones off and speak to me properly? I made you some bread." She found that straight talking with a cranky voice was quite effective on young people.

"I can hear you fine. They aren't plugged into anything and thanks," he said and took the bread out of her hands.

She would remember that later. That he didn't even wait for her to hand it to him, he just took it, and if he hadn't have said thank you, she would have bashed him over the head with her handbag, like she did to that boy who wanted to snatch her purse in the Tesco car park before the earth went to hell in a hand basket and you could still buy an edible potato. Well that taught him.

"Christ it's worse than I thought," she muttered under her breath, looking at the headphones and then the rest of him. He was wearing mismatched socks, one red and one green, poor dear thinks it's Christmas. Did I say that out loud? She wondered. Getting old was a bother.

"I beg your pardon?" He said.

"Nothing," she said and stared at him with a pinched face.

He didn't look like a psycho killer, though they never do, but she was good at first impressions. Always had been. Maybe he had a particular brain condition like everybody else in his generation? Nothing that couldn't be solved with a good kick up the arse and decent nutrition. She stared at him. He didn't strike her as a broccoli eater either.

"Come in. I'm Simorg Wright." He shifted from side to side. It was obvious that she unnerved him.

"I know your name. I'm Eleanor Murphy, but you can call me Mrs. Murphy. I'll come in but I'll just stay for a light lunch as I don't want to be any trouble."

This was the beginning of their short relationship, and even though they both annoyed one another, manners kept them pleasant. Manners and Mrs. Murphy's sense of duty.

She considered herself an undervalued civil servant for keeping such a sharp eye on him. When the council moved Mr. Wright into a smaller house two streets away, Mrs. Murphy was aghast at what she called 'the pure and evil selfishness of the government,' for the streets were cobbled at Mr. Wright's new residence and wreaked havoc on Mrs. Murphy's knees. She was an old woman now for Christ's sake, didn't the council care? It was just another way in which they abused the elderly, but she persevered and made the weekly journey to Mr. Wright's for a cup of tea and a good poke around.

"You have to monitor a person who drinks his tea from a jug and constantly wears a pair of headphones that I've never seen him plug into anything," she said.

She tested Simorg. She wanted to see the shape his anger might take, so asked him about matters that she felt might drive him over the edge like the cost of leeks (a plant she regarded as a wild weed) or the unreliability of the weatherman. All the while she watched the cord to his headphones dangle like a vicious serpent, wondering if he might be ungodly as well as insane. As it turned out he was about to become both.

It was Wednesday at ten to eleven. Mrs. Murphy would arrive at her usual prompt 11:00 o'clock. Simorg Wright filled the kettle and flipped the switch. The tornado sirens had been whistling for over an hour. They were so frequent now that people ignored them like they ignored car alarms. He looked out the window. The air was still and the clouds were grey. Maybe Mrs. Murphy would stay home? Either way, he fancied some pickled beetroot with his salad so went down into the cellar to get a jar. When he was in the cellar he tripped over a bicycle and lost his headphones. He got down on his hands and knees to search, while he was moving his hand across the damp stones, he knocked the shelf with the beetroot jars dislodging the rawlplugs and screws from the wall. The shelf and jars toppled, crashing onto his head rendering him unconscious.

He didn't hear the sound of a train as the grey clouds swirled into a funnel that touched down on his housing estate. The houses collapsed in like a fallen pyramid of playing cards. Simorg finally woke up covered in glass and beetroot juice, he found his headphones and walked up the steps to a changed world.

Simorg's headphones started buzzing right away and had Mrs. Murphy survived, she would have applied her practicality to the situation and determined that a fly was caught in the headpiece.

But, alas, Mrs Murphy had been swept up in the tornado and dropped in a tree a mile from the village. Her khaki mackintosh was fanned out like a nest and her body was purple and contorted like a weak bird.

Simorg was also transformed.

The voice. How could he explain the voice he heard? First, there was a buzzing and static like someone constantly crumpling up paper, but beyond those noises was a constant drip, drip, drip. The dripping was the only thing steadfast and anchoring and when he listened to it he had the strange sensation that the thing that was leaking from him was feeling. Compassion. He tried not to think about it, stayed in bed, put his hands over his head and prayed the dripping would stop. Suddenly it did stop and the voice took its place.

"Get up!" The voice demanded. It was so loud. "Get up and have a bath, you're a prophet now for goodness sake!"

Simorg had no idea this voice belonged to Jude. He didn't even question it, to be frank, he didn't care because anything was preferable to the blasted dripping. Also he was suddenly blessed with the gift of rhetoric. He could roll his 'r's' and enunciate implicitly. He was a baritone and loud. The old Simorg had always been a quiet scientist. He wore the headphones to drown out noise. His voice was unrecognizable to him now.

"Turn on the radio and listen to what I've done for you," barked Jude.

Simorg obeyed and what he heard was remarkable. Two years after he'd been kicked out of mainstream science, they found that the soil had indeed been contaminated and that food grown in this soil was not edible. He couldn't believe it. He had been right. He had predicted the future.

"Put some shoes on, let's go," said Jude.

The voice waltzed Simorg into the main office of the University of Sussex and demanded a formal apology; of course the apology was systematically refused, which forced Simorg to dutifully resort to plan B. Before he knew what he was doing, he dropped his trousers, showed them his bare bum and said something highly intellectual like, "nah nah nah-naa-naaah!" As he left the building he stuck two fingers up at them and felt brilliant. Absolutely brilliant. He jumped up and punched the air, yes!

"See? You possess the rhetoric and unpredictable finesse necessary to be a world-class leader. Or at least a village leader. Now let's get on with the prophet thing. First you have to ask me to stay. You do want me to stay, don't you? After all I've done and how marvellous you feel?" Jude said.

"Yes, yes of course I want you to stay," said Simorg.

"That's all I need," and the voice became a terrifying shape that snaked around filling his whole body.

"Remember me?" Jude hissed horribly.

Simorg crouched in the corner of his brain, small and afraid. He nodded. Yes, he remembered. He trembled. "What have I done?"

21.

Marianne went to check on the pearl the morning after she'd buried it. All night, it had lit up her dreams. It was quiet inside the house and she could feel her ears still ringing from the previous night's sea wind and water. The pearl placed itself behind her forehead like a pulse that spread throughout her limbs, until there wasn't a tired bone in her entire body.

She looked at her palm and rubbed it with her thumb.

She felt that something was changing inside her that was magnificently subtle, like a season. The pearl felt it too and was surrounded by an emptiness that it couldn't penetrate.

She got out of bed and quietly dressed. She couldn't hear anyone awake, so crept downstairs as silently as she could. In the kitchen she took a blue bottle from her mother's medicinal stock and slipped it in her coat pocket.

Her father caught her at the door.

"Aren't you an early bird," he said and placed his hand over hers on the doorknob. "And where are you off to then?"

She was prepared for him, took her hand from under his and removed a trowel from her back pocket. "I couldn't get back to sleep, so thought I'd get an hour in before breakfast."

"Really? I have to say that surprises and pleases me Marianne." He took his hand off the doorknob and patted her on the back. "There is something else I need to talk to you about. Someone told me they saw you talking to Dark Ansley, is that right?"

She gripped the trowel in her hand defensively as she faced him.

"I was only curious, Daddy. What's that saying? Keep your friends close but your enemies closer. Why, you don't think he's contaminated, do you?" This seemed to appease him and his voice lost its previous edge.

"Jude says he isn't, but all the same, I don't like you two talking."

"Okay Daddy," she said and he opened the door for her.

"Off you go," he said.

He stood watching her cross the field. The girl seems to have gained a bit of motivation and allegiance, he thought. That's good; she could use a bit of loyalty. She turned around and waved.

She would have to do some digging now. She went to one of the large vegetable beds and stuck her trowel into the cold earth. If her father were still there in half an hour she'd pretend she needed a wee and enter the woodland. It was early in the morning and the day had yet to warm. Her hands were cold. She knelt down and began digging. The grass was whiskery with frost.

A few moments later she saw Jude parading down the pavement with a group of cherubs. His legs were so long it looked like he was on stilts. Excellent, she thought, as she knew her father would invite him in for a cup of tea, but instead, they stood outside and watched her. Eventually two cherubs appeared with cups of tea.

It was frustrating. If she didn't reach the pearl before breakfast, the field would be too full of people for her to sneak away. Jude was always ruining things. It was as if ruination was his secret intent. Even from the beginning, she had felt something low and sinister about Jude's presence.

She'd never forget the first time she saw him.

It was the night of her father's fishing accident. He'd gone out on his boat and hadn't returned for hours. A storm had come without warning; the sky, the waves all seemed to be boiling and Marianne's mother, Janet, stood at the window picking her cuticles' and chewing her lip until it bled.

The rain lashed against the glass in waves and lightening lit up crazed trees. To distract herself, Janet went to the kitchen and stirred a pot of soup she'd made earlier. Marianne could hear her sucking the blood from her lip.

"Can you see him?" She asked Marianne who had taken her place by the window.

"Not yet."

Lightening cracked and Marianne saw trees bend low and spring forward as though they were made of rubber, their leaves twirled like frantic pinwheels against a thousand shades of black. Wait. There. There was something.

"I think I see a light!"

Janet ran into the living room. The spoon was still in her hands and dripping soup on the carpet. They both peered out the window and when they saw his head torch bouncing like a ship lost at sea, they screamed with relief. Her mother ran out to greet him; she threw her arms around him and then stopped abruptly, when they reached the door Marianne saw why.

He was soaking. His eyes were huge and bloodshot. He was stringed with seaweed and covered in mud. His face was white, pure white and he had no shoes on his feet. He looked possessed.

"You should have seen it, it was enormous and evil, evil it was and it came at me under the water," he muttered in a quiet but alarming voice.

Her mother led him to the sofa and sat him down. She put another log on the fire and went to the kitchen to fetch him some soup. She didn't look at Marianne.

"There you are," she soothed. "Get some warmth in you and you'll be fine," she said and handed him a mug. "What about the boat, Harold?"

The mug steamed inside his sodden hands. They were wrinkled as raisins. He said nothing and stared at the fire.

"The boat, Harold, where is it?" Her mother asked and put her hand upon her father's shaking knee.

"On the rocks, in pieces." Marianne could hardly hear his answer.

"Oh, Harold, can we fix it?" The boat was her parents' livelihood.

Her father threw his mug of soup against the wall. It splattered like an orange paintball. He grabbed her mother by the shoulders and shook her.

"Who cares?! Listen! I'm telling you I saw the devil! The devil himself! It was a snake, a snake, and I've seen him before as a child and now he's come back to me! I knew he would and I'm scared Janet, I'm so bloody scared," he buried his head in her mother's chest and sobbed. His large square back jerked.

"Shhh, shhh," Janet kept repeating.

Marianne went to the kitchen and got a cloth. She cleared up the mess from the soup. She looked at her mother. Her mother met her eye and looked hopeless. She left them alone and went upstairs to her bedroom.

She could hear her father mumbling and her mother soothing him with her soft voice. Her father had always been so strong and now he seemed weak and reduced. She took her sketchbook from under her pillow. Drawing soothed her. She began to draw a rollicking sea, a little boat, and beneath it, a serpent. She knew she was drawing fear.

She understood the evil her father had encountered, had felt it lurking beneath her whilst swimming in the bay when the water suddenly went cold as though death had passed.

The doorbell rang.

She walked down the stairs and there was Jude. He was sopping wet. He took his hat off and bowed to Janet.

"I was just checking for tree damage and saw Harold staggering towards the house. Is he alright?" Janet led him though into the living room where her father sat huddled beside the fire.

Jude glanced at Marianne as he passed. His eyes were as void as space, as an empty eternity. People said that he heard voices that predicted the future and could save the present, so they followed him.

What if he's listening to the wrong voices? Marianne thought as she looked at him. She didn't trust his motives. Who checks for tree damage before the storm is over?

Her opinion didn't have time to matter, for in the morning her father had already vowed his life to Jude and had become a Keeper. Jude, he said, had saved him from the devil, but Marianne could never rationalize this in her mind. She believed the devil was something we created ourselves and, sometimes, she thought with horror, unknowingly invited into our lives.

She looked up at the clouds. They were racing as if in a speeded up movie. She'd never seen them move so fast. Thinking about the past made her feel afraid, even though it had already been lived, there was something about it that seemed dishonest and the dishonesty was what frightened her. Her father and Jude were still standing outside drinking their tea, talking and glancing over at her.

There was something about their surveillance that felt overwhelmingly permanent. As though she might never be truly independent, might never live within her own dominion, making only her own choices and carving her own path. How could oneself be sovereign during a time of famine? Humans needed humans to survive. She looked at her father and Jude. They both waved. No, she thought, you are not my people. I don't belong with you.

But how to break away? Ansley. He knew the woods and he certainly didn't fit into the Keeper community. Eventually he would have to leave. They would never allow him to stay, they would kill him before they would risk cross-contamination. Could she do that? Could she share his life of darkness? She immediately thought of Thumbelina wedded to the mole and felt disgusted with herself.

She shoved the trowel into the soil and sliced through the skin between her thumb and pointer finger. It was a clean cut and it hurt like hell. She held on to it with her other hand. It was dirty with mud. The mud mixed with the blood and fell in clumps on the ground. She would need to clean it otherwise it would certainly get infected. It was bleeding furiously now and warm blood was dripping from her elbow and onto the dirt floor with a small, repetitive, pat, pat.

A panic rose in her throat like bile. She unwrapped her scarf and wound it as many times as she could around her cut. It felt cold and wet at first then began to warm as it mixed with her blood. Her hand was as plump as a tennis ball and within seconds the blood stained through.

The vision of the pearl's waters rose like a gentle cloud inside her. She looked up. Fortunately, Jude and her father had gone into the house. She ran to the woodland as fast as she could.

22.

She knelt, panting, beside the pearl's small silvery pond. It was the size of an open mouth and she peered down its neck. She felt that the pearl would heal her. Everything seemed to be waiting, urging her to do it, and so she dunked her hand inside its pool of water, scarf and all. The pain stopped immediately as the pearl poured its light into her.

Could it be? She thought and began unwrapping her scarf. When her hand was revealed she gasped. The cut had completely vanished.

The water was cavernous deep and black and she could see the pearl resting at the bottom like a white ball. She blew across the water and bounced its reflection. She took her mother's blue medicine bottle from her coat pocket and filled it with the silver liquid.

*

So many things were possible, she thought as she walked back to the castle for breakfast, even the fact that she was just going crazy. Does it happen suddenly? One day sane, the next day mad? She had always thought it happened over a period of time. Like when anger takes a person, of course nobody starts out that way, but events can turn you like a piece of wood and a shape begins to take place.

Was she the shape of madness? She remembered seeing a sculpture in an abandoned garden some years back. She was mesmerized by how its form shaped the space around it. Sometimes what the sculptor removes is more important than what they leave behind.

She'd removed her idea of certainty. It had clung to her, yet when she held the pearl, it fell like a chunk of rock chipped from her eyes. Seeing and feeling are the same thing, she thought, and if the water could heal her hand, what else could it heal?

Apart from the blood on her scarf and arms, she could have believed it had been a dream. She looked at her hand and there was no sign of the cut. What does it mean? Could it heal anyone else? She would have to try. She walked back to the castle in a daze.

Jude met her at the castle door and her heart dropped. He was not the person she wanted to see at the moment. She put the scarf in her pocket so he wouldn't see the blood. The last thing she needed was for him to suspect she'd been contaminated.

"It's a pleasure to see you've developed green fingers and initiative," he took a loud and deep breath through his nostrils. "There is nothing like a good dig in the morning," he took a sip of his tea and looked down at the cherub poised like a side table beside him. "Excuse me? Where's your linen?" He asked and the cherub produced a linen napkin from his pocket and draped it over his head.

Jude placed his cup of tea upon the cherub's head. "Really, I shouldn't have to ask," he scolded the cherub, then turned and eyed Marianne suspiciously. "I saw that you came from the woodland?"

This took Marianne off-guard and she fumbled her words. "Yes, I was looking for mushrooms," she knew that he knew she was lying.

Fortunately it was a lie that she could back up as her mother had taught her all about edible plants and fungi. But why hadn't she just told him she needed a pee?

"Ah a fungi expert, how fascinating. You know I've often thought of training the cherubs to truffle hunt, but where does one find the time? Don't stray too far away from the field. I can't have anyone contaminating the herd. Understand?" His eyes bore into her until she had no choice but to look away.

"Okay, I won't. I need to go and wash my hands before breakfast. Excuse me," she said and walked to the kitchen.

She washed her arms and hands. She could hear Jude talking in a hushed voice to someone, and then the click of his boots as he walked down the hallway. When she opened the door the Keeper was blocking the exit. If he were a dog, he'd growl, she thought.

A window was open above them and there was a terrible coughing coming from inside a dorm room. The cough had a metal quality to its sound like choking up razorblades. It made Marianne's body tingle.

"Who is that?" she asked the Keeper and he just shrugged.

"I didn't see who it was, but Jude said he was keeping her in quarantine until she's well again," he said and sat down in a chair beside the door. He was on patrol.

Behind them a cherub was rattling along the pathway carrying his breakfast. The tray was bigger than his torso. It was piled high with everything, porridge, berries, bananas, toast with butter and tea. He handed it to the Keeper, then spat on the grass, took a pack of cigarettes from his dirty nappy and walked towards the field smoking. She looked at the Keeper with surprise.

"They hate humans," the Keeper explained.

"But they worship Jude and he's human," she said.

"He's a prophet, it's different. Breakfast isn't for another hour, now up you go," he nodded towards the row of houses. "I don't like talking."

She ran home and straight up to her bedroom. She took the blue vial containing the pearl's water from her pocket. It glistened with promise and when she placed it on her windowsill it cast a blue rectangle across her bedroom floor. She washed her scarf in the sink and hung it up to dry.

Her parents were fishing and wouldn't be back until lunch, so she had plenty of time to deliver some pearl water to the coughing girl. What if it cured her? She prickled with excitement.

She had to be quick and didn't want the Keeper to see her, so went out the back door and climbed up over the fence. Within minutes she was standing underneath the girl's window again. The Keeper was six metres in front of her and completely focused on his breakfast.

The sound of dry retching came from the inside. Poor thing, Marianne thought, and scanned the building. A rake was leaning against the wall. Marianne used it to tap on the girl's window. It was almost too easy.

23.

A small girl peered out. She looked as weak as a kitten with dark rings around her eyes and skin yellowed with jaundice. Marianne recognized her from the bus. She had looked feeble even then and Marianne wondered how long she'd been ill.

"Down here," Marianne whispered.

The girl raised her limp hand hello.

"I have something for you," Marianne said. "Something that might make you better, but you have to keep it a secret. Can you do that?"

The girl nodded. She seemed too fragile to speak and Marianne didn't want to press her.

"Good. Throw down your pillowcase," said Marianne.

The girl ducked away and seconds later floated the pillowcase down to Marianne. Marianne opened up the pillowcase and dropped the blue vial inside. She tied the pillowcase to the rake and stretched it up to the window.

Beatrice took out the vial. It shimmered in her hands.

"It's spring water. You drink it. I promise it won't harm you. I've had loads myself. I think it might even cure you, but I can't be sure, so you have to trust me."

Beatrice closed the vial inside of her hand, nodded and shut the window. She was feverish all over and her teeth were chattering. It had taken all of her strength to reach for the pillowcase and she lay down on the bed exhausted inside a hot puddle of sweat.

She closed her eyes and brought the vial to her mouth and swallowed the most delicious liquid. It was cool and sweet without being flowery. It tasted lighter than water. It tasted like a gulp of fresh, snowy air.

As soon as it entered her body it seemed to blow through her limbs and lift them, even the burning hot hand she imagined was constantly at her throat released. Her mind cleared like a path swept of debris and she walked along it towards herself. She remembered herself.

Beatrice, she thought, I am Beatrice and she took a deep breath. She peeled herself from her wet mattress and sat up. Everything spun and purred with life.

She opened up the curtains and the sun poured in.

Outside the breakfast trumpets began to sound. As soon as Marianne heard them she ran to the castle and straight up to Beatrice's dorm room. A completely different child greeted her, a child of vibrancy and health, and Beatrice laughed out loud at the look on Marianne's face. Marianne was not prepared for such an immaculate recovery.

"I know! It's a miracle!" Beatrice grabbed Marianne by the hands and pulled her inside. "I don't know how to thank you," she said and gave Marianne a tight hug and started crying with gratitude.

Beatrice was a beautiful child. She was around nine or ten at the most. Her long hair was black and her skin was flawless with ruddy cheeks. Her eyes were hazel and electric. Her bones looked bird-sized and Marianne loved her right away as one might love a small sister. They embraced for a long time, both recovering from the shock of the water's power. Finally Beatrice settled down and dried her eyes on her sleeve.

What was that?" Beatrice sat on the edge of the bed as if stupefied by her amazement. Marianne sat down beside her.

"I can't really tell you because I don't exactly know. All I can say is that it's a special water, but you must swear you won't tell a soul about it," she touched Beatrice's arm, "I'm serious. Don't tell anyone. Especially Jude. You mustn't tell Jude or any of the Keeper's okay?"

"I won't. I promise," Beatrice said and crossed her heart on her chest. "What's your name?"

"Marianne," she said. "What's yours?"

"Beatrice. Marianne, you saved my life," she said and again started to cry.

Marianne hugged her and stroked her hair. It was like touching an angel.

"You stay here and rest. Have a bath if you feel up to it. I know you feel better now, but you still need to build up your strength."

"What will you do?" Beatrice's eyes were needy, doe-like and full of admiration for Marianne.

"I'm going to find out more about this water," said Marianne.

"Will you tell me about it?"

"Of course I will. I'll tell you all about it this afternoon. We can even work in the field together," she kissed Beatrice's forehead and stood to leave.

Beatrice lay down and closed her heavy eyes.

"That's it," said Marianne. "Just rest and you'll be as good as new soon," she said as she softly shut the door.

She stood in the hallway and took a deep breath. Her head was spinning. What on earth would she do with the power to cure?

Better yet, what couldn't she do?

24.

Ansley ghosted along the corridor from his room. He would have liked to go unnoticed and almost missed the days he'd spent in the woodland. Being nocturnal meant that he seldom saw other people, so he wasn't used to the stares his appearance generated. He wished they would stare at him outright and just get it over with; instead they waited until they thought he wasn't looking and glanced sideways.

It was worse when they were trying not to be obvious because he could feel it, eyes like hot darts trying to quickly take his appearance in, to reconcile it, and familiarize themselves enough to look again without wincing. Or they avoided him and tried to act like his appearance was normal.

He would never be normal.

From his birth Ansley's mother had a sadness that she couldn't shake. She was not bad or weak but the force of her maternal bonds did not flourish and ultimately were set to repel. His father told him how he would perch him on his arms like a scrappy owlet determined to fly one day. Ansley was too young to remember this, but he used the image of an owl's silent predatory grace to bolster his courage from the voyeuristic stares of the other castle inhabitants.

The castle now sounded jovial and alive. People were no longer zombified. It was as if the food had awakened them and Ansley could hear their conversations as they walked down the hallway, their footsteps, the person in the dorm next to him brushing their teeth, the sounds produced a new level of intimacy, which meant community. Ansley both longed for community and feared it, in truth, there was a part of him that felt he didn't deserve acceptance, and so he pretended that he didn't want it.

It was so much easier to be with animals. Perhaps that was why he didn't shy away from Dex, on some level he considered Dex part animal. Animals trusted their instincts and their instincts always told them that he was kind, despite looking like a monster. Dex spent a large amount of time as an animal and had developed that instinctual side of his personality.

Marianne was another story. She just accepted his ugliness in one huge gulp, like swallowing cod liver oil or some nasty medicine that would benefit her in the end. There was something instinctual about her too and although Ansley couldn't pinpoint it, he knew she was, well, sacred. That was the only word that popped in to his head. Sacred enough not to care about the trivialities of the exterior. Or at least he hoped she was.

He took a deep breath and stealthily opened the door to the castle hall. He slipped into the breakfast room. Words and heat and breakfast smells flooded him. It was packed and excited. Everyone seemed to be talking about Jude and the second chances the new world offered and, of course, food. People dart glanced at him as he moved to the buffet table. He tried to steady his breathing.

He stood in the queue for porridge. It steamed from a large silver urn. A cherub stood on a chair and used a big silver ladle to slop it into each bowl. Jude walked up to the cherub and smacked him on the back of the head, "Careful nappy brain," he said.

Jude was wearing a silk peacock blue shirt, black jeans, and a monocle, but no top hat. His tattoo looked like a flat purple toupee until you were close enough to see the tentacles. Jude took a bowl and sat down in a carved mahogany wing back chair positioned at the head of a table. A centipede of cherubs held the chandelier above him while he ate; all around him eyes were watching with idolatry. Ansley wondered what it would be like to be stared at with such admiration.

Marianne was nowhere to be seen and Ansley sat alone at a shadowed table listening to the chatter and rain falling against stone. The wind moaned against the stone. The air was hot, but the walls were cold and at that moment he missed the freshness of the woodland more than he could say.

A Keeper walked in, his rayon tracksuit was speckled with rain and Marianne was following him, when she saw Ansley she looked straight at him, and then ever so slightly shook her head no. Her meaning had been clear. Ansley wasn't to speak to her, so concentrated on eating his porridge.

Marianne and the Keeper sat at Jude's table and when she went up for some breakfast she dropped a note beside Ansley's feet. He stepped on it and waited for her to return to her seat before he picked it up. It was still damp from her nervous hand. To be caught with an illegal note would mean dire punishment for a Keeper's daughter. The fact that she had risked herself for him gave him a joy beyond measure.

The note had been folded into a tiny crane and he squeezed the bird in his hand as he walked back to his room. It was too dangerous to open the note in the dining hall.

He locked his door, sat down at his desk and carefully opened the crane wing by wing so that he would remember how to fold it again.

It was part of a poem:

Out of the night that covers me,
Black as the Pit from pole to pole,
I thank whatever gods may be
For my unconquerable soul.

She had told him that his poetry must be his entry point. To where? He had asked. To the place where you truly live, she had said, your own home. She hadn't laughed at him or made him feel soppy in any way. He read the poem once more. Is that what she thought of him? An unconquerable soul cloaked in darkness? He turned the note over and read:

I'll sneak out tomorrow night and visit you on your shift. Something amazing has happened. Mxx

It certainly has, he thought and turned the paper into a bird once more. He placed it on the windowsill. On the pavement below, Jude was walking back to his house, contemplating the note he'd seen Marianne drop for Ansley.

25.

Jude opened the door to his library. The curtains were drawn and the room was dark but for the glow of his helixes. He lovingly ran his hand along the rows of jars. The little green swirls brightened with his touch.

In the beginning his collecting habits had been random and disorganized. He had worked with quantity in mind, not quality, and this had been a mistake. Over time he realized that if he wanted to direct the evolutionary course of his planet, he needed to be selective. The disasters were a blessing for him as they naturally weeded out the weakest of the species. It was important to observe the survivors and choose the most suitable.

He kicked off his cowboy boots and slumped into his thinking chair. That disfigured boy and his little girlfriend were definitely brave. Did they really think he wouldn't spot the note?

He practically invented body language. He should probably just eat them now, but then he wouldn't discover what they were scheming. It was difficult to get the balance of dictatorship right. On one hand, he needed an evolutionary spark of innovation and genetic capability, on the other; he needed souls he could control.

There was something about Marianne and Ansley's relationship that overrode Jude's greater sensibilities. He knew he should dispose of them as they were taking risks and not living in accordance with his laws. But. But what?

Well, Ansley reminded him of the snake he'd been when he'd fallen in love with Eve. He simply wanted to see how it would end. Curiosity was a sign of intelligence and he was a supernatural genius, after all, so it did make sense. But the whole thing was rather pathetic. Did that hideous creature actually think a girl of her standing would return his love? And after she dumped him, and she no doubt would, Jude might find a proper confidant.

The truth is that he never got over Eve. Not really. He thought he had, for years, until that blasted cherub paid him a visit and all of his emotions rose to his throat like a geyser.

The cherub had come to tell him about the seed. It was their first decade out of the Garden. Ages ago. He still can't quite believe the cherub actually told him, but they were all trying to find their place in the ruined world and he was probably just rebelling against Eve.

The new world was tough to begin with, even for Jude, as he hadn't honed his skills and, to be frank, they were all a little spoiled in the Garden. He always did feel a bit sorry for the cherubs. Once they were out of the Garden they stopped ageing. Imagine being stuck inside an infant's body forever, never getting your teeth, constantly wetting yourself, falling down, zoning out mid-sentence to stare at your feet or hands. Must be a total nightmare. Anyway, sympathy kept Jude from eating him on the spot.

"You're on my rock, kid, move it," he said.

The cherub didn't budge an inch. He just crossed his chubby little legs and lit a leaf filled with tobacco plant. Jude couldn't believe it. The cheek of this one will taste nice, he thought.

"I've got news for you. Something you'll definitely want to hear," it said blowing a smoke ring. How obscene.

"Oh yeah? What makes you so sure?"

"Because it involves the Scripture Tree," he said. He had the voice of a fifty year-old smoker. It was gross, but he was cocky and Jude liked cocky.

"You look ridiculous. Put that death stick out, and not on my rock, I'm sunbathing here, show some respect. What's wrong with you kids these days?"

He needed to be told a thing or two, it was exasperating and Jude was losing his patience. The cherub stubbed his cigarette out and accidently wet himself.

"Ahhh! You've pissed on my rock, butterball! That's it! You're dinner now!" Jude lunged forward, fangs out and squirting. What was the harm in scaring the cherub a little when he'd already emptied his bladder?

"No! Wait! The Scripture Tree, remember? The Apple Tree? There's a seed left! I saw it! I promise you, I saw it!" the cherub was whimpering. Once a baby, always a baby, thought Jude and he stopped squeezing. "What did you say?"

"I saw it. I did. It rolled down her cheek like a big white tear."

"You mean Evie?" He felt a lump in his throat, heck, he was all throat. He felt a lump in his body.

"The one and only. She let it drop into her hands and clasped them together like this," he demonstrated the hands-in-prayer, tight like a clamshell position. "Then she walked into the sea. We all begged her not to go."

"What? She walked into the sea! My Evie, you mean she's gone?" Turns out he had a soft spot for her still, you see. She was the first he'd ever corrupted.

"No. No. She came back but, well…" He seemed to be searching for the correct word.

"But what?! But what?!"

"But she's different," the cherub said.

"Different? How?"

"She was underwater for a long time. We all walked to the water's edge and held our breath. Then bubbles started to rise, one by one, and the angels started circling overhead. They were singing when she rose to the surface. He opened the clouds and there was a pool of light. She walked calmly up to the sand and smiled at us. She had no hands. Her hands and the seed inside of them were gone. They'd completely vanished! The angels began to cry. Feathers fell from the sky. 'What have you done?' we asked her. 'I've given them another chance,' she said, rising in a beam of light. It was the seed. A seed from the Scripture Tree."

They fell silent for a while and thought about the blank planet at the bottom of the sea. It made him sick to think of her without her beautiful hands. He wanted to weep, but regained composure and snaked around the cherub's neck.

"Why are you telling me this?" he squeezed.

"Because I know you can find it," he said.

"And if I did, what good would that do you?" He squeezed harder.

"I'm hoping that you can change me, you know, let me age," he gagged.

Of course Jude ate him, even though eating smokers is downright disgusting, but the cherub had left him with no choice. He couldn't have him hanging around and cramping his style. Besides he liked to remain indebted to nobody.

Jude searched for a while, but to be honest he wasn't entirely convinced that cherub was right about the seed. Eve was prone to dramatics over the teensiest thing. That was an eon of moons ago and while he'd never forgotten about the seed, he believed it was probably just a myth, so kept it in the back of his mind along with the Golden Fleece and all the other miscellaneous quests.

So imagine his surprise when, centuries later, he stumbled upon the cove.

He saw what looked like big amazing birds circling in the sky as though they were attached to the sea with invisible string. That's strange, he thought and then he heard them. Angels. You hardly ever heard them anymore but their sound was unmistakable. It was like the wind with a song in it or the ringing of a wave. It was not really his thing, but he appreciated that it was beautiful because he was not a total philistine.

The sun was setting and a light shone through an opening in the clouds that lit the cove like a radiant pink bowl. There was a feeling present, he guessed it was peace, anyway it made him incredibly uncomfortable and he knew, he just knew he'd found the cove with the seed. The angels saw him then and came swooping down like attacking eagles. What a bunch of harpies. That attack told him all he needed to know. It was true. God damn, it was true. A whole world contained in one little seed.

He slid off. He needed to come up with a plan and a body, preferably the body of one who was meek. Weren't they meant to inherit worlds or something like that? He thought of all the people he'd planted scales in and Simorg sprang immediately to mind.

The last he knew he lived in the area and had little soul of his own. Too much soul burnt him but in a delicious mouth-watering way, like chilli-chocolate, so he sucked out their souls before eating and collecting their helixes. It was a bit of a pain, but it kept him fit, so he was not complaining.

This, however, was different. It was his dream come true. If he wanted the new world the seed offered, he'd need to populate it with followers. This would be his greatest plan yet; he couldn't just slide in with a plague or a band of murderers. No, he needed to be subtle, delicate and completely consuming.

Ahh, Evie, he thought, thank you for this chance. To you, my star, my princess, to you, I give my skin.

He rose from his chair and flung open the window. He took a deep breath of fresh air and smelled something absolutely delicious. What on earth is that? He thought and promptly followed his nose.

26.

Beatrice could hear a radio. It was like all of her senses were alight and amplified. It reminded her of her parents, as they used to listen to the radio in the evenings. They liked words in a room, not images. She remembered how their mugs of tea clinked against the countertop, remembered their hushed voices and her mother's humming.

She might have made up the humming, she was not sure, the memory was so far away now, it was almost unreachable. A thing like grief never leaves; it remains embedded, but eventually, it learns to step to the side, allowing other emotions to take residence. Overcoming her illness was the catalyst Beatrice needed to push faith into view.

Marianne was right, she was still weak from her ordeal, and it would take some time to get her strength back. Well, she had plenty of that, plenty of time and something new as well, something inside of her that hadn't been there before her illness, like a coin shining at the bottom of a well. A wish was inside her.

She was gazing at it when she heard someone on the other side of the door.

Swiftly her wish shot up into her throat like an alarm.

*

Jude had tried his best. He really had, but he could smell her soul from up the road and there was something magnetic about it, something slippery and mouth-watering, like melted chocolate only lighter, fluffier. It was hard to be good when you were bad.

And just one little slurp, just one, wouldn't hurt, would it? She was already ill, so it wouldn't raise suspicion if she went missing.
How often do you find a scrumptious soul with a deathly cough? These opportunities are rare, he justified to himself, and sometimes you just have to accept your true nature. He heaved a sigh of resolve, checked to make sure nobody was looking and slipped under the door.

*

She heard him before he appeared. The noise was sticky, slimy. She sat up
and looked around the room. It was as if someone was shoving mincemeat
under her door. Living mincemeat, like red worms, it congealed together
and formed an enormous snake. It smiled at her and flicked its tongue as if
testing the air. It slithered around positioning itself and began sucking. The
sucking caught her mouth like a fishhook. It pulled the air from her lungs
and squeezed. Her whole body became rigid and unable to move. He sucked
and sucked and she could see herself tunnelling into him like gold dust.
All the while the wish hung on to one of her ribs like a bit of paper blown
against a lamppost. It refused to let go, and when he stopped sucking, the
wish fluttered slowly back down to the bottom of her. It was the only thing
moving. Perhaps it's my soul, she thought before she felt herself go.

*

He didn't always eat them. You don't last long in this business without a
touch of resourcefulness, so he implanted the ones he thought would be
useful in future. The ones he felt had found reverence in his presence,
however grotesque. They were born bloodthirsty and he could smell that
heat.

Simorg the microbiologist had that smell. He was a little piggy that had
been rolling in stink. He stank of neediness and the desire for acceptance.
Jude could smell him halfway across the world. He hardly even needed his
locator.

Jude had skins waiting for him all over the world, just in case the seed was
found and he needed to slip into a meek body. He was surprisingly picky
about whom he'd use to populate his world, considering he needed them
soulless, and that didn't generally equate with good character. But the world
was increasingly superficial and he had his choice among people.

It was interesting to lead Rye as a mock community before he implanted
his own world. He was learning how to speak to the carbon forms, how to
govern, and on the whole it was a sociology experiment that he was enjoying
immensely.

Simorg should consider himself lucky, thought Jude; actually all the skins should consider themselves lucky because they hadn't been eaten right away. He prolonged their lives and wasn't life the greatest gift? Not that he was some bleeding philanthropist; mind you, more of a ventriloquist that preserves its puppets. And there have been a lot of puppets.

He'd inhabited and discarded bodies many times throughout eternity, yet he felt, even from the beginning, that Simorg's body was different. It was almost as if they were a team. Almost. Simorg had never been as repulsed by Jude as his other hosts, rather he was like a scared little pea that just rolled into the corner of his own brain. Jude nicknamed him Bird's Eye.

"Hello, Birds Eye!" he'd shout at him, but Simorg never laughed. It got on Jude's nerves. It was funny, damn it! The other thing that was different was that Jude could feel Simorg thinking. God, it was annoying. If Jude could have put his finger on him he'd have squashed him. Why do you need to think when you have me? It's not like you're going anywhere, but Bird's Eye was clever, too clever maybe, and stayed just out of reach.

It's not easy work and Jude dreamt about how glorious it would be to throw his skin off completely and bask in the sun like the old days. He had to keep Simorg's body around to give him an air of authenticity, but as soon as he had enough DNA to populate his new world, he'd let the skin go but, honestly, he wondered if he wouldn't half miss the little pea brain.

He didn't know he had it in him. It'd been handy to have another character around, like an extra heat, an extra blanket. He felt the cold now that he's older, the actual temperature, but also the world's frigidity of spirit. It wears on the elderly, you know. Simorg is his human touch; he needed to be believable, for without him, everybody just might've smelt a snake. C'est la vie.

27.

Jude felt that he could do anything now that he'd sucked out a lovely soul. It had been ages as so many of the trusting and delicious were the first to perish. And while, he supposed, it couldn't be avoided, it was most certainly a shame. He was hungry and it was hard to be around all of these souls without eating a few. Cherubs just tasted nasty.

Have a bit of control and fatten them up first, he scolded himself, make them strong and then devour. It made him sweat just to think about it. He'd been living off cherubs lately and that had completely put him off his food. It was definitely what you'd call a mixed blessing.

And then, there she was, a little ping-pong ball of pure delight bouncing around in his cavity like an echo. "Say hello to Birds Eye," he told her. It raised his spirits no end and he was whistling the Jolly Green Giant as he entered the breakfast room.

A Keeper put his podium in place and cherubs flew around the ceiling clapping their hands to get everyone's attention. He started speaking when the chandelier was in place.

"Good morning, my fine people. The day is clean and fresh and my lungs consume it for they can't help themselves. Whose breath isn't deeper when the air's clean? We are creatures that consume purity. That's our world. Consume or be consumed. Like it or not, the fact that you're standing here means that you've chosen to consume purity. As have I! Aren't we lucky? For we stand over the last patch of uncontaminated soil and today our hands will grow dirty with it. Tonight we'll sweep it from our floors, wipe it from our knees and we'll pick it from our fingernails. Don't be complacent about the soil you tread upon. It represents power in an evolutional race where Homo sapiens are losing, but not you, not us, oh no. Those that stand here will win the last and most important battle the Lord has ever sent us. The battle for existence!"

Cherubs floated around with 'Applause' signs and everyone put down their cutlery and clapped. It enlivened Jude as he loved an audience.

"I told them. I told the so-called scientists: if you bury BSE it will contaminate the soil. But did they listen? No! How can you grow pure food in a ground riddled with disease? Now they've all lost their minds! Who's laughing now? Huh? My laugh is the laugh of a human. Their laugh is the laugh of a madman, a psychotic hyena! That's right, our brothers and sisters around us have become animals, so we will recreate our family here, in this little community, with our simple hands in the earth, gritty and moist with life, we will remain the uncontaminated breed!" He shook the podium and stomped his cowboy boots.

"Keep your minds earnest and swift. Keep your hearts wholesome and spirited and we will rise into the next millennia as a new species. Together! Humans have seen dark days and we aren't past the darkest yet, but do not pity the fallen for they have been reduced by their greed! They have been reduced by their sins! They are on the descent and don't you go with them, don't you let them drag you down. There are still a few wondering psychos out there, so be careful and cut off, cut your old selves off. Imagine cutting the old world ties that bind your hands, your mouth, your legs, and come closer to us, closer still," his voice softened and he raised a palm to the ceiling, then pointed.

"You. And you there. You, child, come here, wrap your arms in mine. We are your family now, that's it, wrap your arms together and sway, like boughs on a tree we will ride out this storm. We will hibernate through this rebirthing together, like pure babes in the womb of this fertile valley. We will rise out as one. Come and let's take back our earth."

Once more, the cherubs floated with their 'Applause' signs, but they weren't needed as Jude was given a vigorous standing ovation. There was a simmer of energy in the room that rose up and tried to lift the roof. Jude felt the need for action and did a few star jumps in the air.

"Now let us march to the field that will save us!"

He swayed his arms and marched out the door. Everyone scrambled to follow him as though he were the Pied Piper. He went straight to the greenhouse and started handing out gardening supplies. People were split into teams and given tasks of hoeing, harvesting or mulching. Marianne looked up at Beatrice's room. The curtains were drawn and stillness radiated from the window. The little angel needs her rest, she thought.

28.

It was dusk when Marianne's mother walked into their small yellow kitchen. Her cheeks were red and she smelled of fresh air. She took a baked potato from the oven and sat down across from Marianne looking completely invigorated. Marianne was finishing her dinner and still reeling from the shock of Beatrice's recovery. Her father was at the castle.

"I love a day of gardening," her mother said, a little breathless. "Daddy is at a meeting this evening so it's just us two," she began cutting up her potato. "You seem quiet honey, is everything okay?"

"I'm fine; just tired from today's work, I guess," Marianne said.

Her voice was an echo that bounced around her mind a million miles away. She couldn't stop thinking about Beatrice and her emotions changed from exhilaration to panic with each passing minute. She was beginning to comprehend the responsibility behind the power she'd been given and it terrified her. Her mother sensed something was wrong.

"I've been meaning to ask you, have you made some new friends?"

"No. Why?" Marianne felt her mother's tension and sat up straight in her chair.

"Well," her mother said. "I'll just be honest. I've seen you sneaking out a couple of times and I was wondering where you're off to?" Her mother put her knife and fork down on the table and waited for an answer. "Now it's your turn to be honest with me, honey."

Marianne thought for a moment and then decided it was best to tell the truth.

"I've become friends with Ansley and he can't go out during the day," she said and felt a small leap of triumph in her heart. It felt good to tell someone, like a release, but it certainly wasn't what her mother was expecting.

"You mean Dark Ansley?" She said, shocked and nearly choking on her potato.

"Yes. The sun burns his skin so we have to meet at night," said Marianne. "Which is why I sneak out."

"I see," her mother was processing the information. "How did you meet?"

"On the survivors' bus. He's kind and interesting and about the only person I can talk to in this place," Marianne crossed her arms over her chest.

"You can't talk to me?"

"That's not what I meant. Of course I can talk to you, but he's my age and we have similar ideas about the future," Marianne said.

"Really? Such as?" There wasn't sarcasm in her mother's voice, just curiosity.

"I can't think of anything specific, just stuff you and I talk about. Seriously, he's really nice," Marianne said. "You'd like him. He's like us, he knows plants and fungi. He survived on them after his dad died. He writes poetry."

"Poetry? Who would have guessed?"

Marianne didn't want to be completely honest, although she felt that her mother would understand her visions, she wasn't prepared to broach the subject yet. Her mother looked at her hands with a contemplative gaze and sighed.

"It is important for you to have friends your age, especially since Joan's tragedy, but do you know what the Keepers are saying about him?"

"I can only imagine," said Marianne.

"They're worried that he might be contaminated."

"That's ridiculous," said Marianne. "You don't believe that, do you?" She leaned forward across the table.

"No, actually, I don't. He's survived, hasn't he? He's just different," she said.

"Different is good," agreed Marianne.

"Yes, but it can also bring about apprehension. You need to be careful and so does he. I'm not crazy about you sneaking out at night to meet a boy, any boy for that matter, but I trust your judgement," her mother said and placed her hand on top of Marianne's. "Your father can never find out."

"I know," said Marianne. "Believe me, it's nothing sinister, I usually just help him with his shift. We talk a bit and then I come home." She could tell her mother didn't entirely believe that, but was going to let it slide.

"Listen, whatever you do, I want you to be extra vigilant; okay?" Her mother said and Marianne nodded.

She should have told her mother the entire truth, but there was so much to explain it was overwhelming. She felt a bit buried.

"Especially now, because everyone's scared and adjusting to their new way of life. It makes them paranoid," her mother continued.

"By scared you mean brainwashed," said Marianne.

"Maybe," her mother sounded exhausted and leaned back in her chair. "But we're safe here and we have enough to eat. How else could we make it through this time? I admit it's not ideal and I don't agree with everything that's said or happens, I just don't see another choice," she reached out and lovingly brushed a strand of Marianne's hair out of her face. "Hang in there."

"So, you promise you won't tell Daddy about Ansley?"

"I'm not comfortable keeping things from him, but I'm afraid he wouldn't understand, so I won't tell him. Like I said, he can't find out because I'd hate to think what he would do if he did. However, your father is not himself these days and I'm overriding his judgement because you need friends. I'm happy you have one, whatever the package," she stood and hugged Marianne.

"Thanks Mum," Marianne said.

"Sure. It will all work out, you'll see," she said and walked towards the hallway. "I'm going to have a bath, honey. My muscles are aching from digging all day," her mother said and climbed the stairs.

Marianne just nodded her head yes and stared at the wall. She was tempted to tell her mother about the pearl, but where in the world to start? It was almost as if saying it aloud would somehow jinx the spell and reverse it's powers. She looked down at where the cut had vanished on her hand and felt panic and wonder at the same time.

Her thoughts flew around her head. She thought of Beatrice alive and well. It was true. The water could actually heal, she kept repeating in her mind. She touched the empty pouch around her neck. She was beginning to comprehend the pearl's real power; it sat inside her and held the weight of knowledge. She knew she needed to make the right decisions.

She could hear her mother walking around upstairs, and as soon as the bathwater started running, she went outside into the garden shed. She had to be quick. She stuck the trowel into her back pocket. The safest way to the woodland was to cut through the village.

29.

If you could call it a village. It wasn't always this small. It had been shaped by a succession of hurricanes and floods. All that was left now was a winding High Street from which a few roads twisted like tentacles towards the castle. The grey floodwater came right up the castle. The harbour was around the corner and its waters covered most of the old town.

For a while, when the tide was low, you could see the drowned rooftops and the mists rolling over it looked like smoking chimneys. It was quite unsettling, but eventually everything rotted away and was forgotten. The sea could claim anything, even memories.

The uncontaminated field looked empty, but all the same, she kept at its edge to avoid being seen. You never knew who was lurking about and Jude had the propensity to turn up at inopportune moments.

It was strange that Jude had decided to lodge Ansley. She didn't completely understand it as he often talked about the risk of contamination and obviously the Keepers were wary. He constantly warned them about the need to keep the population pure and unpolluted, so Ansley's acceptance seemed to contradict Jude's own philosophy and from that angle, she could understand the Keepers' point of view. There was no question that his presence could be disconcerting and even she had had her reservations at first. Would she have befriended him without the pearl's influence? She wondered.

He was unattractive by all conventional standards, but he compelled looking and considering. In that way, he was quite stunning, plus he had an exquisite mind. His poems were beautiful and frighteningly powerful. It was as if he had a secret knowledge that he drip-fed the world through his words. He was still largely a mystery to her and she often thought of him as a white mummy that she alone had exhumed and was unravelling. But to reach the end of the undoing and live with the human beneath, could she cope with that?

Every time she entered the woodland she felt as though it were enchanted and tonight was no exception, like a single living creature, the colour was visceral, the colour grabbed her by the breath and pulled, but it was not hostile. It was smelling her, judging her like a dog recognizes a friend or foe. The crows announced her to all.

In her pocket she carried the trowel. She walked to the beech tree and gasped when she saw how much the pool of water had grown. She knelt down. The pearl greeted her, rose and bobbed to the surface of the water like a white ball. She picked it up and it felt slick and cool in her hands.

She laid the pearl in the centre of her palm; it rooted down into her hand and felt Jude's scale inside her like a sickness. The pearl mourned her loss of innocence, but understood that there could be no other way, for in order to receive great power she mustn't be entirely void of the dark world. To combat evil she needed to empathize with it's source, and although the pearl accepted the scale was of benefit, it still scraped it like a claw. It knew the snake was close and it would have to warn her.

*

In the castle Ansley was dreaming of Marianne. He woke with a poem at his fingertips.

> *Past her reflection*
> *there spreads a field*
> *half shrouded*
> *like a world left*
> *unfinished.*
> *We are given the tools we need*
> *to save ourselves.*

In his dream they were standing in a misty field of red poppies. The sound of stalks and vines growing and surrounding them was like someone twisting braided rope.

The plant species that grew vigorously were called multipliers, for it wasn't that the crops no longer grew (some did in abundance) it was simply that humans couldn't eat them because they carried a strand of BSE. When you change the element of something you don't always kill it. Poppies were an example of this, as well as rapeseed, and the only difference they had to their originals, apart from aggressive growth, was that their stems were black. The patchwork of red and yellow gave the land a kaleidoscopic quality that looked plentiful, but any nourishment to be had from it was purely illusionary.

Certain animals flourished too. Crows were BSE resistant and multiplied in flocks as large as rainclouds that cried through the air and blocked out the sun. Rats, termites, cockroaches and ants were all disease resistant. The flooding loosened once compacted soil and large ants' nests were cropping up on high ground like condominiums. The rotting vegetation gave them the food necessary for a population explosion of insects. In his dream, all of the multipliers had gathered beyond the mists and Ansley could feel them humming as they approached him like a huge vibrating shadow. He understood it was the shadow of obsession and he felt himself inside its clutch of painful ecstasy. He finished the poem.

And you
Breaking me
As morning
Broke the song
Through the window –
Pain and more.
More.

He looked out the window. Dusk had fallen and it was nearly time for his shift. The woodland stood beyond the field like a half-imagined entity, buttoned against the pale night, as if waiting to be undone. He wondered if Dex was out there, as a deer, a fox or a field mouse. He put his shoes on and left.

The atmosphere of the castle seemed strange and somehow nervous. He went into the hall to grab a bread roll and some cheese. It was surprisingly subdued and everyone spoke in hushed whispers. They seemed to stare at him more than usual, so he took his bread roll and walked out into the night.

In the distance Jude was speaking earnestly to a group of solemn faces. Jude was in a chariot composed of salvaged bicycle parts and an old bed frame that had been spray painted a metallic gold. The chandelier hung above him from a hook attached to an old flagpole and on top of that was a large black deck umbrella. Four cherubs pulled the chariot and Ansley could hear Jude shouting to one of the Keepers as he dismounted. "Find me some small buckets to attach to the cherubs will you? They're worse than bloody horses!" Then he swept inside with a twirl of his magenta cloak. Ansley moved out of Jude's way.

Beyond the empty field, Hastings burned like a boil of blue and yellow daylight on the horizon. He dumped the remains of his bucket onto the compost heap and the slugs fell out like bloated tongues. He felt disgusted as he knelt down in the broccoli patch to begin picking off the living predators, and it was a relief to see Dex. They worked in the far corner of the field so that Jude couldn't see them talking. Even though everyone was inside Dex was still wary of being pulled into what he called 'the regime.'

They were picking slugs and chatting when Dex hesitated, put his finger to his lips and hissed, "Shhh!"

"What is it?" Ansley whispered, alarmed.

"Someone's over there," Dex pointed to the woodland.

Ansley turned around and saw a small hooded figure with a torch kneel down in front of a large beech tree. It was Marianne checking on her pearl.

"Let's get a closer look," said Dex. "Come on."

They walked quietly towards the tree and noticed a small and luminous pool of water between the knotted roots of the trees base. It was the thickness and colour of mercury.

"Stop!" Marianne jumped up and threw back her hood. She held her trowel towards them, guarding the spring.

"Marianne!" Ansley said. "It's me," he stepped closer.

"Ansley?! What are you doing here?"

"What do you mean? I'm on slug duty, you know that. Jesus! Marianne, relax will you?" He reached towards the trowel but she flicked his hand away.

"So I take it you two know each other?" Dex asked and stepped between them.

"Who is he?" Marianne pointed her trowel at Dex and he laughed.

"Is she serious?" He asked Ansley then turned back towards Marianne. "Miss, I am going to have to ask you to put your weapon down."

"Don't you dare patronize me," she was seething mad. Ansley stepped forward.

"Let's start this all over again okay? Dex, this is Marianne. Marianne, this is Dex," he introduced the two of them.

"Right," said Dex as he rubbed his hands together. "Now that the formalities are over, what in the world is that?" He pointed to the pool. "It looks amazing."

Marianne put the trowel at his throat. "Who sent you?"

"Marianne," Ansley spoke in a soothing voice. "Be reasonable. Nobody sent him. He's my friend. You can trust him, honestly," he reached forward and lowered the trowel.

"Phew," Dex said sarcastically.

Marianne stared at him for a few seconds and Ansley could tell that she was deciding if she liked him or not. He felt her mood shift from anger to excitement, possessive excitement, but better than a trowel in the throat, he thought.

"It is amazing, Ansley, just amazing," she said and looked at Dex.

Ansley sensed she didn't want him to hear what she was about to say.

"Seriously, Marianne. You can trust him," he reassured her.

"Have you told him about my pearl?" Marianne said.

"No. Why would I? You're really starting to freak me out now," said Ansley.

Marianne looked at Dex and then at Ansley. "Don't you think it's odd that he's suddenly here? Where did he come from?"

"Hastings," said Dex.

"We met in the woods. If you just let us explain... whoa! Dex! Dex?!" said Ansley, but Dex had vanished.

Marianne and Ansley looked thunderstruck as they stared at the small pile of clothes Dex had dropped on the ground. Ansley kicked Dex's shirt and revealed an empty trainer. A second later, Marianne screamed.

30.

"What the hell?!"

"He's shifted!" Ansley panicked and picked up Dex's clothes and shook them.

"Shifted!?" She stabbed her trowel at invisible predators in the air.

Ansley grabbed her torch and shone it through the trees, but there wasn't a single animal in sight, then an awful thought occurred to him.

"Oh no. Don't move Marianne. Just bend down and collect all the bugs you can," he carefully dropped to his knees and began sifting through the bracken and moss.

"What? Can you please tell me what is going on? Now you're freaking me out!"

"Look if you are not going to help, fine, but just stay completely still, okay?"

"It's fine now, Ansley, I'm back." It was Dex. "Just a little indisposed, if you know what I mean," he laughed from behind a tree. "Could you just pass me my clothes please?" Dex stuck his bare arm out and Ansley handed him his things.

A few seconds later Dex appeared fully dressed. He looked at Ansley with new admiration. "Thanks, mate," he said.

"I thought I'd stepped on you," Ansley said and punched him in the shoulder. He was visibly relieved.

"It's one of the hazards of our friendship I'm afraid."

"Look I hate to break up your little moment, but could someone please explain what just happened?" Marianne interrupted.

"I was an ant," said Dex.

"A what?"

"An ant," he said defiantly with a hint of mischief.

"Yeah, I heard you, but what does that mean?"

The pool glowed bright silver and began to expand before their eyes and distracted her from Dex for a moment.

"Look," she knelt down beside it, mesmerized.

Another puddle appeared and rose in soft ripples like a gentle geyser between the tree roots. The roots acted like a cup and held the water in. The ripples spilled over the sides in one corner and created another pool. The pearl was the source of the geyser and it was rapidly growing. The three of them stood together and peered down at the water. The pearl decided it was time to warn them.

"It looks like a moon," said Ansley.

He looked up at Marianne. She was smiling. Her skin shone. He felt like a planet between two moons.

"Is this the amazing thing you mentioned in your note? Thanks for that by the way," Ansley said.

"Yes," she said. "I wanted…"

"What is that thing?" Dex interrupted, pointing.

Ansley looked down again. The pearl sent a snake slithering around its moon as though it were going to eat it like an egg.

"A snake? What does that mean?" Marianne accusingly spoke to Dex.

"What? Don't look at me! I'm no snake!"

"Well it's a pretty strange coincidence that you appear on the scene just as a snake coils around my pearl!" She was upset.

"She's just like a bird," Dex said to Ansley.

"And he's a sexist! Ansley! Seriously do you even know him?!"

Dex didn't give Ansley time to answer.

"No, I meant that literally, birds can get pretty frantic. It's because their hearts' beat so fast. If I could just put my hand on your chest…" Dex reached his hand forward.

"Stop!" Ansley shouted. "Stop it, both of you. Dex, Marianne does not appreciate that kind of humour. Marianne, Dex is only half joking about the bird thing. You see, he has actually been a bird."

Marianne looked skeptically at Dex.

"Tweet tweet," he said and shrugged his shoulders.

"He is a Shape Shifter. That means he shifts into different animals," explained Ansley.

"What?" Marianne whispered.

They gave her a while to process the information. Ansley loved it when her brow furled. She looked like an evil comic book character.

"But that's impossible. Isn't it?" She looked once more at the pearl.

A transmitting pearl was an impossible phenomenon, but it had happened right?

"It's called a DNA exchange. When I said I was an ant earlier, I actually meant it," said Dex. "It's just that dropping out of my clothes is a bit of a hazard."

"Marianne, it's true. Honestly. And despite his bad humour, which does become tolerable, after a while, he is a nice guy," said Ansley.

"By tolerable he means endearing," said Dex and bowed.

"You're completely serious?" Marianne asked.

"Yes!" Ansley and Dex said in unison.

"Well, I guess nothing shocks me anymore," her voice was fascinated. "Not even the fact that you might have a single redeeming quality," she said to Dex.

"Ouch, it's like we're dating already," said Dex.

Ansley felt a pang of jealousy and changed the subject, "Marianne are you going to explain your secret now?"

"Yes, but you have to swear you won't tell a single soul. This is the world's greatest secret, so swear, on your lives."

"I swear," said Ansley, crossing his heart and Dex did the same.

"Let's sit down," she said and led them away from the tree.

She flattened some bracken and sat in the middle of it like a deer. She crossed her legs and looked up at the sky. The stars were swallowed by clouds, thick and tin coloured. Where could she begin?

"Right," she said, took a deep breath and concentrated. "When I get my visions it's like being awake and asleep at the same time."

"Like when you had the vision of the cave?" Ansley asked.

"Exactly like that. Like I just know, I mean I know something is going to happen. I dreamt this pearl before it came to me, but the dream was alive, just like it was alive for the cave," she said and Ansley nodded. "Just like it was alive for this tree. It wanted to be buried here, I don't know why, but as soon as it was underground the stream appeared, it cracked through the surface of the ground the night after we went to the cave and then a miracle happened. I cut my hand and it healed it," she held her hand up to show that it wasn't cut.

"What do you mean 'healed it'?" Ansley asked.

"I mean I put my hand in the water and the cut entirely disappeared," she said. "But that's not all. I gave Beatrice, a girl with tuberculosis, some to drink and it cured her. It cured her completely."

Ansley and Dex were speechless.

"It healed her, Ansley! This water healed her! She was almost dead and it cured her! Can you believe it?" She was grabbing him by the shoulders; she was ablaze as though she'd swallowed a light bulb.

He stood there staring at the water, considering.

"I think I can believe it," he said in a soft voice and then whispered. "What about me? Can it cure me?" His face was imploring and white.

"I don't know," she said and squeezed his shoulders a final time before she let him go. She took a blue medicine bottle from her pocket and handed it to him. "Here. Fill it up and see."

He bent down and collected the water. His skin was a taunt drum that his heart beat against and the pearl could feel him pumping out hope. He put the bottle to his lips, drank, and then he sat back and waited.

31.

He could feel the water as it worked its way around him. He could feel it as it mixed with his blood and swished along his veins like an icy solution. It spread though every nook in his body trying to find a way to cure him, but there was no way to break through his condition and regret sank it's cold stone through Ansley. Something powerful was blocking the pearl.

"It was a stupid idea," he said and choked back his tears.

Marianne put her arms around him. "No," she said, "it wasn't." She held him, but his face was expressionless, and he made no move to hold her back.

Dex had been quiet, and now when he spoke his voice was full of reverence.

"Ansley," he said, "it won't change you because it needs you as you are."

"What do you mean?" Marianne asked and unwrapped herself from Ansley "Do you know something about my pearl?"

"Maybe," he said.

The pearl saw his awestruck reflection in its silver waters and felt him thinking. Not yet, the pearl beckoned him, first show them what they're up against and he shook it out of his mind. "I think it might be a type of seed, but I'm not completely sure. I'll let you know what I find out. Have you told Jude?" He asked Marianne anxiously.

"Of course not!" she seemed insulted.

"Good. He can't find out. He's an evil man. I was in his garage last night," said Dex.

Marianne and Ansley glanced at one another.

"Why?" Ansley asked.

"I could smell food. He has a stockpile of it," Dex said.

"Maybe he's waiting to divide it between the survivors," Marianne said.

"Yeah right," Dex spat sarcastically. "Most of it was rotten."

"How did you find it?" Ansley asked.

"I was a fox following my nose and ta da. Those dogs gave me a run for my money though, they're vicious. There is something else you should know. There are loads of other survivors setting up camp just outside of Hastings now that the last wave of contamination is over," he said.

"Why are they coming to Hastings?" Ansley asked.

"I'm not sure, but I think they are following the light, the fires or something, but they are all starving. I've been thinking about it all day and if I just stole a little bit of food every week, he wouldn't even notice and I could save lives."

"I'm helping you," said Marianne with bold conviction. "It wasn't meant to be like this. The whole point of growing food is to feed the uncontaminated. Do you think he knows how many survivors there are? Maybe I should tell him and we could take the bus to Hastings," she said.

"Are you kidding? He knows exactly what's going on. Don't be so naive. I've seen his little men," said Dex.

"The cherubs have been in Hastings? Are you sure? What were they doing?"

"Raiding an off-licence for alcohol," Dex said.

"That sounds like the cherubs alright," said Ansley.

"I can't believe this! I know Jude's a liar, but to knowingly keep people starving is, well, it's murder!" Marianne was furious. "I am definitely helping you steal the food."

"So am I," said Ansley.

"Are you sure? You have more to lose than I do. This is your home now," said Dex.

"I can't stand back and let people suffer and nor can Ansley," said Marianne and Ansley shook his head in agreement. "Thursday night is the best night to do it," she continued, "because there is always a Keepers' meeting and they usually run late."

"I do love inside knowledge," said Dex and winked. "You're in."

"Okay. Thursday it is, but we should meet tomorrow night and come up with a plan. Somewhere less exposed," said Ansley.

"I know just the place," said Marianne. "We can take a midnight picnic."

"Wait," Ansley interrupted her. "Are you really sure it's a good idea for you to come, Marianne? Your father is a Keeper and what if we get caught?"

"We won't get caught. I can't explain it, but I finally feel like I am on the right path. The world is on our side. I don't know how or what it all means at the moment, but I feel I am going forward, I feel it. Trust me. Let's meet at the New Harbour tomorrow at midnight. Ansley, I'll come early to help you with slug duty so Jude doesn't get suspicious. I need to get home, but remember, tomorrow at midnight and be thinking of a plan," and she turned and walked away, leaving Ansley and Dex with their thoughts.

"She's right," said Dex. "The world is on our side."

He stood watching Marianne until she had completely disappeared. When he finally turned and looked at Ansley there was something in his eyes that made Ansley want to hit him.

*

Back at the castle, Ansley sat alone in his room replaying Dex's face as he had watched Marianne walk away. He played it again and again in his mind until he was certain he wasn't creating emotion where emotion didn't exist.

Thoughts of you
compress like sediment.
I bore into my chest and pull
out a cylinder of stacked losses.
Careful, I say to my weak, white hands
careful not to smash yourself.

32.

What Dex remembered about his parents was not wholly accurate. How could it be? Over time, the shape of who they were had altered to fit the mould he'd created for them inside his slipping memory.

His mother was always digging. Her fingernails were never clean. He saw her brushing dirt off her jeans and laughing. She carried seeds everywhere. He remembered his father's hand on the small of her back and her gaze up at him.

They were happy, which is why it was such a shock when they died. Apart from the utter loss and ripping love that he felt for them, there was something else, something unimaginable about the fact that kind and happy faces could vanish. It scared him to the core, but also, it made him brave.

The kind of bravery that comes only from intense fear, a controlled bravery, not a foolish or reckless bravery. It's the reason why he'd survived. It's why he eventually picked himself up and decided to live. Now that his life was his choice, he wanted to use it for a greater good and realize his potential.

He had lived in the lock-up since his parents died. Of course nobody checked to see if he was paying rent. Who was around? Half the town was wiped out in the earthquake. The earth just swallowed them up. All their seeds were stored in the lock-up. There were thousands, in sacks and boxes, he wondered if they would even propagate. "A life can lay dormant for years," his mother used to say.

He had been at the community swimming pool when the earthquake hit. It was sudden. He was swimming a lap when the water began to rock so violently that it flung him to the side. He'd actually laughed because it had felt like that comedy sketch where the goldfish is thrown from the fishbowl as the table is knocked over. That's what he thought; who knocked the table over?

He has always felt guilty for that laugh, but that's the way it is with humans, they laugh at inappropriate times, as though there's a switch between tragedy and humour that our brains flick when necessary. He picked himself up, dried off and walked to the front desk. He found the staff underneath the desk with their hands in the bracing position.

"Get down!" They shouted. "It's an earthquake!"

He ignored them and walked outside.

They called after him but he felt immune to natural disaster, as though his shifting had insulated him somehow.

He couldn't believe his eyes. Everything was smashed and upside down. He remembered going to a county fair once and seeing a display of a miniature town. It was a model village. They used Astroturf and green glitter to represent grass. It smelled like burning plastic. He felt as though he'd become a miniature figure trapped inside a demonstration town. It was as if someone had smashed his ideal. A giant pair of scissors had come and cut through everything, cracks ran down the centre of the street and set the alarms off. Not a living soul was about.

The only people he could see were the ones he couldn't stop himself from looking at. They didn't seem real. Their bodies were in all the wrong positions. Their eyes and mouths were open as if stopped mid-sentence.

Had there been any notice? Who else survived?

He began to run to blur the images of black and red, to blur the smell of hot tarmac and engines, the sounds of alarms against silence. He didn't stop until he got to his road. The trees were still standing outside his house. It's okay, he thought, and began to breathe again until he looked around.

The road and all the houses appeared to have been chain sawed in two. His neighbour ran up to him and hugged him. Her face was puffy with tears. He ripped her arms away and started running towards his house. His heart was pounding as loud as his feet. "Don't go in!" someone shouted. He heard running behind him. A hand grabbed his arm forcefully. It was a policeman. People were starting to emerge, contemplating the destruction.

"It's too dangerous," he was panting, "I'm sorry, but I can't let you go inside until we know there's no gas leaks."

Dogs were running around piles of rubble sniffing out survivors, but there were none. Dex began clawing the air and making loud noises. Sometimes he heard those noises in his dreams and woke up sweating, but mostly; there was just a hole.

Living in his lock-up was like living in a garage. He'd spent a lot of time camping so really he didn't mind, at least it was dry and warm, well, warmish. He drilled some holes in the wall and made a basic chimney so that he could at least light a fire without suffocating. The only thing that bothered him was the lack of windows.

After they'd removed his parents' bodies from the house, he was allowed to sift through the remains. There was something about the things they had touched: they seemed to carry a heat in them, a hum. He took only a few objects from their house with him to the lock-up. A vase that hadn't been broken. A hairbrush full of hair. Odd tea mugs. Their seed diary. His father's chair. A picture of them all at the seaside. His mother was wearing her favourite yellow floppy hat. Her face was covered in freckles. His father's face was full of stubble. His hair was grey at the temples and wavy. He was holding Dex to his cheek. He had wanted nothing more.

"Take what you like," he had said to his remaining neighbours.

Their mouth's opened and closed like fish. Times were difficult, but they didn't want to knowingly take from an orphan, all the same, when he came back almost everything was gone. It seemed appropriate. There had been too much and empty was better.

His parent's had liked to travel with only what they could carry. It's how they felt free and he wanted, above all else, for them to be free. It's what he hoped. The things he had of theirs were simple and personal, and when he touched them memories fizzled through him like an evocation.

For a long time he didn't want to be human and found himself shifting more and more into animal form. In fact the desire to leave his body forced him to learn to control his shifting. He tried, but could not stop being human, no matter how many animal disguises he adopted he could not erase his true form. It was always there waiting like a small ember inside of him.

He still liked to sleep down foxholes where it was lovely and snug. He added to their dens when he was in his fox form. He'd leave a soft bit of moss or once he even found a piece of insulating foam, but he spent more time as a human these days, which of course had to do with his friendship with Ansley.

Ansley and Marianne were the first people he'd really spoken to in a few years. It just felt good to laugh and joke around; to be light-hearted in this world was rare. It was like wind to his human ember.

Humans are wonderful he thought; just look at Marianne. He'd never met someone so fierce and stubborn and spirited before. She reminded him of what it felt like to be a horse. He knew his mother would have liked her instantly.

It hadn't stopped raining all day. The steel walls of the lock-up were cold and while they weren't damp, they had the clamminess of keeping water out. He sat down in his father's armchair. The boxes and stacks of seeds were closing in on him.

His father had been one of the greatest seed collectors that Wakehurst Place had ever known. Of course it was his father's treasured ability of animism that aided his collecting. They used to send him on the most dangerous jobs, like to the top of some canopy in the venomous wilds of Borneo to find a seed the size of a pinprick. Easy-peasy, he'd say squeezing himself into a tiny fluorescent orange frog and leaping up the tree.

He'd find and swallow the seeds in the morning, then spend the rest of the afternoon swimming in a cloud-shrouded orchid, shaped like some glorious organ. By evening he'd hop down the tree, shift into a man and spit the precious seeds into a small muslin bag. Of course he insisted on always working alone.

He'd walk back to camp and place the muslin bag on the table with a bit of arrogant nonchalance. He knew he amazed them. You could say he was famous among a particular crowd, those with blue-rinsed hair mainly, but it was a time when the young didn't recognize the importance of seeds.

"You tell the story as if you were actually living on top of the mountain, so vivid, so detailed," they would remark during seminars.

He'd changed into a mountain goat and had picked the flower delicately with his rubbery lips whilst perched on a cliff top. "It was nothing really," he'd bemuse leaving them fascinated. He had collected most of Wakehurst's endangered seed species. Life, he told Dex, was a ludicrous and whimsical game that he enjoyed playing it immensely.

Dex looked around at the boxes of seeds and felt a great sadness for how it all turned out. His father would never have believed his precious seeds were in this place. His mother would never have believed her careful labels were smudged and ruined. She had been a botanist at Wakehurst.

He remembered the tornado that took Wakehurst's Seed bank. By then many of the seeds were contaminated but the scientists who worked there were hopeful for a future cure, and so continued to store them. His parents risked their lives to save as many seeds as they could. They left him in a cellar with a neighbour. As his mother was closing the door her hair was blowing wildly, so wildly that he couldn't see his father's eyes, but he could see hers, inky blue like a stormy sky and intense.

"We'll be back. Listen to me, we will be back soon," and she closed the door. He didn't move from that spot and when the hurricaine went over their heads like a train, bits of plaster fell on his scalp.

That night in the bath his mother picked out the white flakes of plaster and explained that the world was changing in ways that could no longer be prevented. That there were things he needed to know how to do, like make a fire, like pick a lock and so on, just in case.

Like find another world, just in case, he thought. But seriously.

What if?

What if the seeds could be cleansed? What if they could use them again and grow their own world? An uncontaminated one, a secret one. Nothing is beyond impossible, he thought to himself and picked up some boxes. If the pearl water cured Beatrice then why couldn't it cure the seeds?

He looked at the wall of boxes. Thousands, tens of thousands of little lives just waiting to open and take shape. It was time to let them go, grow, he thought, it was time to finish the work his parents had started.

"If not now, when?" His mother was fond of saying.

Now, he thought, now.

*

He didn't know how many trips he made that night but by morning the lockup was empty. The seeds made the water multiply. It was like the pearl had been expecting it, as though they should've been feeding it all along, so that what was a stream had become a large pond. Each bag, each box of seeds that he dumped into the water immediately began to move in a swirling dance.

The pearl glowed and the pond became a lake, in the middle of which the beech tree grew from an island. The water was completely translucent and the island had no base to it, rather seemed to float like a water lily holding up the beech tree while underneath it the pearl waited like a white flame. You could see the tree's roots protectively anchoring like bars around the pearl.

The seeds orbited the pearl. They were little black shoals of fish or planets around a sun. He sat like a cat on the edge of the pond and watched them. They are organizing, he thought, but organizing what? Could it really be an original seed?

*

The pearl knew it was the seed for a new world and that it had a duty to make that world grow. What it didn't know was how the world was going to manifest or the role of those facilitating its creation. It relayed what it was able to intuit from the universe, but more often than not, it was simply a part of the mystery.

However, there were ideas that it trusted because it'd had the experience of eons, so understood a great power prevailed with no name suitable for human utterance. It also understood that there were minor powers knotted together in reliable, eternal patterns. They carried simple names with complex histories – good, evil, death, rebirth – that attracted yet repelled one another like entangled magnets.

Our basic human experience comes from our relationship with the minor powers, yet inside the ultimate power there reigns complete synergy, so that is where the miracles take place. That is where a star explodes to create a universe by returning us to dust. That is how small particles can build planets.

There are a few people that can attempt to find the infinite inside the particle, inside dust. It is said that anyone who endures to create honestly and behave courageously in spite of judgment or oppression, is born needing only the right catalyst to peak his or her intuition.

Through Marianne's clairvoyance and Ansley's poetry they acquired intuition and the pearl was able to communicate to them, but it was not the ultimate conductor. It had only the ability to keep them listening to a story that had been playing from time immemorial.

It meant only that Jude was evenly matched; yet the pearl knew that the mere spin of a magnet could change the course of the new world indefinitely, and this scared it.

33.

Throughout the day, Marianne pilfered small bits of food, berries, pears and bread. There were strict rules about stealing food and taking it beyond the garden or eating outside of mealtimes.

"Stealing, smealing," Marianne thought, wrapping the food up in a towel and tying the towel to her mechanical arm. Like a hobo, she thought as she looked in the mirror. Already she was adopting the position of one who had been abandoned. It was a defence mechanism that worked to ease the pain, and now that she had friends who understood her struggles, it didn't seem to matter so much.

Abandoned by her father, who was alive, but disconnected to her world in an absolute and deadening way. She realized this when she listened to Dex and Ansley speak of their fathers' devotion and love, which left her with a bizarre dose of envy. She couldn't remember a single grain of wisdom presented by her father, no praise, no interest, no guidance, no sense of worth, so that the love remaining between Dex and Ansley and their two dead fathers seemed more real than her father's physical presence.

So, yes, the hurt of this was lessened by Dex and Ansley's friendship. Their acceptance and companionship was a healing balsam that thickened as her father's power over her dwindled. She knew that someday, by the strength of her new alliances, she'd no longer need him to want her anymore.

She snuck out as soon as she could hear her father snoring and helped Ansley clear a section of slugs before they ran to the New Harbour to meet Dex. He had arrived early and his hair was completely wet.

"I nearly lost my head," he said and dried his hair by flipping upside down and shaking himself like a dog. "I'd forgotten there was a wind farm down there," he pounded his head to get the water out of his ears. "No place for a fish, I can tell you."

"Oh yeah," said Ansley, "I remember it now. There were hundreds of turbines here. My father called it a field of hope," he felt keenly aware of Dex's good looks, but Marianne was staring up at the sky and seemed not to notice Dex at all.

"There still are hundreds of turbines, they're just under water now," said Dex.

"You mean they are still moving?" Marianne came back to the conversation.

"It's like swimming through a maze of propellers," he said.

"Were you human or fish?" Ansley asked.

"Fish."

"Well, you're lucky you survived because we have a surprise for you. Don't we, Ansley?" Marianne said with a voice full of mischief.

"Really?" Dex smiled at Marianne. His white teeth beamed against his dark skin.

"It's in the pack," Ansley pointed to her towel.

He tried to control his growing jealousy by taking deep breaths and reasoning with himself. Marianne wasn't his. She was worthy of admiration and that's what Dex had been doing. They were becoming friends.

"I thought you were finally going to run away with us, right Ansley? Spain beckons," he put his arm around Ansley's shoulders.

"That is," Ansley remained casual, "assuming Spain still exists."

"If you can dream it, it exists," said Dex still looking straight at Marianne.

"It's just a picnic," she said. "But I imagine it has been a while since you've had a peach," she grinned.

"A peach? Seriously? It's been ages. Lead the way!"

They left the harbour and walked down the middle of a hedge-framed road. There were deep cuts in the earth along the bank and mice occasionally scurried between the roots as messy and twisted as snakes. The moon was a dim spotlight above them. Streams of water zigzagged silver lightening bolts around fronds of bracken that punched through cracks in the unused tarmac.

Tarmac will become just another layer of sediment to mark a time, like dinosaur fossils or lava, thought Marianne, and the idea of timelessness made her feel impermanent and afraid. She was here now, she thought, under this sky, with these friends, and on the precipice of when history crashed into the future.

A fox screeched somewhere and on the horizon hills were lit blue, brown and orange with distant fires. There was devastation everywhere. It could interrupt her if she let it, perhaps it could interrupt her forever and she felt the gravitas of that notion.

The pearl glowed inside her then as it could feel her thinking, sinking. The pearl had learnt when it was drifting there is no such thing as absolute death; our life experiences maybe fleeting but the influences that we have make us infinite. She was just beginning her cycle of influence and there was greatness in her, the pearl felt it and gave her another glimpse of herself. A drop of rain sent to a skin of desert.

She looked at Ansley. She knew he had feelings for her and she had feelings for him too, but it was complicated, because she felt as though she were just waking up from a life-long and lonely hibernation. She didn't know the direction her life was going to take, let alone his place inside it, but how she approached that role was entirely up to her. She decided to choose strength and dignity. Ansley was her friend and his importance went beyond his skin. He was important because he was alive. She didn't want to hurt him. She put her hand in his.

This made him so excited that he jumped up and kicked a stone down the road towards Dex. They kicked the stone backwards and forwards all the way to the New Shore.

They were happy then. They felt the weight of colour in Ansley. The creatures void of colour store it inside their minds. He held the influence of the sun, of growth and blossom; she felt it and smiled up at him. He walked in sepia like the spectrum of an old photograph, but if you could unzip him and turn him inside out you would find the vibrancy of day. He's like a planet, she thought, that never turns, that stays pressed against the blackness and still.

They were greeted by an army of herons patrolling the New Shore, footsteps made the birds lift effortlessly through the sky, large as fruit bats. The water was like liquid metal that swirled between the reeds. They poked around the edge of the water. Marianne removed seaweed from a bicycle wheel and found, inside the spoke, a black Ace of Diamonds, brown and disintegrating, but still recognizable. Ansley removed it and wiped it on his jeans. Somehow it felt lucky.

"Keep it." He gave it to Marianne and she put it in the pocket of her army jacket.

"What is this place?" Dex asked and Marianne explained how it used to be the old village. "I don't know if it's creepy or peaceful," he said and pulled a curtain rod out of a mound of mud. "Now that's what I call a staff."

They found shoes, batteries, an old cowbell and, bizarrely, an acrylic bug. Dex fished the cowbell out of the water with his curtain rod and Marianne asked him to float the acrylic bug towards her. It was an iridescent beetle that looked as though it had been trapped inside a block of ice. She picked it up and placed it in Ansley's hand.

"And this one's for you," she said and Dex rang the cowbell.

"Feeding time," he said and climbed up to the field of rapeseed. The black stalks were without their yellow heads and looked like pitchforks in the soil.

Marianne spread out her towel and the feast. They sat on the edges and ate in silence. Hastings was a phoenix beyond them and the herons flew black shadows over their heads. Dex was enthralled by his peach and savoured every bite. Stealing the food seemed even more important now and after the silence of digestion passed, they began to devise the perfect plan.

34.

The following night was Thursday. It was ten o'clock and Marianne knew her father would be gone for hours. The world outside her window was cloud covered and pewter black. Her mother was still awake, but if Marianne waited for her to go to sleep, she would be late, so she had to sneak out. Dex and Ansley would be waiting for her. She put her trainers on and pulled a fleece over her flannel pyjamas. Her coat was downstairs. She cupped her hand against the wall and listened. She could hear nothing, so opened it gently. Her heart rang in her ears.

She crept down the steps and over to the coat rack. She lifted her coat off the hook, inched opened the door, stepped around it and soundlessly closed it again. Once outside she took a deep breath. The mist was so thick she could feel it filling her lungs like a milkshake coating a glass.

She ran through the back garden, over the fence and down the side of the road that lead to the woods. If she had looked back at the house she would have seen her mother's face at the window watching her run. Marianne's flannel pyjama legs like bright flags through the mist. If her mother's eyes could etch glass, the window would read: don't go.

*

Ansley's outline waited for her at the edge of the woods and she ran to him.

She stopped to catch her breath. "Sorry I'm late."

"I'm just glad you're here," he said. He was carrying a large cloth bag stuffed with other bags. He wore nothing that would snag. His face was completely blacked out and he wore a black stocking cap, black jeans and a black roll neck. His eyes were still pink and rimmed with pure white. It was strange to see him without his balaclava.

"You look so different," she said. "Does it feel weird?"

"Yeah. Do you prefer it?"

"God no. I like you better glowing. Where's Dex?"

Just then a fox came sauntering out of the mist. He walked up to Ansley and Marianne and the three stood in a circle. He seemed to wink at them. It was just as they had planned.

"Awesome. Let's go," said Marianne.

The arrangement was for Dex to distract the dogs while Ansley entered the garage and filled the bags. Marianne would keep a look out while Ansley passed the bags to her. It all seemed easy enough.

They walked silently towards the sea and the castle's edge, it's huge shadow spread across the water. The night was so still the shadow looked solid, as though it could break off as a whole and float away. The buildings around them were like sleeping giants covered by mist. They took the back path to Jude's house.

The two top windows watched them like black eyes. Dex ran ahead. He turned back once and then started digging a hole under the fence. Dirt sprayed like water. The fence was easy enough to climb over. Ansley just dumped a rubbish bin over and used it to reach the top. He turned and faced Marianne before he jumped.

"Remember, one sharp fox scream if there's trouble," he said, then jumped down and was gone.

Marianne stood there, suddenly cold, she moved out of view of the black windowed eyes. All the sounds were muffled in the fog. She strained her ears to hear something, but there was silence. She looked up and down the road. She thought she could hear footsteps and panicked. Was that the shape of a person? A cat leapt out and crossed the path and Marianne had to muffle her shriek. Get a hold of yourself, she thought.

Within minutes the first bag of food was shoved through the hole under the fence. She looked inside it and was astonished. Fresh broccoli, corn, carrots, leeks and cabbage. There were sugar snap peas. She couldn't believe it. Why was Jude stockpiling this? Who was it for? Another bag was shoved through. This time it was fruit, strawberries, blackberries, a melon and apples.

She heard the dogs. Their barks were mean and fierce and she looked through the hole in the fence. The dogs were chasing Ansley. How would he get back up? He climbed the tree as the dogs snarled and snapped beneath him. Where was Dex?

"Quick, crawl over and jump down," she whispered as loud as she could.

"The branch is too weak, I can't. Throw the bin over."

She picked it up and heaved it over the fence. Rotten rubbish juice slid down her cheek and she gagged. The dogs were still circling the base of the tree and snarling low growls, but the bin surprised them momentarily and she could hear them sniffing around it.

She looked again through the hole. The bin had landed on its side. She would be mauled if she tried to turn the bin around as the dogs were foaming at the mouth and crazed. She tried to look again through the fence hole but they snapped viciously at her face. Now they were after her as well as Ansley.

Finally, Dex darted through the garden and started circling around the dogs like a maniac. He bit their ears and darted off, which outraged them and they chomped, chasing him and barking loudly.

"Now Ansley!" Marianne shouted when she could hear the dogs retreating.

Ansley didn't waste any time. He jumped down from the tree, turned the bin over and climbed it and was over the fence in a flash. Upstairs a light came on and a figure appeared at the window. Marianne jumped. Ansley picked up the bags and made a loud fox cry to warn Dex, but Dex had already seen Jude and had brought the dogs and his fox form into view. Jude opened the back door and saw the commotion.

"Scram, you dirty beast!" he shouted to Dex and waved his arms.

Dex was feeling cocky and ran underneath his legs. The dogs followed and Jude tripped, landing on top of Dex. Dex yelped and darted towards the fence, he shot through the hole, and when Marianne reached her arm out to touch him, he bit her.

It was a savage bite and she grabbed her arm and stifled her scream. Jude cursed the dogs and bounced a torch beam around the garden like a strobe light. Marianne's arm was bleeding viciously. She wrapped it in her coat and stuck her coat sleeve in her mouth to keep from screaming.

Ansley held her close and unstuck the hair from her wet cheeks. He took his own shirtsleeve and wiped the snot from her nose. She seemed too stunned to move. Dex kept his distance. His fox eyes were full of regret.

They could hear the click-flip of Jude's slippers as he walked down the steps and into the grass. The torch shook around the garden like a firefly in a jar and finally landed on the hole under the fence. They pressed their bodies against the fence and tried to keep completely still.

Shhh, Ansley mouthed to Marianne, he's coming, shhh. Relax, breathe, relax.

Jude bent down and touched the newly dug soil. They could hear it crumble between his fingers. The coat sleeve inside Marianne's mouth was dripping wet with spit. She didn't dare to breathe. They could see his hand coming through the hole and moving close to a strawberry that had fallen out of the bag. His fingers were groping the ground and getting closer.

Dex let out a loud bone chilling fox cry, causing Jude to bolt up and bang his head against the fence. Dex took this opportunity to run through the hole, between Jude's legs and towards the other side of the garden.

"Little furry vermin!" Jude said. "Damn you!" Dex led him far from the fence.

Ansley grabbed the two bags and ran with Marianne down the path and behind the castle out of view. They stopped, panting, Marianne slowly unwrapped her coat from her arm and winced in pain. A large mouth sized bite of flesh hung from her arm like an enormous bloody earlobe. She could see her pink muscle. The wound was turning black.

"Let's get you to the pond," Ansley said.

"No! No, don't worry about me, I know what to do. Just go. It's important that you go and deliver this," she nodded towards the bags of food and rewrapped her arm.

"I'm not going to leave you," he said.

"We can't get caught with stolen food, Ansley, be sensible! Look," she nodded towards the field.

It was Dex. He was running towards them.

"Marianne, I'm so sorry! I ran back and got dressed as soon as I could. I don't know why I did that! Are you okay?"

"It was instinct," she said, breathless and dizzy.

"What can I do?" He stood beside her and touched her arm.

"Just take the food, will you. I need to get to the pond to heal this," said Marianne.

"Um, about the pond, I, enlarged it a bit," said Dex.

"What do you mean by 'enlarged it' exactly?"

"Come on, Marianne," said Ansley, he wanted to remove her from Dex. "You can see it for yourself, you're bleeding everywhere. I don't want to risk leaving a trail of blood and you're seriously injured."

35.

They started walking towards the woodland. Marianne could feel herself weakening from the blood loss and a few times she thought she would faint. Dex carried the food bags and Ansley helped Marianne. He was remarkably strong for being so thin.

The woodland closed behind them like a dark green curtain. The pond was huge. It was a hundred times the size it had been and the beech tree was on a small patch of ground that had become an island.

They saw that the island was attached to the pearl with threadlike roots. Its vibrancy radiated a white light that completely illuminated the entire pond as though it were an underwater lamp. They stood dazed on the bank of the water.

"What did you do?" Marianne whispered. It felt like a sacred place.

"There is not much to explain, really," said Dex. "I just put my parents' seeds inside the pond and it began to change."

Marianne's arm was throbbing so she bent down beside the bank and plunged it straight into the pond. She could feel her arm healing and breathed a sigh of relief. What were those churning things at the bottom? She waved and stretched her arm underneath the clear floodlit water and the seeds began to swim in circles around her hand. She tried to catch one to pick it up for a closer inspection but it seemed to dart away. They looked and behaved like tadpoles. She could feel the healing wash her entire body and when she took her arm out there was no sign of the bite at all.

"Thank you," she said to the pearl and looked up questioningly at Dex.

"Those churning things are seeds," he said and knelt down beside her.

"Seeds? But they seem alive like animals," she said.

"They are alive. I thought that if the water could heal people, then maybe it could cure seeds. I felt compelled to try. I started with one box, just to test it, and the water seemed to reach out to me as if it wanted or needed more. The pond grew and churned and sparkled and the seeds came to life, like little fish and the more I poured in, the more vigorous they became, the more hungry until eventually I fed it every single seed I had," said Dex.

"How's your arm?" Ansley asked. He sat down beside them and peered into the pond at the seeds.

"It's completely healed, look," she said twisting it around so that he could see it at all angles.

He ran his hand over where her cut had been. "Incredible," he said. "Does it hurt?"

"Not at all," she said. "Told you," she winked.

"I know, but to see it happen is insane," he said.

"Everything's insane at the moment," said Dex. "Look at the seeds, they seem to know where they're going."

"It's like they have awareness," said Marianne and Ansley hummed in agreement.

They lay on their stomachs and watched the swirling seeds in silence, each assimilating the night's adventure and recovering, until eventually Marianne spoke.

"We need to expose Jude," she said.

"Marianne, you should have seen inside that shed. It was enough to make anyone crazed. I've never seen so much food in my life! And, like Dex had said, most of it was rotten. I could have filled fifty bags or more and just look at this food, it's fresh and uncontaminated," said Ansley.

"He's a criminal and shouldn't be allowed to get away with it," said Marianne.

"I totally agree, but who can prosecute or stop him?"

"The Keeper's," she said.

"No way. They'll never do it. He's chosen them specifically for their inability to think for themselves. He's their brain," said Ansley.

"Then the survivors," she said.

"Most of the survivors are too malnourished to care and just want to be fed," said Ansley.

"I know, but maybe if we organized them once they were stronger?"

"No," said Dex, quietly. It was almost inaudible. "Nobody is doing anything."

"What are you talking about Dex! He deserves to be punished for this," said Ansley and Marianne nodded in agreement.

Dex put his hand into the pond and let the seeds swim in and out of his fingers. He knew about murder. He knew about death, but something bigger was happening, and he felt certain that Jude was immoral beyond their comprehension.

The catastrophes had marked a time of roots. A dark time of searching, scraping, clawing for nourishment. It was as though the world had turned itself inside out and very nearly buried the human species. The earth seemed to feed on human bodies, and so replenishment had a new meaning, it meant feeding the earth with mortals so that the planet might continue to live. People had forgotten that the planet had eons, had many forms beyond the one we inhabited and could renew itself over time. Perhaps she's giving us time, giving us a chance, thought Dex, perhaps she's ready to finish the job and heal.

He looked at his friends. If he told them what he thought now there would be no going back. His chest banged with indecision.

"Dex? Dex, don't you agree? What is it?" Marianne put her hand on his shoulder. He still didn't answer. "If it's about my arm, don't worry, seriously, I know it was an accident." He shrugged her hand off his shoulder and looked up at the sky.

He took a deep breath.

"I don't want us to bring attention to ourselves. I think we should just leave Jude alone. Yes, of course, I think it's murder, of course I do, my God, the people I've seen, the children, all reduced to, I don't know what, to... rabid dogs. It haunts me, the images attack me and if I had nothing to live for I'd strangle him myself. But that's just it. I do have something to live for, something greater than anything I'd ever imagined and so do both of you - the pearl. I think I know what it is. I've heard seed collectors talk about it over the years. I always just assumed it was folklore, but I'm beginning to believe it's true. I mean it's no ordinary pearl is it? What I'm saying is, I think it's an original seed."

*

"An original seed? What do you mean?" Ansley asked.

"I think it's the seed of Genesis," Dex knelt down beside the stream and swirled his finger inside the water. The pearl radiated for him then. Ansley and Marianne moved towards him, listening.   "My parents used to work for the Seed Bank at Wakehurst Place," he said.

"Wait, didn't that burn down in the first fires?" Marianne asked.

"Yes, we were there at the time and my parents risked their lives removing seeds. They stored them in a fireproof lock-up," he looked at Ansley and nodded. "And that's where I live now. It became a family mission to collect and preserve as many seeds as possible for the future."

"Even the contaminated seeds?" Ansley asked.

"All seeds. We were hopeful that science would bring about a new way to use the contaminated seed species to grow food once more. You see we are losing seeds rapidly through destruction, pollution and the take over of Phosforests."

"So you really believe the pearl is a seed?"

"Seed is the name given to something that grows or enables growth and it's certainly done that hasn't it? Who knows how the terminology might have changed over the years, anyway, it's the story that's important," said Dex.

"And the story is…?" Marianne asked.

"The story is that the original seed is a part of the original garden, Eden, and that it can produce a whole new world."

"You mean cleanse the planet?" Ansley asked.

"No. I mean a different planet. A new one. And look at the other seeds orbiting the pearl, it looks like a universe is starting already. Doesn't it?"

36.

Ansley and Dex went to deliver the food to one of the refugee camps on the periphery of Hastings. Ansley had never been so close to Hastings. The city looked calcified and the fires waved around it like blue anemones.

They walked down a footpath that coiled through the South Downs. The wind bit and snagged the bags like sails. The grass was balding in patches and soil kept whisking up into Ansley's eyes. He actually wished it would rain to keep the soil down. Dex pointed beyond the hill and quickened his pace. As they descended the air was warmer and full of ash. They could talk now that the wind had died down, but Dex seemed lost in thought and Ansley was just as happy to stay silent.

Ansley could see a shoal of moon lit cars parked in the field ahead. The field had gone to bracken and Ansley and Dex waded through its infected hip-height fronds. It was a used car lot and looked derelict. The old office building had broken windows and graffiti sprayed along its paint-chipped walls. The door was missing and inside looked like a place where rats lived, yet, oddly, the sign on the building read 'Martin's Used Cars' and was completely legible.

Ansley looked around. The cars were rusted with blacked out windows and covered with twisted vines. The wind still rang in Ansley's ears and could be heard resounding behind the hill like a harpy. In the valley there was the silence that only inhabitance can create. Dex made the sound of a house martin and was answered by a similar birdcall. He called twice more and a car door slowly opened.

A tall woman stepped out. Her hair was grey and long, she wore an old boiler suit and a tattered wax jacket. The bones on her face were strong and her skin pulled around them in high peaks and dark hollows. She seemed both ancient and young, capable of anything and masterly. Ansley liked her straight away.

"Martin," said Dex stepping forward and offering his hand.

"Hello, my friend," she said and pushed his hand aside to embrace him. "Are you well?" She held him away from her to study.

"Yes," Dex said. "Better than last time," and he forced the picture of

Marianne from his head.

"It's beautiful to see you in human form," she said and squeezed his shoulder. "Now, who's your friend?"

"This is Ansley," said Dex.

Martin turned to face Ansley. One eye was dark brown and the other was a pale cataract blue. She took his hand and shook it with a firm two-handed grip conveying the warmth of another member of humanity.

"I'm Martin," she said.

Ansley nodded. "Good to meet you." He said.

"We have a couple bags of food for you," said Dex.

They handed them to her. Martin looked through them and put her hands together in a prayer. "Bless you for helping," she said and whistled a bird song into the air.

Another car door opened and another woman in a boiler suit arrived, spoke quietly to Martin, and then took the food away.

"Please come in," she said and opened the door for them.

The inside of the car had been completely gutted and turned into a little home. The space where the opposite door would have been was converted into a tunnel composed of scrap metal. Martin saw Ansley looking at it.

"We are all connected here," she said. "Like a big above ground burrow," she sat on one of the floor cushions and indicated for them to do the same.

The walls were papered with old photographs and torn book pages. There was a long piece of foam and a blanket for a bed. A clothes-line was draped and stapled to either end of the ceiling, from which hung kitchen utensils and drying socks. On a log was a plastic tray and on top of the tray was a cylindrical metal tin with a vertical wick of yellow flame surrounded by a fine metal gauze. It was a crude Davey lamp and provided the only light.

"Now, let me make you a hot drink," she said, taking three mugs and a camping kettle off the wire.

She took an old metal toast rack and placed it over the flame as a stand for the kettle. She twisted the base metal cylinder to increase the oxygen supply to the flame and the soft yellow became a concentrated blue heat.

"How are things?" Dex asked.

"That food came just in time," she said. "Our scouts have been very productive and we've had quite a few newcomers. Though I'm not sure how many will actually live given the state they're in."

"Are they contaminated?" Ansley asked.

"No. Starving. I think they've all decided to come out of hiding now that the contaminated have either died or entered their final stage. It's a paradox of the worst kind. We are grateful that so many have survived, but we don't know how to feed them."

When the kettle was boiling she took a canister down from a makeshift shelf in what would have been the boot of the car and put two bits of bark into each mug. She poured the boiling water over the bark and handed Ansley his drink. She didn't shrink from his appearance at all and seemed to accept him totally.

"So how did you manage and how do you know Dex?"

"He had foraged in the woods. But we met when he saw me shift from a deer," Dex answered and blew over his steamy water.

"Really?" Martin looked at Ansley.

"Really," Ansley confirmed and took a drink.

The tea was spicy and nutty like a cinnamon-flavoured mushroom. Martin and Dex shared a knowing glance. It was unheard of for a regular human to witness a shift.

"Ansley do you have any special powers?" Martin asked.

"I wish," said Ansley.

"Hum," Martin took a sip and was thoughtful. "Well people cross paths for all kinds of reasons that aren't immediately obvious. Anyway, it's nice to have a friend right? It can get lonely without companionship."

Dex didn't want to reflect on his friendship with Ansley. He knew that Ansley had feelings for Marianne, yet he couldn't stop thinking about her himself. He changed the subject.

"Martin, do you know Rye castle?"

"I do," she answered.

"Well there is a field beside it that's uncontaminated and already in production," said Dex.

"A whole field?" Martin nearly dropped her tea.

"Yes," Ansley interrupted. "I work the night shift. Come whenever you want and take what you need," he finished his tea and set the mug down on the tray.

Martin again took both of his hands in hers. Clouds seemed to be gathering in her blue eye and Ansley felt startled in a celestial way.

"The Martin's will never forget your kindness," she said and kissed him on both cheeks. "And don't worry about your own safety, when we come to the field you won't even know we're there," she nodded at Dex and Ansley sensed it was time to leave.

Dex kissed her goodbye and opened the door. They got out and walked to the edge of the fractured tarmac.

"That was very strange," said Ansley, looking back at the silent car lot.

"Yeah, it's how people live now," said Dex.

"Why not a block of flats?" Ansley was trying to lighten the atmosphere between them.

"Too easy and obvious for raids, plus this is surrounded by chalk soil, so it's safe from the fires," he pulled at fronds of bracken absentmindedly.

"So I take it she can shift?" Ansley asked. He knew something was wrong with Dex.

"Yes, but not as easily as I can. It pains her," said Dex. "There are different degrees of shifting."

"Right. Are you okay? You seem upset or worried or something," said Ansley.

"I'm fine, I'm just thinking about the pearl." And whom it belongs to, he thought.

"Why didn't you tell Martin about it?"

"Because I promised Marianne I wouldn't," he seemed taken aback that Ansley would even ask.n"But also, because I don't know who Martin has with her."

"You mean you don't trust her?"

"No. I'd trust her with my life. She was a friend of my mothers, but I am sceptical of everyone else. We can't afford not to be," said Dex. "Listen, I need to be on my own for a while. You know the way back, don't you?"

Ansley nodded. "Okay, that's fine. Are you sure you're all right?"

"Seriously. I'm fine. I'm just pent up and need to run," he said, shifting into a fox. He picked up his clothes with his mouth and darted off through the undergrowth of bracken, leaving Ansley all alone.

37.

A new world. That's what Dex had said. A new world. Marianne's mind was
animated as she was walked home. How would it emerge? Would they all
be transported to a different planet? What a mad idea! Surely it could never
work, she thought, I mean logistically, the pearl was small and they were big.
Not to mention a lack of food, water, air and so on. Or perhaps the people
would shrink? She thought of herself as a dust mite or a firefly.

Maybe the pearl would grow and rise up into the sky, like another moon,
or even bigger, a visible planet that dwarfed the moon. Well, the pearl
was growing and she had seen swirling clouds, but no, it was completely
improbable and ridiculous and it hurt her brain just thinking about it.
On the other hand, what about the last few days hadn't been completely
improbable and ridiculous? Why not create a new world? Why not? She felt
like her life was out of control.

She couldn't go home yet, even though she was exhausted, she needed
to think, so she went to the New Shore. The fires were intense and moved
the skies from bluish purple to orange. It seemed a juxtaposition to the
endless wind and rain. The streams and flooding actually helped spread the
methane by delivering fresh kindling to the flames. An aerial view would
have showed the fires glowing along the waterways and down to the sea
where they became rafts of flame that eventually extinguished. The earth
oozed methane, had become as slick and greasy as wet skin.

She could see the fire rafts on the other side of the bay, still thirty or more
miles away, like floating dragons. She swallowed her fear as she searched for
objects from the past. Fracked oil swirled around the reeds and her waders
in greasy rainbow shades. She waded past a group of cutlery, like a shoal of
silver spoons and forks. A black iron garden gate. Red wooden Christmas
baubles. Coasters. A white light socket. A child's metal train. She picked the
train up and put it in her pocket. It seemed wrong at sea. Of course nothing
there seemed right, not even her, wading through the refuse of others.

Her time in the world had begun to feel rented, like something she had
never owned, but that was true of all life and nothing is kept indefinitely.
Except the will to make your own decisions and that's what she'd done, she'd

decided for herself. She was rebelling against Jude's regime, once and for all, she was leaving. Although it felt like the right decision she was still afraid.

So let the fires come, she thought with trembling lips and legs. She knew what she had in her. A strong heart that had no need to follow and the pearl's knowledge inside it like a glowing confidence. But still, she would miss this place, miss everything about it and what it once was, so she wanted to take something with her into the new world.

The grandfather clock was silent. She took the hands from its face and put them in her pocket. It would be one of the first things to burn when the fires eventually reached it. She felt scared of the devastation to come and the premonition of evil that twisted alongside the awareness of change. A small part of her wanted to do the easiest thing, to close her eyes and melt into the shape of those around her, to believe in Jude and things that were permanent.

What if she weren't the right one to fulfil the pearl's purpose?

She was flawed. She had always been flawed and full of weakness. She imagined a deep gorge full of her deceits, the lies she'd told, the uncharitable thoughts, bad wishes, secret little hates and everything she'd done that she felt ashamed of and it was full to the top. Putrid and blistering like a swamp, it dwarfed her with its size. How could she possibly jump over it? Without falling, without drowning, how?

Even with strength in her heart, it was hard to believe she was worthy of something that felt so great and noble. She put her head in her hands and cried. Worthiness is always the hardest thing to accept. The pearl burned in her then. Beautiful girl. It burned a pair of wings.

*

The sun was just about to roll over the horizon and the earth had turned a deep purple in preparation for the beginning of light. She longed for home and bed. She carried the weight of purposeful change. She wished that she could just fly through her window and curl up underneath her duvet. She closed her eyes and brushed her fingertips along the wispy tops of the knee-high grass and a remarkable thing happened. One minute her feet were touching the ground and the next she was floating above it, with wings.

She had shifted into a moth.

38.

She screamed, flittered and fluttered towards the few remaining stars. How glorious! She was flying! She shifted! But how could she shift back? Her clothes lay in a pile beneath her. She started to panic at the thought of getting down and then saw a swanky red fox walking through the field below. She knew it was Dex.

"Wait for me, Dex," she beckoned and flew towards him. It was an enormous effort and she was puffed out when she reached him.

"Dex!" She hovered above him and then landed between his little pointed ears.

He growled at her. His clothes were in his mouth. He'd been running since the delivery to Martin and it took him a few seconds to register her voice.

"Marianne? Oh my God, is that you?" The one he'd been running from.

"It is! I can't believe you can hear me! I'm a moth, Dex! A moth!"

"How is this possible?!" He cocked his ears and scratched himself.

"I'm not entirely sure, but I'm guessing it has something to do with the bite you gave me," she said and landed on his ear.

"Of course! We swapped blood! The DNA exchange! I've never bitten a human before so I had no idea," he said and ran around in circle.

"I can't tell you how breathtaking it is," she said, lifting off and flying. "Shocking and scary and, well everything, it's all my emotions in one, everything, everything! Dex this is me! Can you believe this is actually me?!"

She hovered above him, then landed between his pointy little ears, closed her eyes and fanned her wings. Her body had been so heavy. It felt miraculous to be without it, miraculous and free.

"What was it like when you shifted?" Dex asked.

Marianne thought for a few moments.

"Everything went black and I heard soft noises, like distant thunder or gurgling. It was like I'd woken up inside a cave where water was dripping."

"Like waking up inside a stomach," Dex agreed.

"A stomach, yes, like that. I hadn't thought of that before, but you're right. It sounded like the inside of a body, then there was a flash of light and the next thing I knew I was flying! I knew I was a moth right away. This is so extraordinary, Dex. Do you think I'll always be able to shift?"

"I don't know. I hope so. That is exactly what happens to me and it would be brilliant to have someone I can talk to about it. On the surface it's an incredible thing to be able to do, but it does separate you from everyone else," he said. Nature seems to be bringing us together, he thought.

"I can only imagine. I already feel completely different to my previous self now, as if I've broken out of my skin. What next? What will happen to me?"

"I don't know. We'll just have to wait and see," Dex walked her to her house while she flew above him.

She didn't want to be separated from him yet, there was too much to learn, and she was beginning to feel apprehensive and scared.

"Will you help me get down?"

"Sure," he said. "Is that your bedroom?" He pointed his snout towards her open window.

"Yes, what will you do?"

"Ever seen a fox climb a tree?" He asked.

"No," she said.

"Me either," he said and shifted into a monkey.

Still holding his clothes, he scurried up the tree, swung from a branch through her window and into her bedroom. She flew up and joined him.

"See what fun we're going to have?" He said.

A table lamp dimly lighted her bedroom. Her wings flicked against the light bulb.

"I don't know why I'm scared when this feels so wonderful," she whispered as she fluttered around the light.

"It takes a while to get used to it," said Dex. "Pretty soon it will become second nature, believe me. Sometimes I feel more comfortable in animal form than human form."

"How do I shift back to a human again?"

"I'll talk you through it. You have to will yourself to change. Choose something you like about yourself and focus on it until you start to feel movement," said Dex.

She hovered above the light bulb.

"Movement? What kind of movement?" Marianne's wings singed.

"It's hard to explain, but it feels like something is wiggling through your brain, it's a bit uncomfortable, but over in a second," he said. "Turn away and I'll shift and get dressed," he said.

He turned off the light and put her dressing gown on her bed.

"I'm facing the wall. Start shifting whenever you're ready," he said and stuck his nose in the corner. "It will be okay; don't be scared. Just trust me."

Marianne thought of the pearl, she thought of the fisheye, she thought of Ansley and Dex and her human body returned to her as abruptly as a brick dropped inside a pillowcase. She felt heavy and rough.

She began to cry. The change was too overwhelming. She put her dressing gown on and Dex turned around, watching her. She was slender and hollow in the morning light. He took a step forward and wrapped his arms around her. She shook like something trying to break out of itself. He engulfed her with his chest.

"You did it, well done," he said. He touched her hair.

Her bones were hard under her skin and he thought of shrapnel, of steel. He'd never met anyone so immensely strong. He nuzzled his nose into her neck. It was wet with tears, snot and sweat. She smelled and tasted like the sea. He couldn't help himself. He kissed the spot where her neck became her shoulder. He kissed behind her ear. He lifted her hair and kissed the back of her neck and down to her shoulder blades where he stopped and gasped.

"Marianne," he breathed and held her away from him. Her face was flushed and full of surprise. "Your back! It's bleeding."

She just stood there and stared at him. She was too besieged to speak.

"Wait here," he said and searched around the bedroom.

He grabbed a sheet from her bed and pressed it against her back. She felt light-headed and took hold of the window ledge. The room began to shadow and lose its focus. She stumbled to her bed, lay down on her stomach, and let him investigate her wounds. She could feel blood trickling down her sides and into the folds of her armpits. A shiver went through her. He dabbed the sheet softly against her shoulder blades. She was immensely tired.

"Does that hurt? Marianne?" He shook her gently and when she didn't move, he put his ear beside her mouth. She was fast asleep. Dex stared at her. Seared into her shoulder blades and covering the whole of her back, were the red patterns of wings.

39.

Ansley went to his emergency camp after he and Dex had delivered the food. It was strange to be back there again, nothing much had changed, but the time he'd spent there felt lonely and far away from his present life.

He was a different person now and didn't want to return to the hermit he'd been. Dex seemed lost in his own thoughts, but that wasn't strange considering all that was happening. He was still Ansley's friend; and Marianne might be more than a friend as she had taken his hand.

He fitted what he could inside one of the now empty food bags, buried the rest and bid his past goodbye. There was a new world waiting for him and he was filled with optimism.

He entered Rye and although the sun was beginning to rise, he couldn't help passing by Marianne's house and peeking up at her window. He looked up just as her light switched off and saw Dex.

What was he doing there?

The outline of Marianne appeared and Dex embraced her. He began to kiss her. Ansley shut his eyes and clicked them open again. It was true. They were still embracing and Ansley winced with pain. Dex picked Marianne up and carried her out of view.

Something metal ripped into his chest and grabbed the good in him.

He ran back to the castle. He could feel the sun's heat just breaking through the clouds. Burn me, he said to the fireball invading the sky, go ahead and burn me. I no longer care.

When he got home his heart released its dogs and they hacked through him and tore open little bloody creeks. He turned on the shower and stepped inside. He turned the water as hot as he could stand and let it run over his head.

How could she?

He looked at his reflection on the glass. How could she not?

The steam rose and he placed his hand where his face had been. The anger subsided to sorrow. What was he thinking?

There had never been a declaration of real love or anything of the sort between himself and Marianne, but so much, too much had been left unspoken inside moments where words seemed unnecessary, as if they might clog the air vibrating between them.

He had feared that if he spoke her eyes would change. The mere fact that she even looked at him that she didn't turn away in repulsion was a miracle and to be seen, truly seen as a human and not as a monster, had felt like a vow of love.

They were a fortress, not just against the village and the castle, more than that, against the servitude it represented. That was it; she made him feel free and what was love if not the liberation of one's self?

He should have told her how he felt.

But how? It would have ruined their connection because if it weren't reciprocated, it would have always been between them. It didn't matter now. She was never going to care for him in that way. He was ugly and although she called him beautiful, he knew he wasn't and she wasn't meant for him. He was confined to the house. She was adventurous and shouldn't be locked away from the sun.

She was on the light side of the moon and he was on the dark.

He was destined for loneliness. It had always been this way. He had always been a root, had always lived away from the light and knew scraping. He knew isolation and had never seen the sun apart from a few dappled moments of warmth.

It's a peculiar thing to be awake while others are sleeping. You don't know loneliness when you're always alone, until, that is, you lose companionship. They were his only friends, yet how could he be around them now?

But... how could he not?

He slammed his head down on his desk and closed his eyes. He just wanted to stop thinking.

Ansley's mind practised the worst of himself and he only saw that he was ugly. He only saw that his skin was fixed, his body and its organs were fixed. He forgot about his mind and its unique ability to unfasten and sluice poetry past the razors of life. He forgot that this made him beautiful, which is different from handsome, but better, worthier.

You place your soul inside the thing you care about the most, so while the true beauty of him lay within his poems, his talent, his value sat in ugliness, small, diminished, like a tiny flame inside a monsters hand. He let his anger crush him.

40.

When Marianne woke up in the morning she thought first of her wings and then of Dex. He had kissed her and she had liked it. They could both fly and he had given her this ability. She looked at her back in the mirror. The wings were printed with a deep burgundy and, in some places, black like a tattoo.

Marianne felt that she ought to eat breakfast in the castle as usual. She didn't want her father to suspect anything. Her back wasn't bleeding, but it felt as tender as sunburn. She liked the feeling; she liked the hurting because it reminded her of wings. Wings. She had unthinkable, miraculous wings imprinted on her back.

Ansley ignored her in the dining room like he always did when a Keeper was around, so that wasn't unusual, but he did seem more withdrawn than normal. She stood in the queue for porridge until the Keeper on duty touched his earpiece and left the dining room in a hurry. Now there were only cherubs patrolling breakfast and they didn't care about her actions at all.

They didn't care about anything. Without the Keepers or Jude to reprimand them, the cherubs smoked while they served the food and tipped their ash inside the porridge pot. Disgusting.

She pushed the guilt she felt about Dex aside. It was in the heat of the moment and she couldn't wait to tell Ansley about her wings, so grabbed a tangerine and sat down next to him.

"I had the most amazing night," she said and when he didn't reply, "is something wrong?"

He shrugged his shoulders. Was she really going to tell him about her night with Dex? Had he made up the sentiment between them? His eyes filled with tears.

"Don't worry about talking to me. Jude has taken advantage of the nice morning and called a big meeting," she rolled her eyes. "Building an ark probably," she said as she peeled her tangerine.

He wished she'd just be quiet. Hurt and resentment began to swell in his throat. He was just about to speak when a small boy put his tray on their table.

"Good morning," Marianne said. The boy looked up at her, noticed Ansley, quickly stood as though he were frightened and took his tray elsewhere. "What's wrong with him?" Marianne asked.

Ansley steadied his eyes on his porridge. "At least he's being honest about his feelings towards me. At least he's honest about his repulsion," he said.

Marianne didn't seem to understand that he was talking about her.

"Are you saying that people have been avoiding you?"

"Nobody wants to be near me," he cringed at how pathetic he was sounding. She was turning him into some drivelling cretin.

"Since when?" Marianne seemed genuinely surprised.

He looked up from his porridge. "Nobody has ever really wanted to be near me Marianne. Ever. I don't know why I thought this would be any different," his voice was cracking and he was furious with himself for sounding so weak.

They stared at one another and he tried to infuse her with meaning, but she seemed at a flabbergasted loss for words. She slammed her hands down on the table and stood above him.

"Get up," she demanded. "Get up and show me," she said.

She was angry, but her anger wasn't directed at him, rather at the whole preposterous idea that vanity still mattered in the midst of extinction. She walked behind him, took him beneath the arms and lifted.

"What?! Stop it!" Ansley wiggled free and pushed her away.

People had stopped eating and were watching them. The cherubs were glancing and smiling at one another. They loved a fight.

"Go on," she shoved him towards a full table. "Show me what happens when you get close to someone." She wasn't going to have him feeling sorry for himself, hating himself when he was a good person and people liked him. She hated how contemptible he was acting. It disgusted her.

"Why are you doing this? You, out of anyone, should know what happens." He was on the verge of tears, but he knew she wouldn't give up.

She was torturing him for some reason and he went along with it because he was bent on torturing himself. "Fine," he said, despising her. "Watch."

It was true. She watched in horror as those he approached scattered from him like scared birds, some even left the hall altogether, holding their hands over their noses as if he were contagious. What had she made him do? She was gutted. She had wanted him to see that nobody cared about his appearance when food was at stake, but she had been wrong.

He sadistically liked causing distress and growled like a monster, pounding his chest as he chased after them and looking back at her with hateful satisfaction. It was unbearable.

It dawned on her that they were acting as if he were contaminated. She stood up on the table and clapped her hands.

"Hey!" she shouted. "Listen up everyone!" she brought her fingers to her mouth and whistled. The castle hall went quiet and everyone was looking at her.

"I don't know what you heard but..." something whizzed through the air, stung the back of her leg and stopped her mid-sentence. "Ouch!" she cried and everybody turned all at once, like a sail, towards a cherub poised on top of a large fruit bowl.

"You shot me!" Marianne screamed as she yanked the arrow out of her leg.

The puncture was like a small bee sting. A young girl in the back began to cry.

"I have my orders," said the cherub reloading another arrow in his bow. "That was just your warning shot." He positioned himself like an archer and drew back his bow.

"Your orders for what?!" Marianne rubbed her leg.

"To shoot trouble makers on sight," he spat his cigarette out on the table and stubbed it with his dirty toenail.

"Trouble maker?! I am trying to problem solve! Which you'd realize if you'd just let me speak!"

"I told you that was a warning shot. You can speak, but don't get out of hand," he said and calmly aimed his arrow at her chest. "Go ahead and continue."

Ansley moved closer to the cherub. Despite how deeply she'd hurt him, he wasn't going to have her shot. He could feel Marianne deciding her next move and choosing her words carefully.

"Right," she breathed to clear the air around her. "I just wanted to say that you're all acting like Ansley," she pointed to him, "is contaminated and he's not. Why?"

The cherub drew his bow further back.

"I just want to know why! Please!" Marianne said.

Ansley could hear real fear inside her plea. Why was she risking herself for him when she wanted to be with Dex? He felt torn and confused. He inched closer to the cherub. A lifetime of being invisible made it possible for him to move without arising suspicion. Take it slow, he thought, take your time. The cherub seemed to be relishing his new position of power and considered her question. The crowd waited on a stunned tenterhook.

"Fine. Answer her," said the cherub but they were all too afraid to speak. "I said answer her!" the cherub stamped his little baby foot and squashed a bunch of grapes.

The small boy who had left Ansley and Marianne's table cleared his throat and stepped forward. "We heard that somebody was contaminated and needed to be removed," he said. "He seemed most likely because, you know," he trailed off and wouldn't look at Ansley. "And then he wasn't at dinner last night, so we thought…"

"There wasn't anyone else missing," someone shouted from the back.

Marianne scanned their strange and frightened faces. A cold understanding froze through her. Someone was missing actually. The cherub sensed her change right away, mistook it for mutiny, and let his arrow go, but he was too late. Ansley yanked the tablecloth from beneath him and the arrow shot up through the rafters. The cherub tripped and tumbled over the spilled fruit, cursing and reloading. The commotion broke the crowd from its spell and everyone ran in all directions like scared wildebeests.

"Run!" Ansley shouted to Marianne and she did, she ran to the room of the person she knew was missing. Beatrice.

She ran up the stairs to her room and found it empty. Where had Jude taken her?

41.

Ansley suffered twenty-four shots before the poison made him pass out completely. He woke up inside his dorm room. The shadows on the wall told him it was late afternoon.

"Marianne?" he called.

"You're fond of her, aren't you?" Jude stepped into view.

He was wearing a green and gold striped waistcoat over a white button down shirt. The sleeves were rolled up and his arms were hairless, glossy and muscular.

"Love," he said with distaste, "I've only let it trouble me once. I loved her and she cast me out," he walked up to the bed and Ansley could feel the air grow colder. "Load of rot and rubbish," he put his hand on Ansley's shoulder. "Don't fall prey to it. Never. Ever. Be prey."

Ansley tried to move, but couldn't. His eyes were open and he could hear what Jude was saying, but his own voice and body seemed buried under rock. His mind shouted at his arm to lift, but it was cold and stone heavy.

"But that's just it, isn't it?" Jude's voice took on a light detective tone as he walked to the window.

Ansley noticed he had a shiny black cane that he twirled like Charlie Chaplin as he peeked beyond the side of the blackout blind.

"Look at them out there. Easy prey really and where is the fun in that? Lambs, but not you," he returned to Ansley's bedside and for every word he spoke he poked Ansley with his cane. "What. Is. It. About. You?" He scratched the octopus on his head. "I'm curious and that is why you are alive. We are closer than you think, Ansley. I understand you in ways you don't even comprehend," he sat at the foot of the bed.

"I'll let you in on a little secret. I'm older than you know," he pointed his cane towards the window. "The sea outside the window is infantile when compared to me and all this time, eons, I have never once forgotten the abandonment, the banishment I suffered because of her. Never once. It made me who I am today. Not holy, as you have already guessed, but certainly, certainly great."

Jude rose, took a golden coin out of his pocket and rolled it along his knuckles.

"Yes. There is no denying my greatness. And all of it, Ansley, everything, the result of feeling powerless and needing it to be otherwise. So should you want to feel otherwise, flip this into the air and ask me to catch it," he slid the coin into Ansley's pocket. "I can give you all the power you desire," he leaned down and spoke directly in Ansley's ear. "I can give you colour. I can give you her," he said and stood straightening his lapels.

"Right then. I'd better get going. I'm glad we had this little chat. Don't cause trouble, Ansley, okay? I don't want to hurt a fellow outcast, but trouble makers are like wolves and I am a shepherd that will kill for my flock," he fluttered his eyelashes, then walked to the door.

"Don't panic," he said. "The venom will wear off in a couple of hours, but the heartache, ah, the heartache! Now that, my friend, is there for good," he said as he closed the door behind him.

Ansley was locked inside his body and a great terror constricted his mind. He couldn't think straight. Marianne had stood on the table and defended him. She had taken an arrow for him. No, he thought, she had pushed him into humiliation and run away. She had let him take the arrows for her. Jude was a monster, but maybe he had a point? Maybe he'd been prey? Sleep squeezed him into blackness and he let the lid close over himself. He let it.

Jude stood on the other side of the door. Perfect, he thought and slipped one of his scales into the soft folds of Ansley's brain.

42.

The castle was packed. Jude had called for a special meeting before dinner and even though Marianne was desperate to see Ansley, her father had volunteered her to serve the evening tea. It was difficult being in the kitchen with the cherubs. They spat everywhere, smoked, and ignored her completely.

She was doing her absolute best to keep busy and unseen, but her heart was sick with worry about Ansley and Beatrice and also incredibly nervous of spontaneously shifting into a moth. The teacups clattered as she handed them out. Her father sat in the front row talking to Jude. They both glanced up at her occasionally, which made her feel even more panicky.

"Careful dear," said her mother. "Why don't you take a little break and get some fresh air?"

"Thanks," said Marianne and she left the kitchen.

She stood by the open door and took a deep breath. Why were Jude and her father looking at her? They couldn't possibly know about the stolen food, could they? She was paranoid and worn out, plus the thought of Dex made her even more shaky. He had kissed her and she passed out.

The bandage on her back was itchy and she was scratching it when her mother appeared. Her mother wiped her hands on her apron and placed them on Marianne's shoulders.

"I take it you must have heard about the little girl?" Her mother asked.

Marianne closed her eyes and prepared herself for the worst. Her mother could only be talking about Beatrice. He must have kicked her out and said that she was contaminated or something. Well, I'll find her, vowed Marianne.

"What happened?" Marianne asked.

"A little girl named Beatrice died this morning," her mother said.

"Died?! But that's impossible, she was cured! I saw her and she was cured!"

"Sometimes it's difficult to tell if someone is contaminated or not," her mother said and hugged her.

Marianne pushed her away.

"She was not contaminated! I know this for an absolute fact!"

"It's okay to be upset, honey," her mother said.

"No! It's not okay! Nothing is okay! It's far, far from okay!"

Her mother went to hug her again but Marianne stepped back.

"It will never be okay again," Marianne said quietly. They stared at one another.

"You're right," her mother whispered. "I know you're right. Something is wrong, I can feel it, I don't know what it is, but it's there, it's here, it's happening. Everything is a mess. And all of these poor children, my God, what will become of them?" Her mother held the sides of her head as though she feared it might explode.

He'll kill them, Marianne wanted to say, but the pearl stopped her with a vision. She saw Beatrice's soul rising and twirling from her mouth like a ribbon and it terrified her. She knew she needed to keep silent.

"Mum, I need to speak to you alone," said Marianne and wrapped her arms around her mother's waist.

A glimmer of understanding passed between them.

"Not here, not now," Marianne said. "But soon, I promise," she squeezed her.

They could hear big boot's plodding across the hallway. The door opened.

"Everything alright back here?" It was Jude. He glared at Marianne and she went completely cold. The pearl guarded her against his malice and the scale inside her singed.

"Yes, Jude," her mother said, on edge.

"I went to get a cup of tea and there was no one there. Are you ill, Marianne?"

She shook her head no. She couldn't speak to him.

"She's just upset about the little girl," her mother answered and held Marianne close.

"Little girl? Ah yes, Beatrice, dreadful business, but she was contaminated and the sickness got her, but don't worry our flock is safe."

"We are all upset about her, but it is for the good of the village." It was her father. He was standing right behind Jude.

"Quite right, we need to stay strong for one another," said Jude.

"Harold…" her mother protested.

"Honestly, Janet. You pander too much to her," her father said.

"Harold a small girl has died! Marianne knew her. It's only natural for her to be upset!"

"May I interrupt?" said Jude.

"Yes, of course, Jude," her father said.

Pathetic worm, thought Marianne.

"Maybe, during Marianne's sensitive phase, you should keep her at home, so she's not exposed to life's necessary and inevitable misfortunes. I'd be happy to visit on a daily basis and offer her my guidance," he said.

And slowly devour you, he thought.

"That's very generous of you, Jude, but she needs to be exposed to life's misfortunes so she can learn to cope with them." Her mother kept her arms defensively enclosed around Marianne.

"That's enough! Enough nonsense. Jude is right. Thank you, Jude. I think we could all benefit from some guidance," Harold said as he frowned at Marianne and her mother.

"My pleasure. Now, ladies, can I get a cup of tea?"

"I'll get it," her mother said. "You go to the toilet and clean yourself up. I'll see you soon okay?" Her eyes told Marianne that she loved her and Marianne returned the knowing glance and ran inside.

Her stomach felt chopped in two with grief.

"She seems better already," her father said to Jude.

"Hmmmm," Jude agreed. "I have amazing powers," he said and put his hand on Harold's back. "I like the way you handled that, Harold. Well done. And now for a quick cup of tea before I begin my speech. I think you'll find it hugely motivational."

The cherubs adjusted Jude's chandelier and lit a candle on his podium. He finished his tea, handed it to Harold and left the kitchen. He was wearing his top hat and dressed head to toe in black denim. He walked to centre stage and put his arms out, so the cherubs could adorn him in his long red velvet smoking jacket. He pulled a small torch out of his top pocket and aimed it like a gun to the crowd. There was complete silence.

"Now," he instructed calmly and the lights went out.

43.

It was entirely dark, but for the candle on his podium, which flickered his face like an ancient movie reel. His skin looked grey, taunt and chiseled.

"Who remembers their soul?" He asked as he turned on his torch and shot a beam through each of their chests individually. "Remember that tunnel of pure and bright light like a passageway to paradise?"

The beam of light bounced to each chest with illuminating interrogation. He let the effect take hold.

"Well someone, perhaps more than one, has jumped off the Soul Subway and into the pit of darkness," he said and turned off the torch.

The room became one big heartbeat, an animal crouching in the dark.

"Now," Jude commanded and the overhead lights came back on, exposing him in his full regalia.

The steam of power rose from him. His kohl-lined eyes bore into the sockets of the crowd without blinking. His red jacket shimmered like velvet liquid. It might have been petrifying were it not so intoxicating.

"Who has committed this act of moral suicide?!" He thundered the words and shoved his finger, long as a ruler, into the air as though he meant to pop something.

"The crux of this sermon is honesty. Now, when I ask you a question I expect you to shout the answer," he cleared his throat and his voice became soft and coaxing. "Do you agree with stealing?"

"No!" Everyone shouted as if in a trance.

"Good! That's good! So you will be appalled to know that there is a thief amongst us. A thief of the worst kind. A food thief. I tell no lie," he said and everyone started murmuring amongst themselves like a hive of insects.

"Silence!" He lost his temper and the room went deathly still.

"Now, I'm a reasonable man and I admit that none of us, myself included, are free from sin, but I know, and you know, that we can free ourselves of guilt through confession. I believe in the power of confession and I personally invite you to liberate yourselves. Liberate your souls! Your channel to paradise! Tell me! Who stole the food? Tell me and feel your soul lighten!"

Marianne stood as still as a mannequin, yet inside of her, currents of fear and rage trilled like wasps. The pearl told her, beckoned with her to breathe and keep quiet. Nobody said a word.

"Nothing?! Not a single suspicious thing?!" Jude stomped his foot like an angry Rumpelstiltskin, then regained his composure and resumed his sick coaxing. "Will no one display the necessary courage? Help us weed out the weak spirits so that we might enter the new age as warriors. Tell me," he said.

In her mind, Marianne saw the black fingernail they'd found at the cove. He is as cold as that, she thought and the vision of an enormous black snake slithered around her brain stem. It was terrible and she wanted to scream, wanted to punch and expose him for the liar he was, but somehow she knew that she'd die if she didn't keep still and quiet; like prey, she thought, he's stalking us.

"A bad omen is amongst us, I feel it lurking, waiting to sneak in and destroy all that we have worked so hard to achieve. A hero casts aside his doubt, come forward, my heroes, and arise!"

"I saw something," said Harold. He stood up and took his hat off. It looked as though he were under a spell. "I saw Robert stealing carrots from the field yesterday evening."

Robert was another Keeper. He was the only other Keeper who was married and had a family. Marianne didn't know them very well as they tended to keep to themselves and his wife was overwrought with the children. Marianne sometimes saw her standing at the top window, as though she were an apparition, with a baby in her arms and staring out to sea.

"Is this true? Did you steal from us?" Jude asked Robert and Robert's face collapsed.

"I, well I. It was only a few carrots! We were hungry! The children are growing and I just thought a few extras would be good for them. I'm sorry, really, I am, I just..." Jude stopped him mid sentence.

"You just thought nobody would notice, right?" he said.

Robert nodded his head and rubbed his tattooed knuckles.

"Take him," Jude pointed to Harold and another man named Sean.

They each stepped forward and grabbed one of Robert's arms. He tried to fight them off, but they twisted his arms behind his back and manoeuvered him through the door.

"Daddy, no!" shouted Marianne and stood. "What're you doing!?"

"Sit down, girl!" Harold's voice slapped her. "This has nothing to do with you!"

Her mother yanked her back down and kept her from running after her father. Everyone else just sat in a paralysed stupor.

"Shhh, now," her mother whispered, "shhh, we'll figure something out."

Jude continued his speech. Outside the sounds of Robert's beating were heard. Marianne winced at every punch, every kick, every moan or bloody cough that Robert made. She could hear the men grunting from their effort and it sickened her. She swallowed back the bile in her mouth and pushed her fingernails into her palms. Her mother squeezed her hand. Tears were falling down her scared face and dropping onto Marianne's arm.

How could her father do this?

Eventually the groaning stopped and gave way to the sound of dragging, then to nothing, to silence. Nobody moved or spoke; they were in the stunned and breathless coma of horror. Jude clapped his hands. In the distance a bird began to sing.

"I think we could all use some light refreshment, don't you? Tea, ladies?"

Marianne and her mother rose in unison and walked methodically into the kitchen. The cherubs were smirking and cutting up cucumbers for sandwiches. Marianne put the kettle on, put the cups in saucers and the sugar in a bowl, all the while silently mourning and wiping her eyes on her sleeve.

She looked out into the crowd of zombies scraping themselves from their chairs and approaching the kitchen. Ansley was nowhere to be seen.

"I'm scared," she whispered to her mother.

"I know," her mother answered.

Jude was first in the queue. He took a cup and saucer.

"I just want to say how much I appreciate your husband. He is a fine man," he told Marianne's mother.

"He's dedicated," she said.

She could feel him crawling under her skin. She couldn't meet his eyes for fear of spitting at him. She set the kettle to boil and began serving the teas. Jude stood there watching her and preventing anyone else from reaching the cups.

"But where's Marianne?" Jude asked.

She hadn't noticed that Marianne had left.

"I don't know. The toilet probably. I'll just go and check," she said. Now it was her turn to be brave, she raised her voice and said, "Jude'll help you everyone. You don't mind do you?" She asked him. She had to get away from him.

What could he say?

"Of course not, it'd be my pleasure," he lied.

Where were those blasted cherubs? They would certainly pay for this he thought.

Janet ran to the toilet and knocked on the door.

"Marianne?" There was no answer.

She walked in and looked inside each cubical. Marianne had disappeared. Her clothes were hidden inside the bin. Janet heard a fluttering noise, looked up and saw a moth trapped against the window. She hated to see things trapped and caged, so opened the latch and watched it fly out into the day's remaining blue. Go, she thought, go.

44.

Janet needed to leave as well and walked out into the evening sunshine. The castle felt claustrophobic and fouled by Jude's speech. She pushed her fingers against her temples and tried to ease her headache.

Harold was there with two other Keepers laughing like old friends. Robert was nowhere to be seen but there was a trail of bloody grass leading towards the field. Harold waved at her, turned back and said something to the others, then ran towards her, smiling. His face was glistening with sweat, he looked years younger, and, she thought in disgust, filled with glee.

"Jaaann," he drew her name out sympathetically as if she were a child that just didn't understand justice.

"Where is he?" She was cold. Her words fell from her mouth like rocks. She hated him. "Where is Robert?"

"He's gone. He won't hurt us anymore," he put his hand on her shoulder.

"Hurt us?! What did he ever do to hurt us! He just wanted some extra food for his family! What is wrong with that?"

"Stealing food is hurting us. Stealing is wrong. It's breaking a commandment, Janet, you know that. Now come on," he said and looked around to make sure his friends were out of earshot.

"I can't believe you are saying this, Harold! I'd have done the same if Marianne was hungry, I would have," she noticed his knuckles were bloody and stepped away from him. "Who are you?" Her voice quavered. "What've you become? I never thought you would, you could, hurt someone. It's monstrous. I want to leave this village. Today. You're making me feel afraid, Harold."

"Of what?" It was Jude.

He was standing behind them. They hadn't heard him approach. "What're you afraid of?"

His eyes drilled holes into hers. She felt her retinas splinter and smash. Of you, she thought, I'm afraid of you and she stepped backwards against Harold. He took it as a sign of subservience and put his arms around her shoulders.

"She's not afraid, Jude. She's just confused. She's never understood evenhandedness. But she will," Harold spoke for her.

"Yes. Yes, I'm sure she will. Especially with you as her teacher. You'll teach her won't you?"

"Of course I will. You know I will," he said and squeezed her shoulders, hard.

Janet could hardly believe what she was hearing. Harold seemed possessed by this malevolent man. She must find Marianne. She must take Marianne and flee.

"Good, you know, I find the sea is always wonderful for consideration. It's a beautiful evening for a boat ride," Jude leaned his face down so that he was eye to eye with Janet. "Wouldn't you agree?"

"What a great idea – how about it, Jan? We should take a trip out on the boat, just like old times? We can watch the sunset," he squeezed her shoulders again and she had to stop herself from recoiling at his touch.

"Are we still meeting at the castle tonight?" Harold asked Jude.

"There has been a slight change of plan," Jude glanced back at the castle and smiled. It seemed disturbingly quiet. "I'll let you know. Where are the others?"

"They've gone home to clean up for dinner."

"Good I'll visit each of them right away. Thank you for your exemplary service and honesty today. I think you're ready for greater responsibilities." Jude put out his hand and Harold shook it.

"I am." Harold said.

Jude nodded and walked away.

Janet kept quiet and vowed to maintain a relative peace until she'd found Marianne. She wasn't leaving without her. Harold led her down to the quay. He had his hand on her elbow and was happy enough to whistle. She would leave tonight while Harold was meeting with the others. Marianne? Janet called out in her mind. Where are you?

The sun was beginning to set and the clouds were thin orange lattices in the sky. The pearl tried its best to enter Janet to reassure her that Marianne had escaped, but fear prevented her from hearing. She stepped onto the boat and it shifted beneath her feet, and when she sat down it felt as though she were approaching her fate.

*

Jude was also thinking about Marianne. Now where was that little loose cannon? He was furious. How dare she speak out during his sermon? Expressed opinions were not good for his particular type of leadership. He needed fevered devotion, like her father, why couldn't she be more like him?

Women were such thinkers, blagh, it was enough to try the patience of any evil wrongdoer. Someone had stolen that food, he thought as he walked towards the Keeper's cottages. Who? He was sure it wasn't Robert! Of course there had been no loss there as Robert was weak and pitiful. It had been worth it just to see the fear wash over their faces like the oil of anointment, just to feel the room thump with terror had been enough to keep him focused.

He must find the culprit. He walked up the cottage path and rang the doorbell. What the hell was that in his ear?! An incredible pain banged against his eardrum and pierced his head. He jammed his finger into his ear, pulled it out again and bashed on the other side of his head with his fist.

Peter, one of the Keepers, opened the door. "Are you okay?" He tried to usher Jude inside.

"No! Get off me! I'm in agony! There's a thorn in my ear," Jude savagely whacked his head.

"Settle down and let me see," Peter peered inside Jude's ear. "Hold still, now, I need to get a closer look, wait a minute, there is something, something… coming out! It's a moth! Look! There it goes!" Peter pointed towards the sky.

Jude looked up and saw a moth, white and small as a fingernail, fluttering frantically towards the clouds.

"I've never seen anything like that in my life," Peter revered. "That was incredible. A moth trapped inside your ear. Do you think it's a message?"

Jude just nodded. Of course it was a message. His body prickled as though barbed wire wrapped and snagged around his spine. He'd certainly seen it before, long, long ago. That was once Eve's party trick. She could become a moth or a butterfly. In the Garden, thoughts had wings, he remembered and looked in the direction of the woods.

"Are you alright now or do you have any other creatures hiding inside your head?" Peter laughed.

Jude smiled and felt Mr. Birds Eye slink further into his corner like a dust ball.

"I'm fine and thank you for your help. I've just come to tell you that there has been a change of plans. There has been another outbreak of contamination. I noticed symptoms when I was serving teas. I'm cancelling tonight's Keepers meeting and asking that you all remain inside of your homes until further notice. The cherubs and I will take care of this mishap immediately," said Jude as he buttoned up his smoking jacket. The whole Eve experience had given him quite a chill.

"Is it that boy? The albino one?" Peter asked.

"Who? Oh yes, Dark Ansley. You're exactly right. It's him. It took longer to recognize his symptoms because of his skin," said Jude. "But don't worry, it's already under control," said Jude.

"I never liked him. It's got to mean something bad when you're born like that. You be careful," said Peter and he put his hand on Jude's shoulder.

"I will. I also wanted to personally thank you for your help with Robert today. I'm sure it wasn't pleasant, but your courage is inspiring and I have no doubt that you'll eventually make a great leader."

"Thank you, Jude," Peter beamed at the compliment.

"You're welcome," said Jude. "I'll have the cherubs deliver some food and get word to you as soon as we've decontaminated the castle."

Jude went to the other Keepers' houses and had similar conversations. He'd have to go to the castle and instruct the cherubs before he dealt with Harold. It was a pity to lose Harold as men like him were difficult to find during a mass extinction, but he really needed to rid himself of the whole family. He knew that one bad apple spoiled the lot and that daughter of theirs seemed poisonous. Ah well, every business has to make it's sacrifices, Jude thought and chuckled.

Fancy a treat later, Birds Eye?

Beyond him, Marianne, no bigger than a snowflake, melted into the horizon.

45.

She was small enough to slip through Ansley's cracked window. They hadn't spoken since the arrow incident and he hadn't been to Jude's after-dinner speech. She rested there for a while. She'd never been so exhausted in her life. How had Jude sucked her up like that? His anger just seemed to reach out and pull her inside of him and what she had seen terrified her. It had taken all of her strength to jerk away from the beating black muscle of a snake.

Was Jude the snake in her vision?

Ansley was awake and moving around now. He still felt weak from the cherub's poison, but at least he was alive. He didn't know that Marianne was there.

She watched him sitting at his desk writing. The curtains were drawn and a green task lamp turned his skin a dull golden colour. His figure was thrown in long shadow across the floor. His mouth was closed and his condition was almost unrecognizable. He's handsome, she thought, poor Ansley.

She thought of Dex's kisses on her neck and felt guilty. Too much happening, too much, too fast and all of it overwhelming. The complexities of her heart seemed to pale against the possibility of a new world and the tragic corruption of her current one. There were more immediate things to concentrate on and she needed to focus.

She flew back home, shifted, changed into jeans and a tee shirt and ran to Ansley's. She knew he was writing and it seemed a shame to disturb him, but she couldn't wait. There wasn't time. The door was unlocked and she opened it.

"Hey you," she said. "How are you feeling?"

"Marianne," he jumped and covered up what he was writing with his hand. "What are you doing here?" He said with a sneer, remembering her embrace with Dex.

"I wanted to see how you were," she said, surprised at his hostility.

"I'm fine," he said and turned back to his notebook. "Seems I can withstand poison and paralysis."

"Maybe you're a superhero?" She joked but it was obvious that he didn't find it funny.

"Look, Marianne, if you don't mind, I'm really busy at the moment so…"

"You want me to leave?"

"Yeah. I do." He couldn't look at her. His anger pushed aside his tears.

"What is wrong with you, Ansley?"

"I saw you with Dex," his tone was vicious.

She was speechless and full of shame. She could only imagine what he'd seen and how much it had hurt him. That kiss was a response to the moment, a fleeting, whimsical thing, wasn't it?

"Please, will you just go away, Marianne? Get out."

"Ansley, you don't completely understand. I know I've hurt you but it's not exactly what you think," she fumbled for the right words. "I need to speak to you, but not here, everyone is acting totally insane and I'm scared," she said and walked closer to him.

He put his hands up like a barricade.

"Just stop. Okay? Stop. I think I understand perfectly. I don't want to hear anything you have to say and I don't care about anyone else. Including you," he said and turned back to his work.

She undid her shirt and slipped it down around her shoulders.

"Look," she said and turned around.

He could see the wings burned into her back.

"I'm part moth. I can turn into a moth, Ansley," she started to cry. "When you saw us, I was so excited and that's why we…" Her crying interrupted her sentence. "I'm so sorry," she sobbed, and ran out of the room and into the dusk.

Of course he followed her. The castle was unusually quiet and the rain clung to him like grief. Sometimes he felt as though the rain was just for him, heart like a filter where the waste washes though and the rest of him numb.

Why had she become a part of Dex and not a part of him?

46.

Jude put the survivors to sleep in the castle. His plan was to suck their souls, slowly digest them and make the cherubs extract their DNA.

What else was he going to do?

He certainly wasn't going to stand around serving teas to all and sundry, no thanks, enough was enough, he thought as he started sucking. The cherubs just laughed and shook their heads as though they'd been expecting him to surrender to his hunger all along. They lit cigarettes and watched his performance.

One by one, souls left the survivors like frail birds, they broke through their throats with no more than a hiccup. Jude almost felt sorry for them. Almost. When he'd finished he turned to his cherub audience, took off his top hat and bowed. They gave him a round of applause; secretly pleased they had outlived his feasting.

"Thank you, thank you," he said. "Obviously there has been an itinerary change and we're swiftly moving to plan B. Stack them up now," he said and waved his hand to indicate the soulless bodies.

"I'll digest them one by one, but I want you to put half a dozen or so on the bus. Pull it around to the side of the castle so it's out of view. I want you to position them in lively forms, you know, make it look like they're chatting, eating fruit and light the scene with my chandelier. Choose the stiffest ones as they are the easiest to work with and once you've finished, I'd like you to disappear for a while," Jude said.

The cherubs looked at one another suspiciously. Their numbers were definitely declining, as Jude had made sure that one or two went missing every few days. It had been the only real way to keep them in line. Fear was his true companion.

"It's for your own safety," he said. "The seed releases spores of everlasting life upon extraction," he lied.

The cherubs smoked nervously. Everlasting life was the last thing they wanted.

"A strange trick of fate to be sure," continued Jude, "but Eve created the seed for humans and humans crave everlasting life. I will send for you once the spores have flown away and disappeared. You can join me in the new world and age," he said.

This made the cherubs cheer and fly around like fat little whiskey-drinking butterflies. Gullible, thought Jude, so gullible, still it seemed to work. He had to get rid of the cherubs and he couldn't face eating all of them. If they caught wind of his real plan, they would certainly tell the remaining Keepers and ruin the whole thing.

He needed the Keepers' souls and DNA to remain completely subservient for the new world. Who else would iron his trousers and hold his chandelier? Plus, there was no way that he was sharing the new world with the cherubs and their disgusting habits. The souls inside him were delicious and he refused to regress to cherub consumption. It would have been like eating over-boiled cabbage after a large helping of chocolate cake. No thank you.

The cherubs flew around and sifted through the pile. They chose the most life-like of the survivors and moved them onto the bus. Jude helped a bit, but it was apparent that he was really too unfit for the physical side of the job and desperately needed to get into consulting. Being his own God, his own boss, really suited him at this stage in life. He left the cherubs to do the staging like foul undertakers.

"You can find me later. I'll send word. But at the moment I have some pressing matters to take care of."

He called one of the cherubs over for a private conversation.

"Please take a food basket to the remaining Keepers. I've told them that there has been an outbreak of contamination. Remind them to stay in their houses until I say otherwise," he said and the cherub nodded obediently.

That should give him a day to absorb enough bodies, he thought. He couldn't have those knuckleheads barging in on his feast. He looked at the pile of sleepers and cringed at the task awaiting him. I'll be picky; he thought, after all, there was only so much DNA a single snake could extract. He wasn't after a population boom for goodness sake, just enough strands in the mixing bowl to get things moving.

And now for Harold, he sighed in the direction of the sea. He really could use a non-disgusting assistant and regretted eating them all ages ago. There was one particular vampire butler that had proved irreplaceable. Ah, well. We all make mistakes when we're young, but it was quite unlike him to feel regret; maybe he'd gone soft over the years? It's hard to say. Anyway, a holiday would do wonders.

He walked to the edge of the shore and watched Harold's little boat drifting in the sea. I must learn to take my time, enjoy the sea air, the birds, he thought, I work too hard. He looked around to make sure no one was watching, lifted his arms, cracked out of Jude's body and laid it carefully on the shore.

This would require his full and glorious snake size, he laughed as he slipped himself into the water and slowly swam out to sea. His body grew and grew until he was as big as a riptide. He sank to the bottom and watched Harold's boat swaying keenly above him. It was no bigger than his serpent eye. He started rocking his tail and watched the boat lurch. The water muffled their screams.

He coiled and sprang, just like old times, he thought, as he opened his mouth and swallowed the boat whole. He'd go back to the castle after this and feed. Swimming always made him extra hungry.

47.

Ansley followed Marianne. It was early evening and although he could feel the weak rays of sunlight pricking his skin, he pursued her anyway. She ran into a deep valley north of the woodland. It was cut into a steep hill of the South Downs like a sheltered bowl fringed with moss and trees. Marianne seemed to know exactly where she was going as she raced up the hill and disappeared over the other side.

Ansley trailed her and saw a forgotten house hidden amongst the rocks and trees. Its walls were composed of a crumbling and bleached stone and its empty windowpanes appeared desolate. Brown vines stitched the rooms together and moss overtook the floor like a spreading disease.

Positioned in front of the house was a shallow ditch that transformed into a pond during heavy rains. It's water was chalky white. Ansley entered the doorframe and found Marianne standing next to a hearth with the thatch roof dripping above her. She sat inside a stone gloom. Broken clay pots lay scattered and wild thyme grew between faded and cracked tiles. The spell of the house softened him for a moment and he felt more curious than angry.

"What is this place?" He asked.

It felt like a welcome distraction from the inevitable.

She ran her hand lovingly across the wall and it broke away in crumbs. There was a picture hanging in a grimy glass frame. She straightened it and rubbed it clean with her sleeve. It was the photo of a woman with long, messy dark hair and small, amused black eyes. Her lips were pressed in a smirk and her wrists were long cuffs of bangles. A goat sat on her lap.

"I've never taken anyone here. Ever," she touched the photograph.

"Who is she?"

"She was a writer. A journalist, actually, she used to come here during the summer and lived the rest of the time in London. Her articles were radical, she was an authority on environmental issues and people called her a revolutionist. She predicted all of this," she waved her hand towards the outside world. "They said she was mad, maybe she was, maybe she had to be, but after they banned her from publication, she took to poetry, it was always the thing she loved, like you, and she moved here. Everyone said she had filled herself with too much red wine and conspiracy theories. Anyway, I never met her. I only saw her once."

"What do you mean?"

"It was a couple of years ago and I had been fishing with my father. It was the night of the autumn equinox and the moon was like a large orange planet in the sky. I'd never seen it like that before. He didn't care about it and just wanted to get home, but I wanted to walk over the Downs and watch the moon. I heard a strange sound, like someone shouting a song. I followed it and found her. She was sitting at the edge of the little ditch; it was full of orange moon. She was shouting something from a book and throwing bottles at the moon's reflection. I could hear the bangles on her wrists clinking, the water quivering and the bottles splashing against the water. I'd never seen anything so passionate."

"What was she shouting?"

"I'll never forget it, I wrote it down as soon as I got home. *The birds have vanished down the sky. Now the last cloud drains away*," Marianne recited.

"*We sit together, the mountain and me, until only the mountain remains*," Ansley finished the quote.

"You know it?" Marianne asked.

"It's Li Po. It was said that he drowned trying to hold the moon's reflection," he said.

"That explains what she was doing," she walked past him and towards the ditch just beyond the front door. "I just watched her for a little while and then I ran away. I was too afraid of my feelings. She was so intense. Too intense. We can't always help our spur-of-the-moment reactions and I've always regretted it."

They were silent for a while, both intent on avoiding the obvious thing that needed to be talked about. It felt like once it was said there was no going back.

"It was the same with Dex. The situation – how can I explain it? – was surreal and intense. I can turn into a moth now, Ansley. Dex helped me and we just, it just happened, like a reaction. I'm so sorry. I didn't mean to hurt you and I regret it."

Ansley looked at the ditch. The woman had thrown maybe a hundred wine bottles into the water. Bottlenecks rose from the silted earth like green and brown periscopes and from their mouths the wind lifted a hollowed music. It was a sound he would always remember, not the crash of the ship, not the fury, but the moan of its decline.

He opened his mouth and the words, "I love you," rose like lyrics.

She turned to him. Her hair had been wind whipped into dreadlocks like wool before it's felted or spun and he pulled her close. She let her body fall against his.

"I know," she said. "And when I'm able to, I will love you back, but right now, I'd just run away," she rested her head underneath his chin.

"Is that why you brought me here? To show me the last poet you ran away from?" He was gently mocking her but she remained serious.

"I don't know. Maybe. I don't understand most of the decisions I'm making at the moment," her voice broke midway through the sentence.

He lifted her chin and kissed her lips, her neck and then her lips again. "It's okay," he said. "You don't have to have to have the answers."

He took her hand and led her back to the house. They used a bit of fallen thatch for a mattress and lay side by side in shared warmth and slept. In the morning, birds were fluttering in and out of the rafters as well as his heart. He slowly, carefully, so as not to wake her, moved from the mattress and into a dark corner. He watched the sun inch towards her and alight the side of her face as though she were her own planet waking up.

"Good morning," he said when she opened her eyes. "Over here. I can't be in the sun, remember?"

"Wait here," she said. "I'll get us some food."

She rose and kissed him. Her breath smelled nutty with slumber.

It would be years before he saw her again.

48.

When she was beyond the house, she ran. She ran over the Downs. She was on the verge of crying again. She just couldn't stop herself. He had seemed so monstrous in the morning crouching there in the shadows.

The truth was that she did have feelings for Dex. She tried to suppress them, but couldn't help thinking about him. At first she thought it was because he irritated her so much but then she found herself looking forward to seeing him. He was the reason she could fly. She couldn't tell Ansley, of course she couldn't, she loved him too, but it was problematic love, with Dex it was easy, natural. Nothing about Ansley was natural. Her heart was in her throat.

"Marianne! Hey wait!" It was Dex. He was a dragonfly. "How's your back?"

She let out a small sob.

"What's up? Are you crying?"

"I had a fight with Ansley," she said.

"What about?" He buzzed all around her head and landed on her shoulder.

"He thinks there's something between us," Marianne said.

"Oh. Isn't there?" If he had his hands, he would be clenching them.

"I don't know," said Marianne and she ran off towards the pond, ducked behind a tree and undressed.

She emerged a few seconds later as a moth. She just needed to be free of her physical form. She flew over the pond and Dex didn't disturb her. He knew what it was like to return to your animal self. He waited on a large rock and she joined him when she was ready. They sat fanning their wings in silence for a while.

"Look, I'm sorry about the other night," said Dex. "I know Ansley cares about you, but I just got carried away. It's no big deal," he said, but didn't mean it.

"It's a big deal to me," said Marianne.

"It's a big deal to me too actually, I was just lying to make it easier," said Dex.

"I don't think anything can make it easier," she said and let her wings fall.

*

Jude had been out for a spot of morning exercise. He'd been feeding all night and it was proving a gluttonous task. It felt good to be in his normal form. He heard voices, looked up and saw Marianne and Dex sitting on a rock. It was the moth that had flown out of his ear. It was just like Eve to deploy a parallel realm to keep an eye on him.

Why didn't it occur to him before? He shook his head in disbelief, that woman, she was one gorgeous maverick. He couldn't make out what they were saying and slid closer to the woodland.

Shape shifters would make a brilliant addition to his DNA collection, plus he could coerce them to search for his seed. Yes, a shape shifter would definitely come in handy.

A strange glow emanated behind the shape shifters and he slinked quietly up to the pond. What on earth was this? It was metallic in colour, like reflective glass with a pale silver tree attached to an island that floated in the pond's centre. He'd never seen anything like it in all his years. His eyes followed the tree roots to the bottom of the pond where the pearl oscillated steadily. He caught his breath. He knew what it was right away.

My seed!

The dragonfly and the moth were still sitting together on the rock. Don't be too aggressive, he told himself as he slithered up to them, took aim and smacked them with his tail. He just wanted to knock them out, not kill them. Once he was sure they were unconscious, he manoeuvered a heavy piece of bark over their tiny bodies and glided into the lake.

The pain was instant and unbearable, as though he were being flayed alive. He screamed and zipped his body, like a firework, out of the water and onto the bank.

"You nearly killed me," he wheezed to the seed.

It was hard not to take it personally. The skin had been scorched from his snake body. His scales were burnt. His eyes were blistered. He stared at the seed. He was feverish with longing. It was his single planet. His blank planet. Where he could be everything. My beautiful seed, he thought and remembered his old tree.

"How could you burn me?"

Hadn't he been the one that loved the tree the most? How could it dismiss him so carelessly? He felt his old inadequate susceptibilities rage through him. The ingratitude gnawed like a dog on a wound.

"I'll be back for you, I promise," he bid the seed and flicked his tongue. "Whether you like it or not, you'll belong to me," he lifted himself up and returned to the rock.

Dex and Marianne were still there, one began to rouse and he flicked it back into unconsciousness. He carefully folded them inside his mouth and slipped home.

49.

Dex and Marianne were trapped inside Jude's pantry. He had put them in a jar and when they woke they fluttered frantically against the glass. They were running out of air. Outside they could hear the dogs growling and sniffing the door.

"I feel as though I'm suffocating," Marianne said. "Change into something and break this glass!"

"I'm trying," said Dex. He was still woozy from the Jude's bash on the head.

Marianne stopped and rested her wings near the golden rim of the jar. She looked around. The room was full of jars similar to the one they were trapped in. The jars were full of small, florescent green swirly things.

"Are those glowworms?" Marianne asked.

The jar rattled as Dex turned into a mouse.

"A mouse! You need to be something bigger!" His brown fur pushed against her wings.

"I'm trying, Marianne, but it's difficult under pressure, you know."

The jar smashed as Dex turned into a wolf. They were both gasping for air.

"Excellent, Dex, now let's get out of here," she said.

He whimpered and Marianne noticed that he had cut his snout on the glass. He smashed it open with his head poor thing. She fluttered down beside his cut.

"Butterfly kisses?" She teased.

"Very funny, it hurts," he said and pawed his nose.

"I'm sure it does, but toughen up, you're a wolf for goodness sake. Would you look at these?" She fluttered around row after row of jars. Each jar was full of thumb sized, floating helixes. "What are they?"

"I have no idea. I've never seen an insect like it before," the breath from his nose fogged over the glass.

"I don't think they're insects, although they do somehow seem alive," she said.

"There must be thousands in here. It's like a collector's laboratory," he said.

He was right. The pantry was the size of a small laundry room and was filled floor to ceiling with jars of DNA waiting to mutate. There was one window and through it the afternoon sun gave the jars a disgusting hue. The dogs were still sniffing around the cracks of the door, but they were no longer growling. Instead they seemed curious. The smells had changed. Dex scratched himself, he was hugely impressive and his silver grey hair shone radiantly in the sun. His eyes were sky blue.

"Window or front room?" Marianne asked of their escape. "Personally I'm curious to see inside the rest of the house."

"How do we know Jude is gone? He might be out there waiting for us," said Dex.

"Hey, listen, can you hear that whistling?"

Marianne flew up to the window and saw Jude walking towards the castle with a group of flying cherubs. "He's going to the Castle," she said.

"That's strange. I can't believe he'd really leave us in here by ourselves."

"He obviously doesn't know our supreme powers," she joked.

"Okay, here goes," and he howled and slammed against the door.

That's all it took to knock it down. The dogs just stood and stared at him bewildered. He peed up against the wall and padded around with Marianne resting between his ears. The house was full of hidden jars of helixes. They were inside cupboards, the refrigerator, under the stairs. In every container and pot there were helixes.

"Where's all his food?"

They walked soundlessly through the house as the dogs cowered and whined. Dex snarled at them whenever they moved and they instantly backed off in submission. Finally they came to a closed door, and when they opened it the heat inside the room took their breath away. Heat lamps surrounded a giant nest and inside the nest there was a long and sticky egg.

"Is that an egg?" Marianne asked.

They walked up closer and looked at the egg. It was disgusting.

"That's not an egg. It's excrement and look what's inside," said Dex.

They both bent down and looked inside the black pile of odd bones and gristle. The little green helixes were tucked in like radiant screws.

"I want to leave now," said Marianne. "I don't like this."

Outside the door the dogs began to bark and pace the floor. They could hear a faint whistling and keys in the lock.

50.

"He's back! What do we do?" Marianne fluttered about in a panic.

"We hide!"

"Where?" They both looked at the pile of poo.

"You must be joking!" Marianne said.

"He'll never look there, quickly," said Dex as he shifted into a fly.

They folded their bodies into the poo and listened. They could hear him talking to the dogs as he went to check on his captives. When he saw the pantry door open and the broken glass he screamed and kicked each dog repeatedly in the ribs.

"Idiots! You bloody idiots! Two minutes! I was gone for two minutes! I can put a town to sleep and you can't even look after some insects?! I've had enough of this! I'm sick of natural disasters and body hosts. I'm sick of being an underling… I want a kingdom to rule!"

He stormed through the house knocking down jars and turning over tables. Glass broke and helixes scattered as he trashed the house. He stormed into the nesting room and walked over to a door that appeared to be a closet. He opened it and the sight behind made Marianne's heart freeze. It was crammed full of bodies standing up as if they had been frozen. Their skin was grey and their eyes were open. On their foreheads were two red puncture wounds. Jude shuffled through them, they clanked like wooden wind chimes, "not you, not you," he muttered as he rummaged.

"Ah yes. Perfect," he said as he removed one from the closet.

Marianne recognized him at once. He was a teenager that had gone missing over a year ago. Jude had called him a 'deserter', had said that he had joined the impure. She had been to that lecture and remembered his family had been beside themselves with grief. Jude had told them that their son had come to him and said goodbye. She remembered their sobbing. She looked inside the closet and recognized most of the faces. Marianne looked at him. There was something still alive inside of him. She felt it like you feel a presence in an empty room. His body was rigid and when Jude dropped him on the floor, he fell like a stick.

Jude raised his arms in the air so that they were straight against his ears, then he flung them down and a large crack appeared. He started wiggling and humming. It was a strange kind of dance, intoxicating almost, enchanting. The skin of Jude slipped, fell from him and revealed a long black snake. When Jude had finally taken Simorg's body off he writhed and stretched. It was luxurious to be his full size and to crack out of his human skin rather than just shifting.

"God it's hot in there, even for a snake," he said to the mirror.

With his tail he picked up Simorg's body and hung it on the back of the door. He slithered over to the teenager who lay like a discarded grey flute against the wooden floor. He coiled around him and began to squeeze. Out of his mouth curled a long thin wisp of green smoke and a howl. It's what's left of his soul, thought Marianne and she was right. Jude sucked it up and closed his eyes in delight. Eating the remains of a weak soul was truly delicious, like a treat that had been marinated.

"That's better," he said and then he opened his mouth ludicrously wide and began swallowing the teenager whole. Jude made a sound similar to that of a constipated person with a gurgling stomach. It was disgusting. Jude was halfway through digesting him when Marianne began to tingle.

She recognized the tingle before she changed from moth form to human form. She tried to get Dex's attention and very carefully she flew over to him. Jude was enraptured by his meal and turning the other way. He was humming with his mouth full.

"I have to go, I'm shifting," she whispered, alarmed.

"There's no way out, you'll have to fly to a place where you can hide," he said.

She looked around. He was right. The windows were sealed and the door was shut. The only door that was open was the door to the body closet. Could she?

Could she really? What choice did she have?

Silently, ever so silently, she flew to the back of the closet and nestled down behind their bodies. It was just in time. She shifted. She stood completely still and covered herself with the others. Only one pair of eyes turned and looked at her. Beatrice. She was alive! Marianne rejoiced. Beatrice looked at her, pleaded and Marianne nodded her head slowly, slightly, yes. Yes, sweet girl, she thought, don't worry, there is no way I'll leave without you. Marianne silently unbuttoned a dress from one of the erect bodies and slipped it over her head. It smelled of infected skin. She'd have to go back to the field to retrieve her clothes.

A cherub walked in carrying a glass jar. He went over to the pile of poo and began picking out the helixes and placing them gently inside the jar. They were shining as though they were radioactive.

"Leave the jar here," said Jude. "I'll have another pile of samples for you after my nap. Ugh. It's gruelling work digesting these bodies. Before you leave, can you put on my sleeping music?"

He had finished his meal and was now curling up for a snooze underneath his heat lamps. He flicked the poo aside and coiled in the nest. The cherub put on a CD of thunderstorms and distant explosions. A few minutes later a fly buzzed in Marianne's ear.

"Come on, let's go. He's asleep," said Dex.

Marianne gently pushed the wooden bodies to the side and lifted Beatrice as though she were carrying a small totem pole. Beatrice was stiff and a small sigh escaped her mouth, which Marianne closed and tiptoed out the door. Jude's snoring was the gluttonous bubbling sound of one who had eaten too much. She tiptoed past the nest and held her breath.

She reached the door just as Dex silently turned into a wolf. She nodded her approval. He flung his head back to indicate that she must climb on, which she did after she'd opened the door. The dogs lifted their heads in protest, but Dex snarled and they fell back. They hadn't forgotten Jude's kicking. She held Beatrice on her lap as she rode out of Jude's house on the back of Dex. Thank goodness the cherubs were nowhere to be seen.

"Thank you universe," she said when they got out into the fresh air. "It will be okay," she spoke softly to Beatrice. "I promise."

"Just hold on to my neck in case something happens and we need to run," Dex said. "Do you notice something strange?"

"Where do you want me to start?"

"Well you're riding the back of a wolf with a fossilized girl down the middle of the High Street like Lady blinking Godiva and there's nobody around! Seriously, not a single soul!"

She thought about it and remembered what Jude had screamed at the dogs.

"Quickly, Dex, take me to the castle!"

51.

The blinds were down inside the castle and there was the strange aura, almost a hum, emanating from the building as though it were alive. The sea splashed against the brick wall at the end of the lawn. Marianne trembled and climbed down from Dex. She balanced Beatrice against him and frantically ran from window to window trying to catch a glimpse inside.

"We have to do something! Dex, knock the door down," she said.

"What about petrified over here?" He looked at Beatrice.

"I'll hold her," said Marianne as she ran over. She picked up Beatrice as though she were a rolled carpet and wrapped her arms around her. Beatrice's eyes were scared.

"Don't worry," said Marianne. "I know how to bring you back, trust me. I just have to see if my parents are inside. It won't take long. Come on Dex, hurry!"

Dex crashed into the door. It hardly wobbled. It was reinforced to prevent vandals in the distant past. He tried again and cowered back whimpering. Marianne found a big rock and threw it at the window, which cracked a little and she thought of the window in the bathroom. It was small and probably not double-glazed.

"This way!" She carried Beatrice and went behind the castle.

She took another substantial rock, threw it at the bathroom window and it immediately shattered.

"Excellent," she said.

She leaned Beatrice against the wall, undressed, changed into a moth and flew through the small opening. Once inside she stopped, alerted. A Keeper was sitting on the toilet with his head resting against the cubical wall. She could hear the Keeper snoring and realized that he was sleeping. How strange, she thought and flew into the main room where things got even more bizarre.

Everyone was there, curled up together and fast asleep. She looked closely at their eyes. They were moving rapidly and they all seemed quite peaceful. Some were even drooling. The room was dark with a peach glow owing to the setting sun coming through the orange blinds.

She flew down and landed on a boy's nose. He looked serene. His breath gently quivered her wings.

Where were her parents? She flew around the bodies, under and over arms and legs, but couldn't see them anywhere. Perhaps they were on the boat?

She flew into the kitchen. A girl was hunched in the corner fast asleep with a tea towel in her hand. Broken and spilled teacups were on the floor. It seemed as though people had just collapsed mid-drink, mid-sentence, mid-everything into a sleeping pile.

There were mounds of excrement in the corners alongside discarded shoes, watches and other non-perishable items.

Was that what he was planning on doing to the sleepers? She thought of the closet and a wickedness churned through her. He wanted them living. He wanted them fresh, so he could suck their souls and swallow them whole. If she didn't get out of there, she'd vomit.

She shifted in the bathroom, put on the clothes she'd hidden earlier in the bin and walked outside. Dex was still a wolf and held Beatrice, awkwardly, with his paws.

"What's going on?"

"He's put some sort of sleeping spell on them, like he's storing them before he digests them. My parents aren't in there, nor are the other Keepers," she said, took Beatrice and buried her face in the girl's soft hair.

She could feel herself unravelling. Stay together, the pearl pleaded, you can save Beatrice as well as yourself.

"Jude knows what the pearl is," she said softly.

"Then we'll have to fight him for it," said Dex. "And we'll win. The world is on our side, remember? It's just like you said."

Acidic bile rose in her throat at the thought of fighting, yet Marianne nodded in agreement, for what else could they do?

"First, let's get her to the pond. She's going to die otherwise."

52.

All morning Ansley had waited for her to return. He stayed in the corner. The hours passed and the sun moved a rectangle of light across the mossy stone floor. Birds flew in and out of the rafters. Bugs flew in and out of the windows and a fox had stood in the doorway. Nothing noticed him and he felt as though he didn't exist.

The wind blew across the bottlenecks and the sound haunted him, like a siren, like slow mourning, like grief. His grief. He knew she wasn't coming back. He couldn't chase her. He couldn't leave. He could only sit and wait for the sun to vanish. It was nearly evening and when twilight came, he stood, dusted himself off, and walked to the castle to pack his bag.

He saw the cherubs hanging the chandelier inside the bus. The castle felt deserted, he slipped in unnoticed and went straight up to his room. He threw his belongings into his backpack. His notebook was still in his desk drawer; he took it out and sat down. He wanted to leave her a note and was waiting for the words. From the window he watched the night's approach slowly drain detail from each tree until it had transformed the woodland into a solid shape against a grey sky. Nothing, no words came.

A swooning black mountain, he thought, with stars above its peaks, bright as golden bells. He could hear foxes yipping like rusty hinges against the blue inferno. He could hear the hollowed instrumental call of owls.

What was there to say?

Even if she grew to love him there would always be a part of him that she couldn't possibly understand because she'd never be able to access it. It was his shadowed part, his ugly part that she could know nothing about. That's the way it is between people. A secret, like a layer of insulation, lies between oneself and the interactive world.

He'd spent a lot of time inside his secret because he'd spent a lot of time alone. It was where his poems came from. It was where his dreams fixated. He found his anger unquenchable. If he could just see her again, then maybe, maybe.

Maybe what?

He didn't know. It was pointless, hopeless, everything, just everything, big, small, up, down, love, hate, real, imaginary, just everything to see her again. All of it. Now. All of which he'd never been able to say had risen and lay waiting like a ball of light behind his eyes. He felt certain that if he could see her, even once, his eyes would bore into her like radiant beams and fill her with the knowledge and magnitude of his love. It was a small hope, but small and strong as a bird.

Dex came to mind. He banged his fist on his desk. I wish it were his face, he thought. Faces. He looked in the mirror. His reflection made him recoil. Again, who was he kidding? He ought to just tell her goodbye and be done with it, hit the road, be a one-man freak show or something.

Wait, he thought, listen. He stopped breathing. He was suddenly aware of an abrupt absence of sound, not an owl, not a scurry, not a pheasant's outburst, the night seemed at once alert and pressed against the barbed hook of something. He rose, walked quietly to the window and looked though the field towards the pond. There was nothing but darkness and a horizon of fire. He saw the lit bus parked on the side of the castle like a lighthouse.

What was Jude up to?

53.

When Dex and Marianne got to the pond it had changed again. It was even bigger and darker than before. The pearl still shone in the middle of it and the seeds churned like meteorites. Dex went behind the tree where he'd hidden his clothes and shifted into a boy once more.

The pond truly resembled the universe and had taken on a life of it's own. It seemed to command that it be hidden. Trees Marianne had never noticed arched their wide leafy brims over the pond's edges. Its waters were mirrored black and reflected the leaves perfectly. Animals were attracted to it as well and stood mesmerized by its power. They didn't flinch or run when Dex, Marianne and Beatrice approached.

"We're just going to dip you in here," said Marianne, pushing back a bough of leaves and laying Beatrice beside the water.

Beatrice's eyes grew wide and curious. Marianne could tell she was trying to speak.

"I won't let go of you, I promise. This is the magical, special water that helped you last time and it will help you again, trust me," Marianne said as she lowered Beatrice into the water.

The water swirled up to Beatrice's body and a wave came forward and lifted her in its fountain. The water poured into her open mouth, carried her away from Marianne and out into the centre of the pond, where the fountain lowered and gently floated Beatrice on her back.

Her eyes were open and the seeds were swirling around her head. A ribbon of green smoke trickled down from the sky, flew up her nostrils and she started coughing. The colour of her skin darkened and her movement returned.

She leaned her head back into the water and seemed to fall asleep. The water returned her to the shore where Dex and Marianne lifted her from its hands and laid her on the grass. She was completely unconscious yet pulsed with vigorous life.

"She looks peaceful, doesn't she?" Marianne put her cheek against Beatrice's mouth. "She's certainly breathing."

"Now what do we do with her?" Dex asked.

"I don't know. We certainly can't watch her all night. Jude'll find us and kill us. I'm surprised he's not here already." Marianne said. "I need to find my parents first though. I at least need to say goodbye," her voice was broken with tears and she wiped them with the flat of her palm.

"I understand," he said and hugged her. "Go ahead and fly back to the house. I'll put your clothes behind a tree and watch Beatrice," he kissed her forehead. "Be careful," he said and she took flight.

The field was windy, yet she forced herself through it, all the while, pushing Ansley from her mind and focusing on her parents. Her house was empty. She dipped in and out of its silent rooms. It surprised her to find that she'd already said goodbye, that her motions now seemed a mere formality – as though she'd accepted that she now lived a different life. Outside the cherubs were loading the bus with the sleepers. She flew past the windows and couldn't see her parents. They must be on the boat, she thought and flew back to the pond.

*

The sun was gone, the moon wasn't full, but it was bright. The woodland had altered. Dex sensed it like an animal senses change, there were other smells and unknown creatures looming. He occasionally saw eyes sparkling amidst the deep green bracken and beside the darkening trunks of trees.

The image of two golden coins kept haunting him. Was it the moonlight? He looked down at the pond. The ripples had been scarlet and pink in the sunset. Now they were deep purple and grey. The night raced across its reflective surface, the seeds shimmering at the bottom like stars through clouds at dusk. And the pearl, in the middle of it all like a living, controlling planet.

What were they meant to do? Well whatever it was they couldn't decide here, they couldn't wait here, finding a safe place had to be the first priority. A place where he could think; at present he could only trust his instincts. They needed a plan if they were going to combat Jude. The thought of starting a new world with her was too big for him to comprehend. What did it even mean? All he wanted was to keep her safe.

She flew back and landed on his shoulder. "How is she?"

"Fine, still sleeping like an angel. Any luck?" He asked.

"No. They might be on the boat," she said. "I'll be right back," she flew behind the tree and shifted.

She walked out stretching her arms. "I don't think I can fly to the sea with this wind. I'm exhausted," she said.

"You don't have to. I'll shift into a seagull and you can hang on," he said.

"Thank you."

"What are boyfriends for?"

She looked at him. "Don't say that," she said. "Not now."

"Does that mean 'not ever'?"

"I don't know," she said. "It's just…"

A stick snapped.

"Ansley?" Marianne whispered.

"It's not Ansley. It's an animal. It's been watching us for a while," said Dex, walking in the direction of the broken stick.

"Why didn't you say anything?" Marianne followed him.

"I didn't feel we were in danger," he said.

A black leopard rose from a bed of bracken, approached them, blinked majestically as if to say hello, and walked towards Beatrice.

"He's guarding her," said Marianne. "Look."

A little wooden boat had been hidden inside the bracken.

How did a boat get here?" Dex asked as they turned it over.

"It's in pretty good condition," said Marianne. "Are you thinking what I'm thinking?"

"Absolutely," said Dex and they dragged the boat to the side of the pond.

It was perfect for Beatrice. The leopard watched them without suspicion and then continued his unflinching stare of duty towards Beatrice.

Marianne took Beatrice by the hands and Dex took her by the legs. They carried her to the little boat and gently laid her inside. She was smiling in her sleep and looked snug inside the boat.

Marianne kissed her forehead and pushed the boat from the shore. The pearl held her in its orbit as a welcome satellite and they felt that she was safe. The leopard didn't make a sound or move but somehow managed to infer its approval.

Dex shifted into a seagull and Marianne tucked her moth form between his wings.

"Come on, first your parents, then Ansley," he said.

She sat between his wings as he flew through the woods towards the sea. Behind them the leopard sprawled along the shore, watching the boat, silent as a sentinel.

54.

"I've brought presents!" Jude held up a blowtorch, a Molotov cocktail and a gallon of white spirit.

He collected his last two Keepers, Thing One and Thing Two, he called them secretly, for a bit of housework. These two had no earthly connections, thank goodness. He didn't like to get his hands unnecessarily dirty and he'd eaten the crème de la crème of the pile.

"I'm afraid the contamination outbreak requires us to blow up the castle. Boo. But! Look on the bright side, it's for our own safety," Jude smiled. "The cherubs and I loaded up the uninfected onto the bus. There is a safe house on the other side of the woodland. We'll still be close enough to the field and once we've purified everything, we can start rebuilding our headquarters."

"What about Harold?" Peter asked.

"It's with a heavy heart that I tell you they were among the infected and had to be put down," Jude took off his top hat and placed it over his chest.

The two men looked at one another with shocked expressions.

"I saw their daughter with that albino boy," said Peter.

"It proved a fatal friendship," Jude said and took his chain watch out of his vest pocket. "A tragedy, a true tragedy. The devil is voracious and we all need to watch our backs. Now look at the time," said Jude, thumping his watch face.

Without question the Keepers picked up the explosives and walked down to the castle with Jude. Aww, bless them, thought Jude, they will serve nicely.

"So you are the last Keepers. The bravest. Be proud of yourselves and do good work. We must keep ourselves pure and safe. The challenge before you is a difficult one, but then, all the greatest challenges are difficult." He gave them each a hug. "Finish quickly, everyone is already waiting for you," he said and pointed in the direction of the bus.

The Keeper's looked and saw the chandelier and the illuminated faces of the passengers.

"We'll grab any belongings you want on the way," he said. "Now I'm not meant to tell you this, it's a surprise, but there is nothing wrong with a little cake encouragement," he winked.

"There's cake? Really? I haven't had cake in ages."

"I think we deserve to be a little excessive as we're purging, don't you? It's a time for a celebration after all! We'll join the future together as pure and I, for one, look forward to having you by my side," washing my pants and brushing my fangs he thought and saw a vision of his new world.

It was barren with hot rocks and developing souls. The thought of it made him quite emotional. He wiped a tear from his eye. The Keepers took it as a touching display of gratitude for their upcoming duty and prepared to follow him anywhere.

"Ready?" Jude slapped the two affectionately on the back.

"Yes," they said, crouching low.

Their eyes narrowed in on the castle and their hands tightened around the fertilizer bombs. They felt pride and importance inside their chests.

"Clean up," Jude said with a smile and they snuck down the hill like soldiers.

Of course Jude could have taken care of this business himself, but it wouldn't have been as much fun, also multitasking is much easier if you outsource effectively. Now he could gather the seed and blow up the castle all in one big swoop, plus he was wearing his favourite pin stripe suit and all the dry cleaners in the area were dead. I'll definitely release the souls of the drycleaners and tailors first he thought as he walked down to the woodland. Now to get my seed.

He was tired of waiting. To hell with finding the shape shifter and that Keeper's reckless daughter. To hell with Dark Ansley, he thought as he stomped through the field. Nothing would matter when he had his planet.

55.

Where did those children find a seed anyway? Jude thought it all rather baffling. It's probably their virtue or some likeminded nuisance that allowed them access to a new world. Were they even old enough to drive for crying out loud?!

A new world!

The words choked forward. Oh, he'd do things differently this time, no trees, for instance and no hopeful peace mongers with their stinking placards. No way. He'd stick a sign in the stratosphere that read: No Angels! And definitely no cherubs.

Earth hadn't been completely bad though, come on. He had learnt a liar's rhetoric and a thing or two about greed, plus he'd had fun. Now give credit where credit is due, you are not entirely reptilian, he thought as he swallowed a mouse. He needed a top up.

The pond was glowing ahead of him. There was something floating on top of it and as he got closer he saw it was a boat. Brilliant, he could use the boat to get the seed. He remembered how the water had scorched his skin before and shuddered. This time he felt prepared and pulled a net from his back pocket, attached it to a long stick and walked to the edge of the pond. The seeds hovered close to the pearl and repelled his presence.

He started to tingle and felt a wave of nostalgia. He looked at his reflection in the pond and saw an old snake. He remembered the Garden, faults and all, as his first home. He was no longer young and although he had done great things with his life, he would never know youth again. With his stick he hooked the boat and brought it towards him. Inside he saw Beatrice, full of youth and beauty.

What was she doing here? Wasn't she in my closet? If he ever finds those shape shifters he'll certainly show them a thing or two. He looked at Beatrice. She was asleep to the world, naive to it.

He began to suck. And with a small intake of wind through his round lips, her soul rose and fluttered above her chest like a hologram.

The leopard flung towards him and knocked him into the pond. It was an explosive chemical reaction. Jude screamed as the skin burned and sizzled from his body. Beatrice woke up and screamed at the sight of him.

The seeds began to swirl together, then suddenly burst through the water in a fountain and shot down the throat of Beatrice. The force lifted her body to the top of the geyser and filled it like a sack. She passed out again and slunk back into the water. Jude was shouting and trying to swim towards the boat.

The leopard dove with stealth and precision into the centre of the pond, picked up Beatrice by the scruff of the neck and swam back to shore. She dangled from his jaws as he ran through the woodland.

Finally Jude grabbed the boat and pulled himself inside where he coiled under a seat, nursing himself and cursing. In the distance he heard the first of the explosions. He couldn't move his body. He'd have to wait until the boat drifted to shore. He looked at his skin and saw that he was completely charred black.

Oh my beautiful seed, I shall have you yet, was all he could think; a snake obsessed.

An arrow shot through the side of the boat with a swish. Jude looked up at the triangle above him and groaned. It was shimmering white and a white arrow could only mean one thing.

He felt the boat slowly move towards the shore and with great effort peeked his little snakehead over the side. A cigarette dangled from the cherub's chubby mouth as he pulled in the boat and when he saw Jude he smiled with tar-speckled teeth. Cherubs. They're like blinking rats. It doesn't matter how many you eat, how many you get rid of, they just keep on coming. His little baby hands lifted Jude out of the boat.

"Ah look what they've done to you! You're black and burnt," he held Jude up to his pudgy belly and stroked him like a dog. It was downright insulting.

"Hand's off, nappyman! Don't forget who I am just because I'm a bit under the weather. Look, I can slither, I can hiss and I can certainly eat you," he said.

"Now that's no way to speak to the one that saved you," laughed the cherub.

He took a small whisky bottle from his nappy and gulped back a swig.

Jude groaned again. These cherubs just loved punishment. Cigarettes, whisky and fraternizing with serpents. Well, with morals like that, he might just be useful.

"Saved me?! Hardly! I was just preparing for another swim. Now what do you want?" Jude asked.

"I've come to offer you my assistance," he said and hiccupped.

"Well, you might come in handy," said Jude as he rubbed his wounds against the cooling mud.

"Really?! You mean I can come with you?!" He was so excited he wet himself.

"Not again! That's the second time this century one of you has peed on me! Urrrghhh! Yes, you can come with me but keep your bladder under control, change your own damn nappy and clean yourself up. Disgusting habits are anti-regality and I'm about to be snake almighty," Jude said and hissed.

"Thank you, thank you, thank you," said the cherub as he threw his whisky bottle and cigarettes into the woods.

"No problem," said Jude. "Now come on. I need nourishment in order to devise a plan." He slithered up the hill towards his house.

Just like packing a snack, he thought. Who's a clever snake then?

56.

Ansley could smell the white spirit and hear the Keepers whispering as he crept down the stairs. He snuck into the kitchen, filled his pack with food and entered the castle hall. It was full of smoke. Smoke was billowing from underneath the door and he could hear the Keepers coming through the kitchen.

There was only one way out. He touched the door and his ring singed into his hand. He took it off and rubbed his finger. He was about to burst through the door when the kitchen exploded causing half the hall to collapse. He scrambled over burning rubble and dodged a beam that fell and broke open the door.

Ansley dived through a small gap and rolled his burning body towards the large puddle of sea spray. He put his fire out and ran. The second explosion went off when he was halfway across the field.

It was like an exploding orange mushroom. The hot blast hurled him up into the air and whacked him down against a rock on the ground. His right hip throbbed from this hammering, but he hardly noticed because he couldn't see a thing. The blast had left him momentarily blind, but he knew he had been thrust in the right direction because he could smell the damp woodland ahead of him.

He got up and staggered towards it. There weren't many places that a pure white creature, like himself, could hide. He thought of the footbridge. It was a few hundred yards from the lake. He wanted to be as far from the pond as possible.

The pond meant Dex and Marianne, plus its luminosity could draw the attention of his pursuers. He knew he'd be safe under the footbridge. He crouched down on all fours. He didn't want to be visible. If I kept the heat to the back of me I'll hit the woodland, he kept telling himself.

He was so disorientated that he accidently thrust his face down on the hard ground and his nose began to bleed. He couldn't risk leaving a trail. He lifted his face towards the sky and pinched his nose to stop the bleeding.

He could feel the ash landing on his skin, numerous and faint as dirty cat's feet. He scratched and smeared the ash across his forehead. The blood was running down his throat so quickly that when he took deep breaths, he gargled with it. He had to stop the bleeding. He grabbed fistfuls of grass and crammed them up his nose. He clawed the ground and shoved dirt and small rocks up his nose.

He expected a hand to reach out and grab his throat at any minute. The bleeding hadn't completely subsided but he had to find cover. They might be watching him now. They might be watching him squirm like a white maggot on the charred ground.

He began to see the emerging shapes of shadows as if he were slowly, soundlessly travelling on a boat through a soup-heavy fog. The hazy silhouettes of trees began to appear. With grass and dirt plugging his nose he couldn't rely on smell so he held his breath and listened intently. In the distance he could hear the fire cracking, splitting though his life.

And he left his life behind, he left it and became an animal. It took all the strength he had not to crawl towards the fire. He thought of the stars. He did, but not as objects of magnificence, he thought of them hidden, during the day, as he was hidden; yet remained. He thought of all the invisible things, invisible ideas, invisible emotions, invisible worlds and the stars began to represent a giant map of all he had yet to discover, like his reason for existing. Tempting him to endure.

There are times when we have to belong blindly to our faith.

He heard the water and it sounded intimately familiar as though it were his own water gently sloshing inside his own skin, as though he'd lived through this moment before, he surrendered, while another hand carried him to the footbridge.

It was the hand of seraphic intervention as there was no way he could have made it to the footbridge alone, without scent, without sight and in incredible pain. The pearl floodlit his internal vision with his own desire to live. He seemed to pour easily over the trees' knuckled roots and didn't flinch at all when nettles slapped and stung his face. When he felt the reed grass he knew he was nearly there and finally his hands hit water. Mud oozed between his fingers and soaked his jeans.

He crawled with the water splashing against his knees, wrists and face because he knew the footbridge was up stream. He could feel mossy rocks beneath the palms of his hands and the occasional slick of a small fish. By the time he reached the footbridge, shadows had become defined images and he was able to wedge himself between the muddy bank and the mossy underside of the bridge without bumping his head as he feared he might.

It's amazing how compacted a body can become when it's forced, like a turtle he folded into himself, then with one hand he began to cover himself with mud. His skin went from pale moon to dark sky. He slowed his breathing until it was simply wind and let the mud encase him.

Only his eyes were visible. They blinked like pink planets under the bridge.

The cry of a seagull spooked a heard of deer and when they ran across the bridge, bits of cold, wet and rotten wood fell into his hair. He closed his eyes and went completely black.

*

The Keepers walked up the pathway towards the glowing bus and Jude slithered up the other side of the hill to greet them. He was still in a great deal of pain. A few souls would do him wonders. Good boys, well done, he thought, the victory in you will taste nice. It's amazing how thoughts can affect the feel and taste of a body.

He pursed his lips and began sucking. The cherub saw the souls rise, chuckled and smoked. He always kept a spare pack of cigs tucked inside his nappy. The village was completely empty now.

"Get the jar ready," Jude said as he began to swallow Peter whole.

I hope we go somewhere fun after this, thought the cherub and started blowing smoke rings.

57.

Dex and Marianne circled the harbour. Marianne looked down but couldn't see her father's boat moored in its usual place. The fires in Hastings gave the west a red haze and black waves smashed against the white cliffs, grey shadowed with the night. The lump in her throat plummeted to her stomach. She knew.

"See anything?" Dex said as he landed on a cliff edge.

"No. The boat's gone," she said.

"Do you think they went fishing?" The hope in his voice was false.

"I doubt it."

"Let's have a look around. Hang on," said Dex as he flew off and circled the cove.

It was difficult to see in the dark but she managed to spot it floating on the water. At first she thought it was a bit of kelp.

"Dex fly down to where that bit of kelp is floating," she said. "I think I see something."

It was a plank of wood and on it she saw the hand-painted 'ST' for Stella Marie. Marianne recognized it right away. It was a part of her father's boat. It had snagged in the kelp and was drifting along in the tide. She began to cry. Dex flew back up to the cove and gently landed. They heard a distant explosion.

"What was it?" Dex asked Marianne, she looked devastated.

"It's a piece of his boat," she said.

"Are you sure?"

"Yes," she swallowed back the sick that formed inside her mouth.

Her parents were gone. It was as though all of the air had been squeezed out of her and half of her heart had been pinched off.

"I've painted it a thousand times. I've hauled in a thousand nets. I know it like the back of my hand, they're gone, I feel it, I know it," she said as she sobbed.

"I'm sorry, Marianne. I know how you feel, believe me, I lost my parents too. Is there anything I can do?"

What could anyone do? They were caught in a tide, to decide their actions seemed pointless. She could feel herself rolling.

"I want to go home! I want to be normal again, a human again, I want everything back the way it was – it's all so – so crazy! I don't understand any of it and I hate it, I hate it all!" She flew to the edge of the cliff where the wind picked her up and thrashed her against the stone.

"Come on," he gently lifted her onto his back with his wing. "Let's get you back to the pond so you can shift. Hold tight, it will only take a minute," he said as he took off.

Who was she now?

The fire looked as though it were in the woods. They were both speechless. The second explosion went off and they saw that it was the castle.

Marianne screamed and they flew towards the blast, but the smoke was too strong, and the heat burned their eyes. They couldn't stay so Dex flew back to the pond and landed on the edge of the boat. Beatrice was gone. They searched all around the pond but couldn't find her anywhere. The leopard was gone as well.

"He's taken her, everyone is gone. Even the seeds are gone," Marianne shifted behind the tree, dressed, then dropped into the bracken.

Her body felt limp and heavy and she just wanted to stay there forever. Nothing mattered. Dex came up behind her and wrapped his arms around her neck. She fell forward and started to cry again.

"They're all gone. He got them all. That monster took everyone," her shoulders jerked up and down with anguish.

Dex held on to her and stroked her hair.

"Not me and not you. He didn't get us or Ansley and he didn't get the pearl. Now come on Marianne, pull it together. We can fall apart later, but right now we need to take the pearl and get out of here. It's up to us now. We need to protect the new world," Dex said as he held her by the shoulders and looked her straight in the eye.

He was right. She knew he was right. She wiped her tears on her bare arm, turned from Dex and dived into the pond. The water glowed. It was like swimming through liquid gold. She could feel the water entering her pores; she could feel it seeping in through her eyes, her nose, her ears and mouth. She could feel her body changing as the water filled her and soaked her with its golden powers. I'm alive, she thought, I'm alive. The pearl detached and rose to greet her. She clutched it in her hand and swam to the surface. As she stepped from the pond the last of the water soaked into her skin and up through her feet. It looked like gold lightening and she shimmered.

She opened her palm and showed the pearl to Dex. She put it safely in the pouch around her neck and looked up at the castle. This time when she shifted she became an enormous Atlas moth. The pearl hung from her strong thorax and the apex of her wings resembled a snake's head.

"Looks like I'm ready for battle," she said. "But first we need to get Ansley," she took off and flew towards the poet's house.

Dex shifted into a bat and followed her. When they got there a low moaning was stirring in the wine bottles. Marianne frantically swooped in and out of the rooms. The house was empty. A tormented sickness rose in her as she realized that there was only one other place that Ansley could be, the castle.

58.

There was little left of the castle. The wood was sizzling and some pieces were still glowing orange and slowly dying. Marianne's scanned the ground looking for clues. It sat gleaming like a piece of silver in the middle of the charred scrap and smoke.

It was Ansley's ring. At first she thought it was a shiny nail, but when she looked closer her heart sunk. Ansley was never without his ring.

"Dex," she said as she flew down and landed beside it.

Dex landed beside her, saw the ring and immediately knew what it meant. His head dropped and he took a deep breath.

"I'm sorry," he whispered.

The two of them were silent for a while. Only the wind, making the wood hiss, seemed alive.

This time, Marianne did not cry, instead, something in her turned to stone. I'm a statue, she thought, a statue amongst statues. Dex flew over to her. He could sense that she was emotionally closing down.

"We have the seed and ourselves to think about," he said. "The new world is depending on us. You need to get up now Marianne. Come on. We have to get out of here before Jude comes back and kills us too."

"Will you take the ring? I can't pick it up like this," she said.

"Of course," he dipped his wing and hooked the ring with his claw. "Now let's go," he said and lifted off.

She flew like a robot and couldn't feel herself. She knew Dex was right and followed him across the field. Back in the woodland they shifted and dressed.

"What will we do now?" She felt alone and vulnerable.

"We need to take it step by step. First we must hide the pearl. Then I think we should go back to my lock-up where we can rest and eat," he said.

"Then what? How do we release the new world?" She wrapped her hand around her pearl.

"I don't know," he said.

"Help me," she whispered to the pearl and it gave her the vision of a child.

She heard the baby crying. In her mind she saw a body full of water.

"Shhh! Can you hear that?" Marianne grabbed his arm.

Dex listened and could hear a faint cry, almost like a braying.

"It's a baby," she said and began running in the direction of the sound.

"Where are you going?" Dex followed her. "It's too dangerous to go back into town! Let's just get out of here," he said.

"It's a baby, Dex. Don't you see? It's perfect! Thank you," she said to the pearl and kissed it.

"What!? Are you insane?! The last thing we need right now is a baby!" He chased after her.

The street was a dark branch that the houses perched alongside like dead owls. Only Jude's house seemed alive. His lights were on and the bus was parked on his drive. It was so quiet they could hear their breath as they quickly followed the sound of the exasperated baby. The crying was coming from inside Robert's house, of course, thought Marianne, he had an infant.

The front garden gate had long been missing and tall thistles and ivy covered up the wrought iron. A burst of dandelion clocks flocked around her as she stormed up the brick path towards the steps. The front door and window frames had once been painted a vibrant blue. Marianne turned the doorknob and, remarkably, the door pushed open.

"Come on," she said and disappeared.

The house smelled of hearty soup and old carpet. Marianne ran up the staircase, into the nursery and straight to the baby's cot. The baby's little fists clutched the bars and his face was hot and streaked with tears. She picked him up and gently rocked him. His cry became a whimper and eventually he settled. Dex stood at the doorway and watched as Marianne took the pearl from its pouch and popped it into the child's mouth.

"Swallow," she said and the baby swallowed. "Good boy, well done."

The pearl lit the child up like a lampshade.

*

Jude and the cherub had been watching from their hiding place behind the curtains. Jude had just finished the last of the bodies on the bus and the cherub had stored the helixes safely in the pantry jars, when they, too, had heard the baby crying. It was like the cherry on top of a sundae, thought

Jude as he slunk into the house. To leave with a young soul inside of him would feel glorious.

They had just come in through the window when they heard Marianne running up the stairs. Now they stared at her in disbelief. The cherub dropped his unlit cigarette on the floor and Jude gave him a nasty look.

"Quiet," he mouthed. "Let's listen." These two might give him the information he'd need to access the new world. He couldn't believe how easy it had all been. It was just falling into his hands, as though the new world wanted him to rule it. He was closing in on his dream. They both turned back to the child, rapt with possibility.

The seed was inside the child.

59.

"What are you doing?!" Dex stepped forward, grabbed the baby and started patting him on the back. "Come on. Cough it up," he coaxed the baby, who instantly started crying again.

"Stop it! You've upset him! I hid it, just like you said," she snatched the baby back and began to bounce up and down to pacify him. "Now help me pack some things for him."

"You have got to be kidding me," Dex said and desperately took his head in his hands.

"Think about it Dex. What is the body made of? That's right, water. So in water the seed can protect itself from Jude. Get it? It's a stroke of genius really," she said as she threw some clothes, nappies and a blanket into her rucksack.

Jude and the cherub exchanged looks.

The girl was clever, you had to give her that. I wonder if I could recruit her? Thought Jude, nah, I'll just eat her as soon as I steal the little snot rag. After all, what goes in must come out; it was purely a matter of time. This business was getting seriously dirty, he sighed to himself, the new world has come just in time.

Dex stared at Marianne. She was mad. This was hare-brained madness.

"But how will we look after it?" He asked.

She hugged the baby and whispered in his ear. Dex could see tears on her cheeks. He wanted to tell her that the baby would never replace the people she had lost but it wasn't the right time.

"Him, not it, him. I can do this on my own you know. Nobody's asking you to come," she said. "It will be alright. I promise, it will all be alright," she cooed into his peanut-sized ear.

Dex knew she was talking to herself as much as to the child and it cut him to the bone to see Marianne in pain, but his anger was not the numbing kind, the deadening kind, instead it wanted vengeance, it wanted blood. He made a vow to find the one responsible for her heartache and for the loss of his friend.

He wouldn't leave her on her own. Maybe, he thought, just maybe they could find a place where they'd be safe. They could go to his lock-up for a few days' rest and come up with a plan. Dex touched the child's arm, he guessed he was about six months old.

"Does he have a name?"

"Emoli," she said and managed a small smile.

This is perfect, thought Jude, just perfect. I do so love a dysfunctional family.

He pursed his lips together and began to suck, but for the first time ever, their souls wouldn't release. Eve has changed the rules of the game, he thought, these three are immune to my antics! It's becoming hard work but I'll just have to eat them the old-fashioned way. The main thing is the seed is out of the pond, it may be surrounded by water but it's neatly packaged in skin, so all hope isn't lost. He licked his fangs. The cherub flicked a Zippo with his thumb and illuminated Jude coiled like a rope in the corner.

"Now that was truly touching, really, I'm impressed," he slithered up to Marianne and Dex, who stood shocked in a state of repugnance.

Marianne recognized his voice immediately. He was the snake she'd seen inside of Jude's brain.

"It really is you," she gasped as all the air in her lungs deflated.

"Oh yes," he said. "We meet again. Only this time you have something I want," he said and began to hideously grow.

The sound of his expanding skin was like cracking knuckles with a groan. Fangs shucked out of him and frothed. His eyes were yellow with black slashes outlined in red. He towered over Marianne. Her palm began to throb and Jude realized she had one of his tracking scales inside of her. Now that was interesting, he thought. A scale can only attach to sin. What about this girl is sinful? I guess we all have our secrets, he thought.

"You can't hide from me," he said. "I'm inside you."

She shook her head as if trying to throw off his words. He was losing patience.

"Just give him to me you little witch and I'll think about letting you live," his spittle fizzed against her cheek and Emoli immediately began to scream.

Marianne's heart pumped bile into her throat, her mouth was dry and her tongue was a lump of fabric, but somewhere inside her courage reined.

"No," she said in a small voice and clung to Emoli. "No."

Jude reared back and laughed a sinful laugh. The cherub laughed too and lit the curtains with his Zippo. Fire began eating the fabric like a million red ants.

"Fine," Jude said. "Have it your way," he opened his mouth and attacked.

"Run!" Dex screamed as he shifted into a wolf, howled and sunk his teeth into Jude's neck.

60.

Marianne had just enough time to get down the stairs before Jude flung Dex whimpering into the corner and chased after her. His body was the size of a doorframe and he smashed all that obstructed his way. A piece of splintered banister flung above Marianne's head and impaled the wall like a thrown sword. She ducked, jumped through the front door and ran down the street.

Seconds behind her, Jude grew, like a murderous train, he chased her and pulverized everything he touched. Her legs were burning and her arms were beginning to weaken from the weight of Emoli. Her heart was a bomb in her chest. She didn't know how much longer she could run. She was no match for him. He was too strong.

Please, she pleaded, please help me.

Jude's tongue flicked the back of her neck, his open mouth dripped venom onto her shoulders as it prepared to crush her skull. She held her breath and expected to die.

"I'm sorry," she said to Emoli. "Forgive me."

The black leopard crossed the field in three quick bounds. It was five times its normal size. Its growl was deep and angry as it crashed into Jude and pinned him to the ground. Jude, equal in intensity, roared and lashed his tail against the great black claws that ripped through his scales as the leopard bore down on his skull. Marianne took the opportunity to run with Emoli and hid behind the stone wall.

"Shhh, it's okay, it's okay," she whispered in his small and red from screaming ear. "We will be okay," she said with a sinking heart.

Beside her ruins of the village and castle lay fizzing with embers, her parents were dead, Dex was missing and undoubtedly injured and the evolutionary battle for supremacy between carbon and silicon had begun. She was numb with horror.

Jude's sharpened tail struck at the leopard like a medieval lance. Blood surged from the leopard's back and chest. The air took a coppery stench and the ground was sticky and dark with blood. The leopard kept slipping, but never quit, for his aggression was ruthless. Jude's versatile scales slid over each other to provide protective armour with ultimate flexibility. He laughed at the leopard's attempts, as the leopard's strength could not counter the writhing and slinking attack of suffocating coils and piercing tail.

"What on earth is wrong with you, cat? Can you not see that I am the superior being? It's obvious, you idiot! Give up!" Jude lassoed the leopard, flipped him over and sunk his fangs into the leopards exposed inner leg muscle.

The leopard howled, sprang to his feet, raised his front left claw and smacked Jude across the grass.

"Never!" The leopard shouted. "I will never give up!"

He leapt forward and raised his claw to attack, when two arrows, sunk into the soft underside of his paw. Jude recovered quickly.

"Ah ha!" Jude said. "Outsmarted by a man in a nappy!" He lashed the leopard alongside his head and tore his ear in two.

Jude was right. A cherub, with tattered nappy and blackened wings, turned and flew towards Marianne and Emoli. Marianne screamed, grabbed Emoli and took off running down the street. The leopard bit each arrow, yanked it from his paw, chased after the cherub and caught him in two seconds. He bashed him unconscious and then threw him, like a bouncy ball, all the way to the sea.

Jude chased Marianne and Emoli down the street towards the harbour. The leopard pounced on Jude's back and sunk his teeth into Jude's neck. Jude beat his body like a whip but the leopard hung on with his mouth.

Marianne and Emoli kept running, another cherub caught up and flew behind them with an arrow mounted in his little bow. String poised by the side of his nose, he released an arrow that flew, almost in slow motion, in a gentle arc directly into the back of Marianne's right leg. She went down. She attempted to cushion Emoli by landing on her elbows and they combined in a wail of skin against tarmac. Jude, having finally flung off the leopard, plucked Emoli from Marianne's arms and quickly slipped away.

"Emoli! No!" Marianne screamed and when Emoli heard his voice he began to glow.

The hypnotic beauty of the glowing child caught Jude unawares and the leopard smashed into him. The blood from the leopard's impact splattered into Jude's eyes, blinding him, but he clung onto Emoli and shoved the leopard, once more, against the ground. It was clear the leopard was losing strength and could not win the battle.

Marianne quickly pulled the small arrow out from behind her knee. She knew a cherub's arrow carried a paralyzing potion, but that it took many hits to be effective, still, she felt groggy and pain pulsed from her elbows and leg.

Where was Dex?

The leopard had his jaws on Jude's head and rear paws gathered around his tail, but Jude hung onto Emoli, and used the remainder of his form to coil around and crush the leopard's body. Eventually the leopard had to let go. Jude felt the world order was shifting and was exhilarated by the battle. He rose up to the height of a two-storey building. Fangs exposed. The leopard reared up to meet Jude and Jude saw a flicker of weakness in his eyes.

"Ready to die, stupid cat?" Jude hissed.

Suddenly Jude twisted and screamed. A hornet attacked his neck, laying down a barrage of barbed stings. Only a hornet could fit between those scales. It was Dex! Dex shifted to a great sea eagle with talons scathing the Jude's eyes. Still, Jude clung to Emoli.

"Cherubs!" Jude shouted.

Two cherubs came with arrows whizzing. The leopard caught one in his giant paw and tossed him to the ground. The other cherub chased away Dex and the two of them wrestled in the air. Marianne pulled herself up, took the poisoned arrow and wedged it, tip skyward, into the soil.

"Dex!" she shouted and pointed to the arrow.

Jude returned his attention to the leopard. He whipped his tail around made a sickening crack against the leopard's skull. The big cat sunk low and his coat bristled.

"I am a Protector!" he roared. "Release that child!"

"No!" Jude shouted. "The seed is mine!"

"Then prepare to die!" The leopard grabbed Marianne and expertly pierced her chest with one of his claws.

A bright light torched through the hole and to cut into Jude like a sword. It was her soul, her life force. She felt mutable, stuck in the tension before a shift, but there was pain and the light began breaking open her chest. The light seared though Jude's scales and entered his cold body. Blackness in her exploded, immeasurable as space, but entirely empty, it began to steal her breath. She was too tired to fight it and a part of her detached and began to float towards Jude.

"You would use her?!" Jude shouted to the leopard, disgusted. "You would use her before her training? You must be weak. See, she hasn't the strength to resist me!" He held out his tail to catch Marianne, but the leopard smashed it to the ground.

Shine, said the pearl, shine into the emptiness. She tried. She tried to direct her light and her attempt burned Jude. But what she found when she illuminated the emptiness was fear and loss. It was too much for her and she panicked. The light snapped off and she plummeted to the ground. The leopard stood, bloody and weak, between Jude and Marianne. He was ready to fight to the death.

"Damn you!" Jude slithered towards the leopard. "She won't taste as nice now," he beat the leopard to the ground and rose up to attack Marianne.

"No!" Shouted Dex as he slammed the cherub, heart first, against the poisoned arrow.

He flew at Jude and swiped his eyes with his talons. Jude smacked Dex with his tail and sent him flying across the field. The leopard, half dead with exhaustion, pounced once more on Jude's head.

"Have some self respect," Jude hissed as he flicked him off and began to slither away with Emoli.

Dex, Marianne and the leopard lay whimpering in defeat.

"Get up!" The leopard shouted. "Cut him off at the woodland," he said and began running after Jude. Everything inside Marianne hurt and breathing was swallowing razorblades, yet she lifted her sore and heavy body and painfully followed Jude. Dex flew above. Jude was heading with Emoli across the field. We'll never make it, thought Marianne, for Jude was seconds away from the shelter of the trees. Help us, she pleaded, please.

And above them the world eclipsed.

As though the Earth had shifted behind the moon in fright of the sun's intensity. A black shadow fell over everything as the shrill of a thousand house martins came screaming through the sky like a meteor shower. They descended upon Jude with a feathered vengeance, pierced the spaces beneath his weakened silicon scales with their small beaks, hooked their feet into his body and craned him up into the air. Emoli dropped from Jude's coiled grasp like a glowing ball falling through feathers and shrieking commotion. Marianne caught the child in her scratched arms and covered him with kisses. Above them, they watched the birds carry Jude cursing across the sky until they all disappeared between parted clouds.

All that could be heard were the embers roused by wind and their gasping breath.

Emoli let out a small coo as feathers fell like exquisite ash snowdrops against their stunned faces.

They watched the sky blazing blue and yellow until their daze subsided from disbelief. Marianne turned around while Dex shifted and dressed. It was excruciating to return to his human form. His body was bludgeoned with bruises and cuts and he cursed in pain. Emoli nuzzled against Marianne's neck. She turned to look for the leopard, but found his trail of bloody paw prints led toward the woodland and vanished. Dex limped towards her.

"Are you okay?" He put his arm around her shoulder. He inspected her wounded leg, her arms and the point below her chest that the leopard had opened. She gathered Emoli closer. "Does it hurt?"

She looked down at the spot where she'd opened with light. Where the skin had closed was a tattoo of a ball of fire. "Yes," she said. "Obviously it hurts like hell."

"That's not hell," said Dex. "That is a comet. The tail wraps up around your neck," he traced the tail to her throat and hesitated. "Marianne, I, well, for a moment I thought you..." he stumbled. "I'm so glad you're alive."

She nodded. She understood his emotion, as well as the need to stop it from pouring, as anything could happen now. They were at the edge. "Me too," she said and met Dex's eyes. "I know what you're feeling," she said and he nodded. "So, were those birds friends of yours?" She said to change the subject.

"Oh, we have all kinds of friends you don't know about," he said. "I am full of surprises. As are you," he said and pointed to her comet. "Seems you're a lot more than you realized."

"I can't believe that was real," she said and looked at the devastation around them, burning, demolished and dead. "I have no idea who I am," she said and he took her hand.

The world was a wound that they fastened around themselves and began to own. Together. They took aim for the fires of Hastings, as though its radiance were coming from the North Star, and started to walk.

*

Ansley could see again and sat under the bridge motionless for a long time, reconciling the fact that Marianne and Dex weren't coming for him. Perhaps they were dead, he thought, in any case, they were dead to him. He saw meteors falling between the black branches of the trees and a flock of birds as wide as a tide. Perhaps the world was finally coming to an end. Let it, he thought, let me, end.

He decided to walk to London. He could fade away in London, as only the diseased and insane remained, so it was like walking towards a guillotine.

The pearl did what it could.

But humans become their emotions in the end, when the present has been stripped and the future is too distant to recognize or contemplate, emotions rise like clouds of stamped dry earth and fog their vision. All the pearl could do was wait.

All night he walked and the mud fell off him in chunks until he was once again completely white. He put on his balaclava. The moon moved across the sky with him like a companion.

My only companion, he thought.

He was numb and devastated. He wished to stop and slip into an eternal hesitation but forced himself to continue moving, for he feared that if his legs quit then his heart might also. And despite his desperate grief, he knew he had survived for a reason, as death had spared him too often for his life to be inconsequential. And there was a new planet, the pearl reminded him, where maybe, he dared to think, maybe his father and Marianne might resurrect and he might become beautiful enough for her love. It was a small and deluded hope, but it was something. So he walked until he became just a motion, like water dripping from halted oars, a sound only, an action only, blending into a setting that was, eventually, a vast city.

London, and beyond it, the dark sky falls,
absolute as sudden change.
Dawn begins a weak outline
and the horizon is a thin, white bowstring
that shoots me
into another world.

The Book of Insects

And many of those who sleep in the dust of the earth shall awake, some to everlasting life, and some to shame and everlasting contempt.

Daniel 12:2

1.

The birds pecked Jude's eyes and wedged their beaks between his scales like little hammering syringes. The flock was massive and behaved like a tornado as it lifted the serpent and carried him to the sea. Marianne held the infant Emoli and stood beside Dex. They watched as Jude writhed through the fire lit sky.

All around them buzzed an acute sense of living that a close brush with death delivers, as though their very cells were titillating as they gulped down air, sweet and poignant with spared life. As they walked towards the woodland, a the cloud of birds looped and dived like a single animal carrying Jude above the sea and beyond Hastings. Hastings burned blue in the distance and all they could think about was how they'd been saved, rescued by the birds, when moments before they'd felt the black panic of the end. And, now, suddenly there was life and it seemed at once both fragile and indestructible.

Martin stood camouflaged by shadows at the edge of the woodland. She watched the castle and the surrounding rubble for signs of movement, a cherub or a survivor and only when she was sure that they were alone did she sound her birdcall. Dex recognized it straight away and responded with a birdcall of his own.

"What was that?" Marianne held Emoli protectively to her chest.

"An old friend," Dex said. "She's the one who saved us," he said and walked in the direction of the call.

Martin watched them crossing the uncontaminated field. Dear God, she thought, the infant was already glowing. The seed was more powerful than she had imagined. The urgency to begin the preparations overtook her and she lifted her hands towards the beech tree. The pearl's lake had soaked into the ground and all that remained was the tree with roots as large and exposed as its branches.

Martin began to sing, a low hum that impelled the tree to groan with rapid growth. By the time Marianne, Emoli and Dex reached her, long coils of bark were twisting up into the sky like brown and grey hydras and the tree had nearly quadrupled in size.

"What's happening?!" Marianne stopped where the ground was breaking as the roots expanded.

"I've set the activation in motion," said Martin, standing with her arms outstretched to Marianne. "Welcome," she hugged her and Emoli.

An arrow narrowly missed his ear. Martin pushed them to the ground. Two cherubs were flying across the field and shooting at them.

"Quickly!" Martin said and pulled Marianne and Emoli behind the growing tree.

It was difficult to stand as the ground kept breaking and the bark sounded like gnashing teeth. Arrows were flinging off the bark. Martin grabbed Dex's arm and pulled him towards them.

"Do you remember the way from here?" She asked and Dex nodded yes.

"Good. Go then. I won't be long," she said as she shifted into an enormous fruit bat and flew towards the cherubs, dodging their arrows with ease. She picked up each one with a single foot and flapped in the direction of the sea. Marianne could see Martin carrying the cherubs towards the blazes of Hastings and she shuddered at the thought of their small bodies falling into the blue fire.

"Come on!" Dex shouted over his shoulder.

They ran through the woodland until they reached the cliff tops of the South Downs. Wind bent the grass and spat rain against their faces. Marianne kept looking back at the brewing storm above the woodland. She couldn't tell if it was tree branches or lightening that pierced the clouds with slashes of silver. Emoli cried the whole way but his sobs went untended and unregistered. They could only concentrate on one foot in front of another and safety. They were exhausted, battered and bruised.

Where was he taking her?

At last they reached the used car lot. It looked empty, but when Dex made a birdcall, the rusty door of an old buick opened. He ducked inside.

"Trust me," he said to Marianne and held out his hand.

She took it and they crawled across the seats to the other side where earthen steps lead down into a room that had been carved out of the hillside. Marianne hadn't noticed the woman in the corner until she ran her fingertips along the wall, and where her fingers touched, light flushed. She began drawing pictures of light. Two figures and a small child with a glowing ring around them.

"Welcome," she said. She had the same eerie voice as Martin.

The picture lit the room. Marianne could see small white roots dangling from the ceiling. The woman stepped forward. She was younger than Martin, but wore the same boiler suit and had bronzed passionate eyes with wild hair. She looked at Emoli.

"So it is true," she said and placed the palm of her hand upon his forehead.

Marianne pulled him away, but Dex stopped her. "It's okay. She's reading him."

The woman returned her palm to Emoli's forehead and hummed the low hum that Martin had used. She began to flicker like a hologram and with each flash the transparent image of the pearl surrounding her grew stronger and stronger. When she broke away, she staggered backwards.

"The Seed of Genesis," she said and bowed.

Dismantling myself
Blowing away
Like red and white
confetti,
cells

Night brushes over
the burnt out houses
and deserted places

GPS: 0°44'14"E, 50°57'0"N

Past her reflection
there spreads a field
half shrouded
Like a world left
unfinished.

50.949776°, 0.735572